ARNOLD MARSDEN

Glacier Chalet Surprise

A Bucket List Hike Novel

Contents

Author's Note

This is a work of fiction. The characters are fictional; any resemblances to actual persons are coincidental. I hiked nearly every mile of the trails described in the book (and many more) and visited most of the facilities during my trip to Glacier National Park in 2019. While I have tried to describe the trails, scenery, facilities, and operations accurately, I have made small adjustments to facilitate the story. In addition, conditions of trails and facilities and operational details of the chalets, campgrounds, and the National Park Service change. Conditions described in the book may not reflect exactly what you have experienced in the past or may experience in the future. But then again, that's part of the wonder of visiting wild areas like Glacier National Park; each experience is unique!

Since color images do not work well on many e-readers and to keep the price of the physical books reasonable, I have not included color photos in the book. This is not intended to be a guidebook. However, as a special bonus for you, I have created a **Photo Album** showing many of the key scenes in the book. If you want to follow along as you read, you can download your free copy here.

(https://strivingforsafety.mailerpage.com/fiction)

Maps

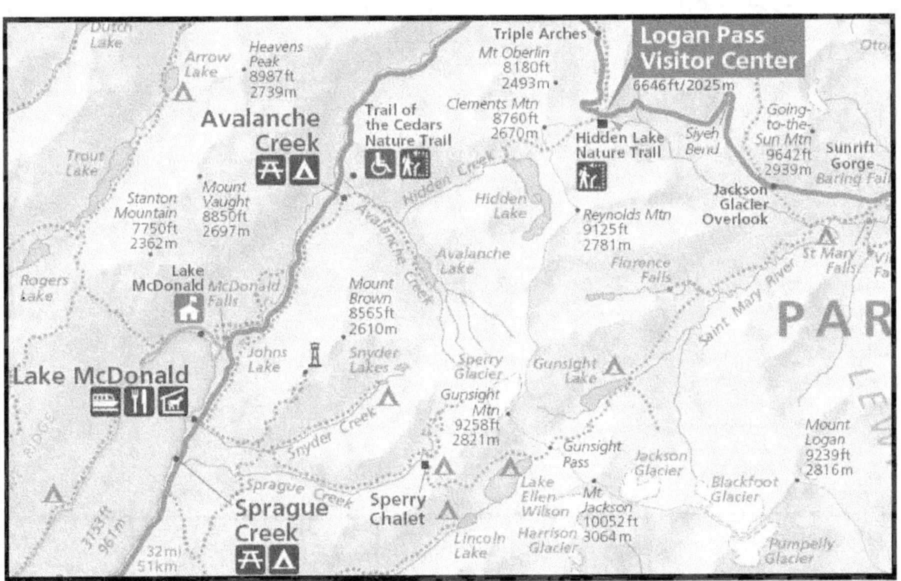

Sperry Chalet and Gunsight Pass Trail

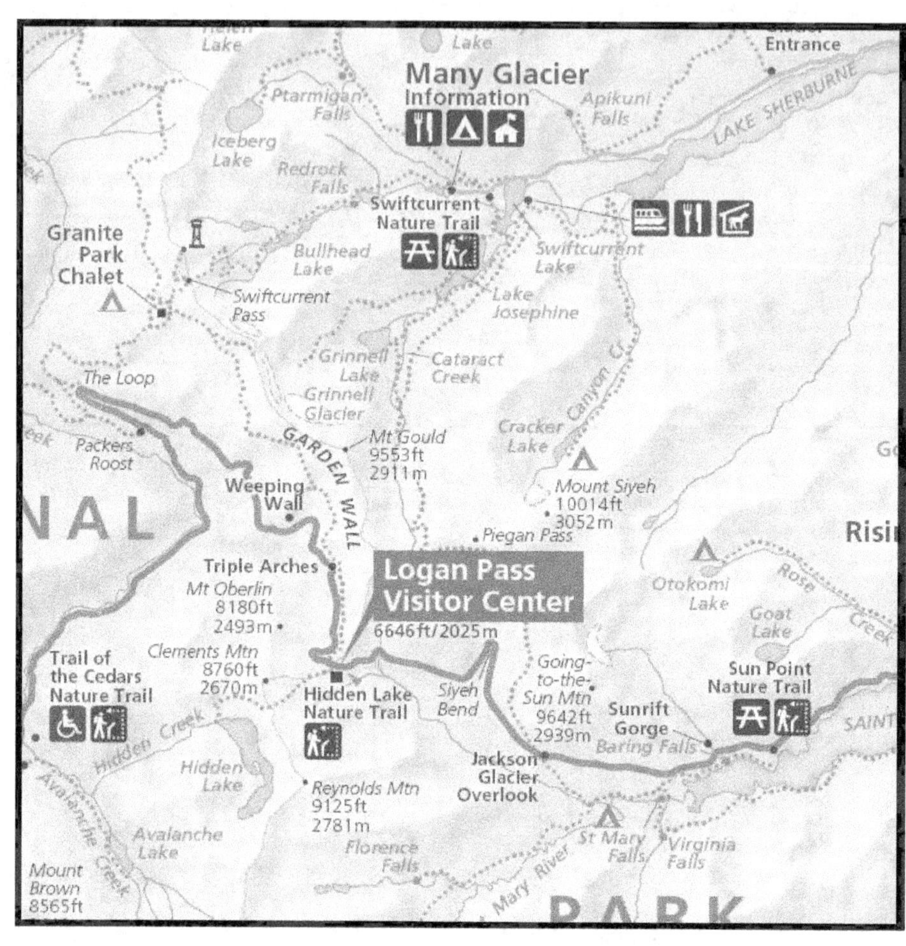

Granite Park, Highline Trail, Swiftcurrent Pass Trail

I

Prologue

August 10, 2017
Houston, Texas

1

Fire

"Fire! Bob! Fire!"

Bob rolled over on the couch, but refused to wake up. His exhausted mind needed the sleep after spending Wednesday night at the plant dealing with the aftermath of a small fire. The plant had shut down automatically as designed, and the alert operators extinguished the fire shortly thereafter. But he had reports to file, an investigation to start, and lots of questions from the bosses to answer. Now the fire was invading his dreams.

"Bob, did you hear me?"

Why was Cathy asking him about the fire? She knew he didn't like to discuss work at home. He gave all he had at the plant every day and needed a reprieve.

"Sorry. I fell asleep. Is the plant on fire again?" he yelled to the other room.

"No. It's in Glacier National Park, near Sperry Chalet."

Bob sat up and paused before he stood so he wouldn't get dizzy as blood rushed out of his head. He walked into the home office where Cathy sat in front of the computer monitor with her hands covering the sides of her head.

"Oh, no!" She lowered one of her hands and pointed to the video on the screen.

"Look!" She covered her mouth with her other hand. "It's awful."

Bob moved behind her and watched the video. Cathy expanded it to full screen.

"Here we go again," Cathy said. She leaned her head back, looked up at him, then closed her eyes.

"Ohhh," said Bob. He grasped both of her shoulders and squeezed lightly.

"It seems like all my trips are doomed to fail before they even begin. Either you won't go with me, or I can't get a permit or reservation, or there's a fire. You name it–it's happened to me." She took a break from ranting to sniffle. "I finally got a reservation at Sperry Chalet, but now they're saying it might burn down. It's such a special place. Now we won't be able to go for … maybe forever!"

Bob released his grip and patted her shoulder. "Hold on, Cathy. Maybe the fire won't reach the chalet. I'm sure they have a plan to fight the fire and protect the chalet. Seems like there's a fire up there every year."

Cathy pointed at the line of people walking on a trail high above a deep blue lake. "Wow! The guests are evacuating on foot on the Gunsight Pass Trail. That's the trail we were planning to backpack. They must fear the chalet is going to burn down."

She stood up and pouted.

Bob wrapped his arms around her, and she placed her head on his shoulder.

"I'm sorry," Bob said as he patted her back. "Maybe they'll give us priority for a reservation next year. If it does burn down, we can try to stay at Granite Park Chalet near Logan Pass instead."

Cathy sniffled again. He tried to hold her tighter, but she pushed herself away and grabbed a tissue from the box on the desk to wipe her nose.

"You could help by setting aside time for us to travel together instead of spending your life at the plant. You should have retired years ago. It's hard enough planning these trips without all your make-believe work conflicts."

She walked away.

Bob looked back at the video and winced when he saw embers raining down near the chalet. It wouldn't last long. The firefighters had no way to shut off the fuel for the fire as they had done for the small fire at the plant. Though he was devastated by the losses caused by the fire and Cathy's disappointment, he felt a twinge of relief. He could stop searching for a way to tell her he had to cancel anyway. The fire at work would set him back for weeks. He couldn't afford to get away now. At least this time, he wouldn't be the one to disappoint her yet again.

II

Day One

July 25, 2023
Glacier National Park

2

Scare

Bob clenched his hands in the pockets of his puffy jacket as he sat on the cold bench on the dark front porch of the backcountry permit center. His fleece hat kept his head warm, but he had forgotten his gloves in his cabin at the Swiftcurrent Motor Inn in Glacier National Park.

A crunching sound ended the peaceful silence. He looked to his left, but only saw an endless black void. As he listened more intently, he heard the rhythmic snapping of dry twigs on the forest floor. He pulled the can of bear spray from the holster on the belt of his nylon hiking pants. Fortunately, he hadn't left that behind in his cabin with his gloves.

Great! I haven't even made it to my first sunrise in the park, and I'm already defending myself from a bear.

Unlike in the Sierra Nevada in California, where he spent the previous summer, both grizzly bears and the more timid black bears roamed this park.

He moved toward the front of the patio so he would have a clear shot at the approaching beast.

"Go away, bear. Get away from here!" he yelled.

The snapping twigs changed to crunching gravel. Bob pulled the safety pin on the canister and held it out in front of him.

Suddenly, a bright light blinded him. He covered his eyes and turned his head.

"Whoa! Don't shoot. It's just me."

Bob tried to face the man, but had to look down to avoid the blinding light. He lowered his bear spray. "You scared me to death. I thought I was about to meet my first grizzly."

The stranger pushed a button on his headlamp, turning the bright white light into an eerie red one which was easier on the eyes. "Sorry about that. I took a shortcut from the campground. They ought to leave a few lights on in the parking lot."

"I guess I'm a little on edge. First day in the park and all. Never been anywhere where grizzlies roam."

The stranger pointed to Bob's bear spray. "Well, it looks like you're prepared. I left my bear spray back at camp. Oops."

The stranger climbed the steps and held out his bare hand. He must have forgotten his gloves as well. "Name is Walter."

Bob shook Walter's icy hand. He felt warmer now that his heart rate was up. "I'm Bob. Are you here to get a backpacking permit?"

"Yep. Why else would I be up this early? They make these permits almost impossible to get."

"You're in the right place. Second in line." Bob walked back to the bench and sat next to the door.

Walter sat next to him. "What permit are you trying to get?"

Bob paused and tried to peer into Walter's eyes below the red light. The Gunsight Pass Trail wasn't a secret, but he didn't want to spur any interest that might jeopardize his chances of getting one of the two remaining permits. The twenty-mile hike could be completed in a long day, but with such beauty and enticing excursions off the main trail, why rush it? His attempts to make a reservation at the rebuilt Sperry Chalet, like he and Cathy had done the year it burned down, had been unsuccessful. Instead, he was here to get a permit to camp for two nights at the Sperry Campground, just up the hill from the chalet, and one night at the Gunsight Lake Campground.

What the heck? I'm first in line. It shouldn't matter. Might as well be helpful.

"I'm hoping to backpack the Gunsight Pass Trail. What about you?"

Walter shrugged. "Oh. I don't know. I'll take almost anything I can get, but someone at the campground also told me that was a great hike."

"Yeah, the Sperry Chalet, a side trip to a glacier, a couple of gorgeous blue lakes, waterfalls, and goats galore."

"Sounds like a winner to me."

Bob began bouncing his knees. "I'd pick a backup or two if I were you. By the time they get to you, I suspect the campsites will be taken. They issue permits at other offices in the park at the same time. Maybe you could hike the Dawson-Pitamakan loop down in Two Medicine. Some people hike it in a day, but it's kind of long–about nineteen miles. Once you climb over the first pass, you have miles of views from a high ridge. And there are a couple of lakes you can camp at."

Walter nodded and finally turned off his headlamp. But the dull red light was immediately replaced by more blinding white light, this time from an approaching pickup truck. Two doors opened and closed, but Bob couldn't even tell if the approaching persons were men or women with the white glow still implanted on his retina.

"You guys are up early," said a faceless female voice. "We'll be right with you. Need to boot up the computer and make some coffee." As the glow faded, Bob saw her male partner tip his tan cap.

"Thanks," Bob and Walter said simultaneously.

Bob stood up and stepped a few feet in front of the door. He let out a deep breath when he saw that Walter stayed on the bench.

Ten minutes later, the door to the office opened, and the female ranger said, "Come on in."

Bob rushed through the door. As he entered, the ranger said, "I'm Teresa. I'll take you over here." She pointed to an empty service window, then looked at Walter. "Sir, my partner, Larry, will help you over there." She pointed to an identical service window to the right.

Once Teresa was behind the counter, she asked Bob, "How long were you waiting out there?"

"About an hour. I heard these permits go fast. I'm trying to make up for a trip my wife and I had to cancel a few years ago."

"Oh, you must have let her sleep in. How sweet." She tilted her head and grinned.

"No, she passed away while hiking the John Muir Trail two years ago. I'm trying to help her finish her bucket list of hikes. She wanted to stay at the Sperry Chalet, but I couldn't get a reservation. I'll have to settle for backpacking the Gunsight Pass Trail. I plan to visit the chalet and eat dinner there."

Teresa's grin disappeared, and she covered her mouth with her hand. "Oh, I'm so sorry. That's a great way to remember her. Let's see what I can do. Hold on just a second. Can't do anything without coffee."

When she stepped away, Walter mentioned the Gunsight Pass Trail to the other ranger. The other ranger's fingers flew across his keyboard. Bob shifted his weight from foot to foot and swung his head from ranger to ranger. He didn't anticipate two rangers working in parallel.

Teresa returned, sipping a cup of coffee. "What itinerary did you have in mind?"

"I'd like to start at the Sperry Trailhead near Lake McDonald Lodge tomorrow morning. Two nights at Sperry Campground and one at Gunsight Lake. Then finish at the Jackson Glacier Overlook Trailhead."

"Let's see here …"

Walter exclaimed, "Really! It's available? I'll take it!"

He looked at Bob. "Hey, thanks for the tip. I got the Gunsight Pass Trail."

Bob's jaw dropped.

"I'm sorry, sir, but none of those campsites are available," Teresa said. "Is there another trip I can try to get you?"

Bob looked back and forth between Walter, Larry, and Teresa.

Teresa continued, "Or you could day hike it if you want. It's a beast, but you look like you could do it."

Bob paused to gather his wits.

"But I was here first, and Walter was just offered the same itinerary."

Walter shrugged and held his palms up. "Sorry, man."

"I'm sorry, sir. That's what the system shows," said Teresa.

"But I was here over an hour before him!" He glared at a smug Walter.

Larry stepped over to Teresa and whispered in her ear. He looked at Bob and said, "Please calm down, sir. You make a good point. Let me check something."

Walter's grin disappeared, and his shoulders drooped.

Bob's heart raced for the second time in the young day. Now he understood why he had been reluctant to disclose his itinerary earlier. He knew Glacier had multiple permit offices, but how was he to know that two rangers would be working in parallel here?

Larry bit his lower lip as he stared at his computer monitor. "I'm sorry, Walter. It's the right thing to do." He waved Bob toward himself. "Why don't you switch places, and I'll get you set on the Gunsight Pass Trail."

Walter glared at Bob as he passed.

Walter and Teresa discussed the Dawson-Pitamakan loop as Larry grabbed Bob's permit off the printer and collected the permit fee.

"Enjoy the hike, Mr. Riley." He looked down at Bob's waist. "I see you have your bear spray. Keep it with you at all times, not just while you're hiking. You may not see a bear, but you're almost guaranteed to see a lot of goats. Keep your pack and poles nearby at all times. They can be aggressive and dangerous too. Do you have a bear canister to store your food?"

Bob nodded. "Great. And some form of water treatment?"

"Yes, sir. I filter every sip. I'm not taking any chances. Used it for three weeks on the John Muir Trail and never got sick."

"I'm glad to see you so prepared. Campfires are not allowed at the campgrounds, or anywhere, for that matter. Each campground has a privy, but if you use toilet paper elsewhere, you'll need to pack it out."

"Understood, Ranger."

"Alright. You're all set."

Bob snatched the permit from the ranger as soon as he offered it.

"Thanks for making things right. My wife's not here, but I can tell you she appreciates it too."

"Sorry about the mix up."

* * *

Bob breathed slowly and deeply to calm himself during the short walk back to the Swiftcurrent Motor Inn. He hadn't expected his heart to race until he was climbing the steep sections of the trail later in the morning.

Over a dozen cars, trucks, and campers lined the shoulder of the road, hoping for a cherished walk-up campsite at the Many Glacier Campground. The crowd reminded him why he had woken so early to get the backcountry permit. He would be camping near a handful of people versus hundreds here at the car campground–and hopefully none like Walter.

All those hours reading blogs, watching YouTube videos, and studying reservation websites had paid off with the permit he sought, but barely. Perhaps he should have saved all the effort and winged it like Walter? It almost worked for him. But no, he had too much at stake. He had to show Sperry Chalet to Cathy, even if only for dinner and even if only in spirit. He had tried his best to make a lodging reservation, but they were harder to secure than his golden ticket for the John Muir Trail last summer.

Bob would have plenty of time to replay the events of the morning on the trail, but first he needed to pack his day pack for a hike on the Grinnell Glacier Trail, a five-star day hike turfed up by his research. A nice warmup for four days of lugging around a forty-pound backpack through the mountains.

3

Solitude

Another reason Bob had arrived at the permit office so early was to get an early start on his day hike. Cathy learned the hard way to leave a buffer day between arrival by airplane and her first day of backpacking when her luggage had been delayed on a previous solo trip. No matter how well you packed, some key pieces of gear like knives and hiking poles could not be taken onboard an airplane.

Bob was grateful to learn that lesson the easy way. Since he and his checked bag had arrived on schedule, he would use his buffer day to hike one of the top three trails in the park, the Grinnell Glacier Trail. Its eleven miles and 2200 feet of elevation gain would test the fitness he had tried to build through training in the flatlands of southeast Texas. Mountain hiking just couldn't be simulated in the gym or on local trails.

He walked to the trailhead, which was only a quarter of a mile from the Swiftcurrent Motor Inn, and was surprised that no cars were in the parking lot. He suspected the lot would be full and dozens of cars would be parked along the road by the time he returned. Perhaps some peace and quiet at Upper Grinnell Lake would help him recover from the hectic start of his day.

He covered the first couple of flat miles along Swiftcurrent Lake and Lake Josephine quickly. He enjoyed the soft, springy trail through the forest while it lasted. The historic and majestic Many Glacier Hotel was barely visible across Swiftcurrent Lake through breaks in the trees. He planned to spend a few luxurious nights there after his backpacking trip. He checked the canister of bear spray on his hip much more often than necessary. Bears loved this area with the abundance of ripe, juicy berries during this time of year. His mouth watered, but he didn't want to linger in the bear feeding zone.

After climbing steadily for about a mile, a bird's-eye view of Lower Grinnell Lake rewarded him on the left. Water from Upper Grinnell Lake, his final destination, cascaded a thousand feet into the lake down a series of rock ledges.

An hour later, he approached a short but steep rise, with the trail splitting in several directions. He saw only an intimidating wall of rock beyond the rise. That must be the Garden Wall, he thought with relief. The lake must be just ahead.

He burst up the last 100 feet of trail and lost what little breath he had left when he saw the green water speckled with icebergs ranging from one to thirty feet across. Or was the water blue? Or turquoise–whatever that was? Who was he trying to fool–he was color blind. He just knew it was gorgeous and not something you found in Texas. He might not know the color, but he did know what caused it–the interaction of light with glacial flour in the water, small particles of the underlying rock ground down by the slow but inexorable movement of the surrounding glaciers.

But what he didn't see or hear was people. How could that be? This was one of the most popular hikes in the park. Where were all the voices, the squeals, and the footsteps? Only the faint rustle of the outlet stream and the water falling down the Garden Wall disturbed the eerie silence. Perhaps the hordes of tourists were waiting for the first boat shuttle across the lakes. In addition to a pleasant ride with the potential for moose sightings, the shuttle allowed hikers to cut two miles off their hike each way. He should savor these last few minutes of tranquility–other hikers would surely arrive soon.

He headed to the left for a closer look at Grinnell Glacier. The ice appeared to be stationary from a distance, but the icebergs floating in the lake indicated otherwise. He wouldn't be getting too close!

The trail ended, so he navigated his own way across the rock. The surface appeared to be smooth at first glance, but upon closer inspection, he noticed the effects of the glacier over millions of years. Parallel grooves scarred the rock, making the traction excellent. Stromatolites, or fossils composed of sediment and ancient algae, formed intriguing circular patterns in the rock.

When he reached the outlet from the lake, he took out his water filter to treat a small sample of the stream. He didn't normally do so on day hikes, but he couldn't resist the temptation of ice cold glacier meltwater, something he only saw in advertisements for bottled water and beer while living in Texas. He swished the freezing water around his mouth but tasted nothing at all–the way water should be. No residual chemical taste like he had at home.

As he moved on, the creaks and groans from the glacier became louder and squashed any lingering desire to climb up on the ice. The edges of the ice hung a foot or so above the rocks, having been melted by the warmer exposed rocks and carved by the water flowing underneath. Cracks near the leading edge of the glacier indicated it would soon birth additional icebergs to roam the lake. He ate lunch by the outflow stream so the rushing water would drown out the loud voices and screams of victory from hikers who would be arriving shortly.

Twenty minutes later, he was still alone and muttered, "Time to head back." The only people he saw were the ant-like figures on top of the Garden Wall. They had hiked up a steep spur trail off the Highline Trail on the other side of the wall. He only noticed them because of their silhouette against the blue sky. He wondered if they could see him basking in the sun on the grooved rock next to the shoreline. No, they were probably counting icebergs instead, a more entertaining endeavor, and also wondering where the infamous crowds were.

Bob had nearly forgotten about Marty, his beloved hiking mascot, still tucked away in his pack. He had given the small plush marmot to Cathy before her final hike on the JMT and now carried him on every hike to keep his memories of her fresh. Instead of setting him on a rock for his typical pose, he placed him on a small iceberg near the shore. He wondered if real marmots did the same thing to cool off their yellow bellies on a hot day. A stiff breeze cooled his sweaty back as he took his photos. When Bob looked up from his phone, the iceberg was five feet from the shore and picking up speed. He gasped as he stepped into the icy water to save his marmot friend. He snatched Marty from his raft of ice but lost his balance on the slippery rocks. Marty went for a wild ride as Bob waved his arms to regain his balance.

"Marty, you must have a death wish." Between his and Cathy's JMT hikes, Marty had been nearly lost or destroyed five times. If he had nine lives like a cat, he was now down to three.

Bob's shoes made embarrassing squishing noises as he walked away from the lake. Fortunately, no one else was around to hear. The dust from the trail turned to mud on his wet shoes.

As he cleared the top of the rise in front of the lake, the buzz of the crowd gathered on the trail jolted him back to reality. No wonder he had the lake to himself. A grizzly bear snacked on huckleberries along the trail 200 feet ahead. The dozens of onlookers holding up their phones and cameras distracted her two cubs. The boldest ones inched forward with their selfie sticks leading the way. The cubs moved closer to their mother for protection, distracting her from her juicy snack. Irritated, she headed toward Bob, then looked back to make sure her cubs were following. Bob took a quick photo and backed away slowly. He put his phone away, pulled the bear spray canister from his belt, and released the safety.

Twice in one morning. This may be a short trip.

The fools on the other side of the bears kept moving toward them.

Bob yelled, "Please back off! She feels trapped."

They kept coming, not hearing his plea over their own chatter and the adjacent waterfall.

"Stop, bear, stop," Bob screamed, as he continued to back up while glancing behind him to avoid tripping on the rocky trail.

Mama bear must have determined the raucous crowd threatened her and her cubs more than his yelling, so she galloped toward him. Bob could feel her feet pounding on the trail. He hurried back up the trail, careful not to bait her by running. The fools down below continued climbing and shooting video.

"You idiots!"

Stepping left off the trail was not an option unless he wanted to tumble 200 feet to the base of the waterfall. Mama bear showed no signs of slowing, so he fought his way through the thick bushes on the steep slope to the right until a ten-foot-high wall of rock blocked his way. The bears were just fifty feet away now, the cubs not straying from their mother. Mama bear slowed and fixed her gaze on him as she passed, making sure he stayed put.

She need not worry!

She breathed loudly and deeply through her open mouth. Fifty feet later, she angled off the trail to the right and headed around the rock face behind him. As the second cub passed by, it stopped, raised its head, and sniffed toward him before scrambling to catch up with the other two.

Bob's heart pounded his temples with blood as the crowd of idiots passed below. Their phones were now pointed at him. His anger and disgust would be obvious when they looked through their photos later.

The dam had burst! The lake would be quiet no longer.

After most of the crowd had passed, he heard, "Hey, Bob. What are you doing up there?"

It was Walter. Was this guy tailing him? Perhaps to steal his permit?

"Trying to survive until my backpacking trip. I'm down a pair of underwear now, thanks to you and your new friends."

Bob slid down the embankment on his backside, not yet trusting his shaking legs.

"What do you mean? I was just sitting behind the crowd, about ready to head back to the trailhead. Those bears were snacking near the trail for about an hour. How many berries can a bear eat in one sitting?"

"That crowd of idiots almost got me killed. Now I know why I was the only one at the lake."

"You're going to have a hell of a time finishing the Gunsight Pass Trail if you can't manage this."

Bob was speechless. No good could come of this discussion. He would rather deal with the three bears. Instead, he walked around Walter and down the trail.

* * *

Back in his cabin at the Swiftcurrent Motor Inn, Bob checked his backpacking gear one last time for anything he may have forgotten. Everything on his list was accounted for, so he put all the gear back in his pack in the designated spots developed through experience on the JMT: sleeping bag on the bottom, bear canister in the middle, and the first aid kit and snacks for the day on top. Rain gear and his poop kit went in the large mesh pocket on the outside. Water treatment gear was placed in one of the side pockets. His tent fit snugly in the larger side pocket made for that purpose.

Though it was only eight o'clock, he laid down in bed. He had a four to five-hour journey in the morning, partly in his rental car and partly on the park shuttle, to reach the Sperry Trailhead. Much of the route was on the iconic Going to the Sun Road that transected the park. The epic views would help pass the time–if he could resist the endless pullouts.

But before he could go to sleep, he had one more task–to leave Cathy his daily update using his voice recorder app.

* * *

Dear Cathy,

Hi Dear. We begin another adventure together tomorrow. Actually, today was quite an adventure in itself. But in the end, I got the backpacking permit for the Gunsight Pass Trail and survived a warm-up hike to Grinnell Glacier despite some idiots harassing a bear right in front of me. Yeah, it only took hours to run into my first grizzlies!

I've realized my guilt for abandoning you just days before our John Muir Trail hike may never relent. You never came back, and I'll never forgive myself. The best I can do is help you finish your bucket list of hikes. I hope you enjoyed the John Muir Trail through my eyes and ears.

So, it's on to number two on your list: Sperry Chalet and the Gunsight Pass Trail, with a side trip to Sperry Glacier. I never told you this, but I was relieved when we had to cancel our previous trip to Glacier due to fire. I'm embarrassed to say I was days away from backing out anyway, but I didn't have the nerve to tell you. You wanted to go so badly. Revealing my betrayal would have disappointed you worse than the news of the fire.

I tried my best to get a reservation at Sperry Chalet, but the openings were gone within minutes of release in January. I've checked for cancelations every week for the past two months, but had no luck.

However, as with the JMT, I'll do my best. The trail will provide plenty of obstacles and pleasant surprises. We'll stay at the Sperry Campground for two nights and have dinner at the chalet. On the second day, we'll hike up to Sperry Glacier if the mountain goats deem us worthy. Then we'll hike over Lincoln Pass, along Lake Ellen Wilson, over Gunsight Pass, by Gunsight Lake, and stay at the campground there before hiking out.

I hope that will be enough for you. I don't know what else to do. As I learned from your death, I can't put off these hikes any longer, or you'll never experience them. And they're not only for you anymore. I now understand why you longed for the mountains, for the wilderness. While they won't remove the guilt, they dull the unrelenting ache and keep my memories of you fresh.

Love, Bob

III

Day Two

July 26, 2023
Glacier National Park

4

Riders

Ding. Ding ding. Ding.

Why did he bring that damn bear bell? He should have listened to the experts who advised that bear bells weren't very effective. They claimed it was better to talk, clap, or even sing instead.

Ding. Ding. Ding Ding Ding.

But this was his first foray into grizzly country. The cautious safety manager in him thought the bell may help prevent an encounter with a bear. He had even bought a proper bell, not the little round ones used to decorate Christmas presents or adorn pet collars. But proper bells made lots of noise!

Ding Ding. Ding.

That's it. The bear bell had to go. Now! The persistent noise distracted him from the peaceful sounds of the trail: the crunching of gravel and pine cones under his feet, the wind whistling through the trees, the chirping of the birds, and the gurgling of the streams. A canister of bear spray hung from his belt. That would have to be enough.

Ding!

Only ten minutes after he had left the Sperry Trailhead, he wiggled out of his backpack and set it on the ground. He unclipped the bell from his pack, stuffed toilet paper inside, and pushed it to the bottom of the outside mesh pocket of his pack. Unfortunately, he now had to carry the worthless four ounces for twenty miles. Leave No Trace principles forbade him from tossing it into the forest, but he might just find another cautious backpacker to unload it on.

If not for the forty pounds on his back, today's hike would have been easier than the one yesterday, but not as scenic. The six-mile trail climbed a whopping 3300 feet to Sperry Chalet, mostly through a dense forest. But unlike yesterday, he didn't have to return to the trailhead.

Most hikers started this hike at the other end of the twenty-mile trail, the Jackson Glacier Overlook Trailhead, so they didn't have to climb this steep slope. But Bob listened to the pleas from his knees to spare them such a grueling descent at the end of the trip.

Bob mostly stared down at the trail in front of him for the first ninety minutes of hiking. The trail was so steep he could almost reach out and touch it with his hand. His calves were already tired, but they would protest even more tomorrow when the soreness kicked in. His calls of "Hey Bear" and frequent glances into the trees for signs of wildlife lasted all of fifteen minutes. Oxygen deprivation forced him to focus solely on the next few steps.

He raised his head, hoping to see a more gradual slope ahead, but only noticed brown fur fifty feet ahead on the trail. He reached toward his belt and pulled the canister out of its holster. Before releasing the safety latch, he looked up again, but this time saw antlers. A huge buck stared at him, just as surprised as he was. They both froze.

I need to pay more attention. What if that had been a grizzly bear?

The buck was in no hurry to move, all the encouragement Bob needed to take his first snack break. He returned the bear spray to its holster and removed his pack. The buck resumed nibbling on the tender underbrush. *I guess we'll be snacking together, big guy. I'm having roasted nuts and dried fruit; what about you?*

Fifteen minutes later, footsteps pounded the trail below. Could that be a bear? They were large animals, but he thought they would step more softly. Then he heard voices. Seconds later, he saw a man on a horse leading three other horses and a couple of mules up the trail, leaving a cloud of dust behind them. The horses carried what appeared to be a family of three, and the mules carried saddlebags.

The pack leader pulled on his reins and yelled, "Whoa!"

The buck scampered up the trail, then bounced into the trees. He was out of sight in three hops.

"What are we stopping for?" yelled the man on the second horse.

The pack leader rolled his eyes and turned around. "A deer was on the trail, and a backpacker is sitting next to it."

"I don't see anything."

"The deer ran off. Don't worry. We're in no rush," said the pack leader.

"My ass is killing me. Let's go. How much longer do we have?"

The man on the second horse, which Bob presumed was the father, leaned over to peer at him around the pack leader. "Oh, I see. Hey! Can you move it? We need to pass."

Bob didn't acknowledge the rude stranger, but noticed the pack leader shrug his shoulders. He was finished with his snack, so he gulped some water and put his food bag in his pack.

"Hey, did you hear me? We need to get to the chalet. I'm getting hungry."

The lady on the third horse said, "Jason, calm down. He's packing up. Unlike you, he's walking on his own two legs and carrying a heavy pack."

Jason threw one of his arms up, causing his horse to flinch. "Well, that's his problem, Crystal. He should have hired a horse like we did if he's too old for the trail."

Bob winced, but continued preparing to resume his hike. The person on the fourth horse tried to hide behind his mother. He appeared to be a teenage boy, perhaps sixteen or seventeen years old.

"Are you still OK back there, Thomas?" asked Crystal.

"Yeah," he muttered.

Once Bob's pack was on his back and buckled tight, he asked the pack leader, "Where are y'all headed?"

"Up to Sperry Chalet. These folks are spending a long weekend there. Now, would you please step to the downhill side of the trail while we pass? If the horses get spooked, they usually bolt uphill. But if you keep still, you'll be fine."

Bob stepped to the side and now had a better view of the rude man he was sharing the trail with. Jason shook his uncovered, balding head. "OK. Let's go already!" The man was lucky most of the trail to the chalet was shaded, otherwise his head would be glowing this evening, and he would not sleep well tonight. He wore business casual khaki pants and a white polo shirt. Bob hoped Jason packed shoes other than the topsider boat shoes in the stirrups. Otherwise, blisters would ruin his long weekend.

Jason sneered at him as he passed. His wife frowned, then moved her lips as if whispering, "Sorry." Sunglasses sat on the brim of the navy blue floppy hat resting on her curly brown hair. The nylon pants covering her slim legs and pink, long-sleeved polyester shirt were more appropriate for the environment than Jason's outfit. The teenage boy stared down at his horse's mane, but peeked at Bob briefly. Black hair barely extended beneath his khaki baseball cap. His pale complexion matched his father's. The poor kid probably wished he could crawl into a saddlebag on one of the mules following him.

Bob coughed as a cloud of dust enveloped him. He turned toward the downhill side of the trail to avoid the worst of it. All but one person he encountered on the JMT last summer had been friendly and respectful. Hopefully, Jason would be the last rude and inconsiderate person he experienced on this trip. Even the man's wife and son appeared to be disgusted with his behavior, and the pack leader was just biting his lip until he could drop them off at the chalet.

5

Rustic

Thomas rushed up the gentle slope from the dining room to the dormitory building on a stomach full of vegetable soup, ham, bread, and chocolate chips. He and his mom had enjoyed lunch in the Sperry Chalet dining room after the brutal horse ride up the mountain. However, his dad had complained about the meal almost as much as the horse ride. He felt sorry for the pack leader and the old man his dad had berated on the trail.

"Be careful, Thomas. It's too rocky to run up here," warned his mom.

He stopped and turned around. His mother and father waddled up the hill after bouncing on a saddle all morning. Thomas walked back to take a suitcase from his mom and a duffel bag from his dad.

As they approached the entrance to the dormitory, Thomas set the bags down on the dusty rocks. "Wow. This is so cool. I can't believe we get to spend three nights in there. Thanks, Mom."

His dad pointed to the redwood rails of the balconies on the second floor. "Are we staying in one of those rooms?"

"No. We're on the first floor," said his mom.

"Why didn't you reserve one of those? We can afford it, you know."

His mother put her hands on her hips and leaned toward Jason. "Do you realize how hard it was to get a reservation here? I called every day for weeks to get this room. You should be grateful."

The stone steps in front of them led to a large redwood porch and a door.

The small lobby contained a few director's chairs for guests to mingle. A beautifully finished wood staircase led to the upstairs rooms.

His mom pointed to a door behind the staircase. "I think that's our room."

She opened the door for Thomas. He dropped the bags right inside the door and stopped.

"Thomas, keep going, I can't get in," said his dad.

He stepped forward and surveyed the room. Two double beds with thin, black metal frames were set against a cedar plank wall. White curtains adorned the window in the rough rock wall ahead. A couple of canvas director's chairs and two wooden tables were the only other furnishings in the room.

"Where's the bathroom?" asked his dad.

"Jason, none of the rooms have bathrooms. I told you that when I made the reservation. No showers either–but the common bathrooms have a sink with running water. And there's no electricity." She pointed to a lantern hanging on the wall. "That's what the lantern is for."

"The bathrooms are in the small building we passed on the way up here," Thomas said.

Jason shook his head and mumbled, "How did I let you talk me into this? That's why I like cruises. They have all that stuff, and they feed you like kings."

"Come on, Dad. It'll be fun. Isn't it beautiful up here?"

"I have to admit it's pretty outside, now that we're out of the trees. But what are we going to do for three days up here?" His dad pinched his lips together and shook his head.

"We can go hiking, get to know the other guests, hang out on the patio–just enjoy being outside for a change."

"That's the spirit, Thomas."

His mom wrapped her arm around him, but he wriggled out of her embrace.

Jason laid down on one of the beds and covered his face with a pillow.

"Come on, let's go sit on the patio and wait for the animals to come," Thomas said. "I've heard we are guaranteed to see mountain goats."

Jason lifted the pillow off his face for a few seconds. "You go ahead. I need to recover from that bone-jarring horse ride."

His mom shrugged when Thomas looked her way.

6

Leftovers

Bob stopped to catch his breath. His hiking partner for the last hour, Sam, did the same. Sam had been following not far behind the mules, and his hiking pace was similar to Bob's. Sam planned to stop for lunch at the chalet, then continue on to the campground at Lake Ellen Wilson.

Sam pointed up through a clearing in the trees to their right. "Hey, look! There's the chalet."

Bob looked up, let out a big breath, and smiled. The well-camouflaged chalet was perched on a rocky ledge which hovered over the long valley through which they had been hiking. When he looked back at Sam, he saw a small sliver of ten-mile-long Lake McDonald over his shoulder. The view was a pleasant break from staring at tree trunks all morning, especially the blackened ones they now hiked through. They must have burned in the fire that destroyed the chalet's dormitory building years ago.

Bob took off his hat and wiped the sweat dripping from his eyebrows with his sleeve before it could burn his eyes. "Good. This has been quite a climb."

"Do you want to take another break or carry on?"

Bob tipped his head up the trail and began walking. He was in a groove. Breaks were nice, but it was so hard to get started again. In most cases, he found it best to plod on at a slower pace.

Thirty minutes later, the trail flattened as it approached a creek. The pack leader and his train of horses and mules approached from the other side.

Bob smiled at him. "I bet you were happy to drop off your cargo."

The pack leader grinned, then mumbled, "Yeah, but not as much as the horses and mules behind me."

Bob and his partner had plenty of room to step aside this time. The pack leader urged his horse across the creek. The second horse hesitated until the rope tugged on his snout.

"Enjoy the ride down," Bob said.

"Oh, I will. Have a good day."

Shortly after crossing the creek, Bob spotted a trail sign. The trail to Sperry Glacier headed to the left into a horseshoe-shaped basin with water falling a thousand feet down a nearly vertical rock wall. Sperry Glacier sat just over the top of the wall. How he would get over it was tomorrow's worry.

The chalet building containing the dining room and kitchen was just ahead and lured them up the hill. Its walls appeared to be made of the same multi-colored rocks as the surrounding mountains. Mortar was applied roughly in between stones of all sizes and shapes. Bob wondered if water entered the building during heavy rains driven against the walls by strong winds. The door, window frames, and rails along the patio were painted the color of redwood. Thin wood shingles covered the roof.

They laid their backpacks and hiking poles against the building and filled their water bottles from the outdoor spigot labeled as 'potable water.' Bob drank nearly the entire bottle to moisten his parched mouth and quench his thirst. He filled his bottle again; filtering water from a stream or lake was not very difficult or time-consuming, but he would appreciate skipping this chore later with so many others to do while setting up camp.

When Bob entered the building, he allowed his eyes to adjust to the dark interior. The dining room on the right contained about eight sturdy wooden tables. Only one was occupied, but the young lady sitting there was writing in a notebook instead of eating. A black wood stove adorned the rough brick wall to his right. An antique cash register sat on the counter just inside the door. He heard dishes clanging as they were being washed to his left in the kitchen. The cloth wicks dangling from the overhead lights indicated the chalet had no electricity.

He had expected to see more people, so he glanced at his watch.

A young man entered from the kitchen area holding a wet rag. "Welcome to Sperry Chalet. Take a seat anywhere."

He waved at the empty tables. Shoulder-length brown hair hung below his Sperry Chalet baseball cap. Sparse long whiskers covered his upper lip, chin, and cheeks. A green apron protected his blue jeans and white t-shirt from the inevitable spills.

Bob and Sam glanced at each other, then at the young man.

"You mean it's not too late for lunch?" Sam asked.

"I think we have just enough for two more. You're welcome to it. My name is Phillip."

"Heck yeah. That was a tough hike," said Sam.

Phillip grinned. He must see pained faces like theirs every day.

"I don't have a reservation for lunch, but I have one for dinner. My name is Bob Riley."

"No problem. You don't need a reservation for lunch. Would you like some lemonade to start with?"

Sam nodded, and Bob said, "Sure."

"And I'll check that reservation for you." He looked at Sam. "Sir, do you have one as well?"

Sam shook his head. "No. I need to be moving on to Lake Ellen Wilson after lunch."

Phillip walked to the kitchen, and Bob and Sam sat at a table against a large window in front of a porch with a view of Lake McDonald.

Phillip returned a few minutes later with lemonade and more. "We had enough soup and sandwiches left for two, but only one cookie, so I'll let you two fight over it. And Bob, I saw your dinner reservation. You're good." Phillip raised his thumb. "We begin serving at six o'clock."

"You don't happen to have any last-minute room cancelations, do you?" Bob held his breath.

Phillip grinned and shook his head. "No, sorry."

Bob's shoulders drooped even though he expected the response. It was worth a shot. He wondered how Phillip responded on the rare occasions when the reply was positive. The ecstatic responses from those customers must be one of the best parts of his job.

"I understand. Thanks for lunch, and I'll see you at dinner."

Bob pushed the cookie toward Sam. "You've still got some hiking to do, and I'm done for the day. Plus, I need to eat some of the candy stashed in my bear canister to make it lighter."

Sam broke it in half. "We can split it."

Bob shook his head.

"Thanks."

* * *

Bob squinted as he and Sam stepped out of the dining room into the bright sunshine. Bob veered to the right when the trail approached the dormitory building just up the hill. He stopped and admired the masonry and carpentry work. The walls were made of the same types of rock as used for the dining room, but here, they were more randomly arranged. Some rocks were a foot thick and several feet long; others were mere inches on a side. A few slender rocks extended six to twelve inches beyond the rest. The rough rock texture and redwood railing blended well with the surrounding scenery. Some may have thought the masons were being sloppy, but Bob figured every stone was intended to make the chalet invisible from afar.

Bob had removed Marty from his backpack while in the dining room and placed him in a side pocket, knowing he needed to take a photo here. He reached back, pulled Marty from beside his water bottle, and set him on the railing of the patio near the entrance. Marty fell off the round railing after Bob had taken a couple of photos. He retrieved the little marmot and stuffed him in the side pocket again. Surely he wouldn't get into trouble during the short hike to the campground. Before joining Sam again, he whispered, "Sorry, Cathy. This is as close as we'll get to sleeping at the chalet."

Sam and Bob headed up the slight incline of the Gunsight Pass Trail. Bob stopped five minutes later at a sign pointing toward the campground on the right. He offered his hand to Sam. "This is my stop. I don't envy you having to hike on with a full belly. Lunch was fantastic. I may take a nap after I set up my tent."

Sam grinned and shook Bob's hand. "Thanks for the company. I guess we won't see each other again since you're spending two nights here. Enjoy your hike."

"Stay safe."

Sam was probably correct, but you never knew what surprises the trail would bring. After all, he thought he had seen the last of that scoundrel, Walter, at the permit office.

Unlike on the JMT last year, most of Glacier's campgrounds had designated campsites. The Sperry Campground had four campsites for Bob to choose from, though one of them was already occupied. It also had an enclosed privy and a separate eating area with an expansive view of the valley below, even better than from the chalet. While exploring the area, he also discovered the water source for the chalet. A hose from a pond above the campground headed toward the chalet, but did not supply running water to the campground.

Bob yawned several times as he set up his tent at site number three. Four hours on the road, a steep hike to the chalet, and a filling lunch conspired to force a nap. He ducked into the tent, blew up his sleeping pad and pillow, and laid down.

Bob was surprised, yet grateful, when he awoke and looked at his watch two hours later. Based on his experience on the JMT, he didn't expect to sleep well the next few nights, so a little in the bank would help.

7

Introductions

When Bob entered the dining room for dinner, the atmosphere was warm and alive versus dark and empty as it had been when he entered for lunch. A fire flickered in the wood stove, and the wicks from the overhead propane lights glowed. A dozen simultaneous conversations created a buzz. Some of the larger tables were full, one was empty, and a lady sat alone at another. She looked from the full tables, to the door, to the kitchen.

Bob guessed she was about his age, about Cathy's age, but he would never share that with her. Her straight gray hair was cut in a chin-length bob. She was dressed in polyester like he was, so he figured she might be backpacking as well.

Bob imagined her muttering, *Please, can you keep me company? Sitting alone with so many people here is very awkward.* Despite her discomfort, he detected a subtle smile when their eyes crossed. He hoped to meet trail friends like the wonderful ones who had made his JMT hike special, so he ran his fingers through his wavy white hair and walked up to the chair across the table from her.

"Hi, I'm Bob. Do you mind if I sit here?"

"No, please do. You can't believe how awkward I've felt sitting alone."

Bob smiled and pulled out the chair.

She extended her arm across the table. "I'm Liz. Liz Baker. Pleased to meet you. Are you staying here alone too?"

Bob grabbed her fingers lightly and shook, then sat down. "Alone, yes, but I'm staying at the campground just up the trail. I would love to stay here, but I couldn't get a reservation. And you?"

"I'm one of the fortunate ones. Must have had a lucky finger on the computer mouse back in January. I had hoped I would meet a travel partner in the meantime, but I'm up here alone as well."

Her smile disappeared as she pinched her lips together.

"Well, good for you. I've learned the hard way you can't take the future for granted. I started the John Muir Trail alone last year, but I hung out with some wonderful people along the way. I'm sure you'll do the same here. How long are you staying?"

"I arrived this afternoon and plan to stay for two nights. I'm hiking across the Gunsight Pass Trail and wanted to take a break after the steep hike up here."

Bob puckered his lips and said, "Ooh. You were behind me. You must have been really hot."

Liz pinched her shirt above her shoulders and pulled it up several times. "My shirt is still a little wet."

"Yeah, that was a leg and lung burner, but better going up than down for me. I'm hiking the same trail, but staying at the Sperry Campground for two nights, then Gunsight Lake Campground on the last day. The rest of the trail is mostly downhill and is supposed to be beautiful. We're in for a real treat."

Phillip arrived and placed a basket of homemade bread and two cups of lemonade on the table. "Hi Mr. Riley. Welcome back. I hope you saved room for dinner."

"Hi Phillip. No problem. Bring it on. That 3300-foot climb set me back a few calories."

Phillip looked at Liz. "And you are …"

"Liz. Pleased to meet you."

Phillip nodded and walked to one of the other tables.

Bob took a roll from the basket after offering it to Liz. He watched the steam escape when he tore off a bite-sized piece and sniffed the yeasty aroma while taking a deep breath.

"Where do you put it, Bob? You don't appear to have an ounce of fat on you."

Bob puckered his lips as he took a sip of the tart lemonade. "Good genes and lots of walking, I guess."

He paused, thinking of returning the compliment, but didn't want to tread on that thin ice either.

Their conversation was interrupted by an unpleasant memory from the morning. Jason pulled out the chair next to Liz and lowered his shoulders when he looked down at Bob. "Oh, you again."

His wife and son appeared on his side of the table. She asked, "Mind if we join you?"

Liz said, "No, go ahead. I'm Liz, and this is Bob."

"I'm Crystal Coates. This is my son, Thomas, and husband, Jason. We saw Bob on the trail earlier today."

Crystal and Thomas sat down. Thomas was taller than both his mother and father. His pale face was accentuated by the short black hair matted on his head after spending all day under a hat. His arms didn't have the same chiseled tone as his mother's, indicating he spent more time behind a computer than at the gym.

Jason reached across the table, pulled the bread basket in front of him, grabbed a roll, and nearly inhaled it. He looked at Bob. "Glad to see you made it up the hill. I didn't know if you would make it the way you were sprawled out on the trail earlier."

"Come on, Jason. Be nice," Crystal said.

Jason jumped as if he had been kicked underneath the table.

Good for her. He sure felt like doing so.

Crystal looked at Bob, then Liz. "Are you two together?"

Liz looked at Bob and giggled. "No, we just met a few minutes ago."

"Could have fooled me. You look like you've been together for years. How long are you staying here?"

Liz blushed. "Two nights for me."

Bob added, "Two nights for me too, but I'm staying at the campground."

"Then why are you eating dinner here?" Jason blurted. "I thought dinner service was for guests only."

Bob opened his mouth to reply, but Crystal tried to defuse the building tension. "Jason, they allow backpackers to eat dinner and breakfast with reservations. Don't worry, I'm sure they have enough food for all of us."

Phillip returned with three more cups of lemonade and a couple of bowls of salad. He started to leave, but Jason grabbed the bottom of his shirt and said, "Excuse me."

Phillip stared down at Jason's hand as he released his grip and tried to hand the cup of lemonade back to Phillip.

"I'd like a glass of wine instead of lemonade."

"I'm sorry, sir. We don't serve alcohol up here. I can bring you water or tea if you prefer?"

"No alcohol! You're kidding, right? We're paying $600 per day, and there's no beer or wine? I need some after being on a horse all morning."

"Sorry, sir. Getting supplies up here isn't easy."

Thomas looked at the other tables as if trying to find an empty seat to escape to.

"Enjoy the atmosphere, dear. We came up here to get away from our normal routine."

Liz looked at Bob and frowned.

Bob tried to change the subject. "Thomas, what did you think of the horseback ride this morning?"

"It was pretty neat, but I'm looking forward to doing some hiking up here. We're staying for three days, and I hear there are some nice trails nearby."

Bob leaned toward him so he could hear Thomas's soft voice.

"Great. There sure are. You can get a magnificent view of Lake Ellen Wilson with a short hike up the trail you came in on. And there's a longer trail up to Sperry Glacier. I'm planning on hiking that one tomorrow. But watch out for the mountain goats. They're all over up here."

Thomas raised his eyebrows. "Goats. Cool. I've only seen them in pictures."

"Goats! They're filthy. They better not come close to me," Jason said.

Thomas cut off his father. "Bob, where's the campground? What's it like? It must be neat to stay there."

"It's just up the trail, maybe a quarter of a mile. I saw a resident goat patrolling the area. Big ole thing. Must be used to getting scraps."

"Sounds cool. Mom, maybe we can check it out tomorrow on our hike?"

Phillip returned with two platters of roast beef and vegetables covered in brown gravy.

Bob waved his hand at Liz and Crystal. "Dig in."

Liz grabbed the serving spoon. "Smells delicious."

Jason sighed. "I was hoping for fresh mountain trout, but I guess this will do."

Liz, Crystal, and Bob savored the tender beef and nodded their heads at each other since their mouths were too full to talk. Jason and Thomas nibbled on their servings, but said nothing.

Phillip came by again and asked how everything tasted. He kept his eyes on Jason and stood just out of reach.

"This is cold. Could you warm it up for me?" said Jason.

Liz put her fork down and turned toward him. "Jason, he's trying his best, and you're ruining a wonderful experience for the rest of us."

Jason pushed his chair back, stood up, and stared down at Liz.

"Wonderful! You think this is wonderful? No booze. Cold food. No power. No showers."

Liz pushed her chair out and stood up. Bob jumped up, ran around the table, and stood next to her. He placed his hand on Liz's shoulder.

"Jason, she's just saying what we're all thinking," said Crystal.

Jason looked down at his wife and son, then rushed toward the door. Bob let go of Liz's shoulder and started back around the table. Liz grabbed his hand and let it slide through hers as he walked away.

"I'm so sorry," Crystal said. "Not only about this, but how rude he was to you on the trail, Bob. Thomas and I just want to explore the beauty of the outdoors. He hates it, but I thought this might be a safe introduction with the easy ride up here and a stay at such a wonderful chalet. Perhaps I was wrong." She moved the carrots and green beans around her plate with her fork.

"Give it a chance, Mom. We have three days."

"You should go exploring tomorrow, with or without him," said Bob.

"Mom, let's try to hike by the lake tomorrow. If it goes well, maybe we can go up to that glacier the next day."

"Good plan. Thanks for the tips, Bob."

Crystal and Thomas stood up.

"You're not staying for dessert?" Liz asked.

Crystal looked at Thomas, who shook his head. "I'm not in the mood anymore," he said.

Crystal put her arm around her son, then looked at Bob and Liz. "Have a good night. And be careful over at the campground."

They walked out the door.

Liz opened her eyes wide. "Wow. That was intense. What did they do to you on the trail?"

"More of the same. Jason was in a hurry to get by me while I was taking a break on the trail–while sitting on a horse, of course. The pack leader probably felt like poor Phillip here. Thanks for standing up to him."

Phillip brought out five plates covered with chocolate cake, looked at the empty chairs, and said, "Oh."

Liz smiled at him and shrugged.

Phillip set down two plates each in front of Bob and Liz and held on to the fifth one. "Have at it. Otherwise, it will go to waste."

"Thanks, Phillip," Liz said. "We appreciate what you do here. I know most things are a lot harder up here."

Phillip gave a quick nod to Liz, then returned to the sanctuary of the kitchen.

Liz pointed to the two plates in front of Bob. "Can you handle that, big guy?"

"No doubt."

"Good, I just asked in case you needed help."

A man much older than Phillip walked into the center of the dining area. "Excuse me, ladies and gentlemen."

He timed his interruption perfectly as the serving of dessert had transformed the raucous discussions into murmurs. The man wore the same hat as Phillip, but no hair extended below it. He must be balding or shaving it close for easy maintenance. He wore khaki cargo pants and a navy blue sweatshirt with "Belton" in large white letters. His gray stubble was about a week old.

"Hi. My name is Chet. I'm the manager here at the chalet. Did you enjoy dinner?"

Over half the room nodded. Others said, 'thanks,' 'wonderful,' and 'great.' Some did both. Jason had missed his opportunity to dissent. Too bad.

Chet meandered around the tables so no one needed to turn away from their dessert for long. A few held their plate so they could watch Chet and enjoy their cake at the same time.

"Great. You can thank Raphael, the cook, Paula, the baker, and your two servers, Phillip and Claire."

Bob and Liz clapped, and everyone else followed suit.

"Why, thank you. We do our best with limited cold storage and twice-a-week supply runs. Welcome to our new guests. I'd like to give you a brief history of this wonderful chalet and a few tips to enjoy your stay. Those who were here last night can tell me if I miss anything, or worse yet, get something wrong. Or you can leave. You won't hurt my feelings."

No one left, but someone seated by the wood stove said, "You were right about the earplugs." A quarter of the room laughed–they must have been on their second or third night.

Chet smiled. "There you have it folks. Tip number one. The interior walls are much thinner than the sturdy exterior walls would lead you to believe, so feel free to grab a pair from the counter as you leave. Does anyone–anyone who wasn't here last night–know what the *GNRy* outlined in white rock on the dormitory building stands for?"

The murmuring returned. Liz looked at Bob and held her palms up. Bob knew the answer, but he didn't want to steal Chet's thunder.

"Well, Sperry Chalet was completed back in 1914 by the Great Northern Railway–get it now?"

A collective "Ohhh" spread through the room.

"But what does the 'y' stand for?" asked someone. After the person sitting next to him whispered in his ear, he said, "Oh. Never mind." The others at his table laughed.

"To entice visitors from the East to what they called the 'American Alps', they built a network of chalets, lodges, and tent camps approximately a day's horseback ride apart to mimic the popular trekking adventures in Europe. Originally, there were nine chalets: Belton, St. Mary, Sun Point, Many Glacier, Two Medicine, Sperry, Granite Park, Cut Bank, and Gunsight Lake. Only three remain as operating chalets: Sperry, Granite Park Chalet over by Logan Pass, and Belton Chalet in West Glacier, just outside the park. Belton Chalets operates Sperry and Granite Park—now you know who paid for my sweatshirt."

He ran his finger over the white letters on his sweatshirt and paused to encourage laughs, but only got a couple.

"The Two Medicine chalet has been converted to a general store. The others were destroyed by avalanches and fires or removed after years of disuse during the war years."

"Here at Sperry, this building and the dormitory were two of the original structures, but obviously, much renovation has been done. And other buildings have been added, the restrooms, for instance. As many of you probably know, the dormitory building was destroyed by the Sprague Fire in 2017. Guests were evacuated fourteen miles via the Gunsight Pass Trail shortly after the fire was reported. Fortunately for you and others who love the park, the dormitory reopened in 2020."

Chet clapped his hands. "OK, enough history. I'll let the staff give you a few tips to enjoy your stay and keep safe. We are in the wilderness, after all."

Phillip spoke up from near the counter. "Hi, I'm Phillip, but many of you know that already." Several people chuckled. "I hope you enjoyed your meal. There are some wonderful hikes in the area if you are spending two or three nights with us, and if not, you can enjoy one before you head down to the trailhead tomorrow. In my opinion, the best one is the trail up to Sperry Glacier. If you came up from Lake McDonald, you passed the trail junction just past the creek on the left. It's about four miles round trip and 1500 feet of elevation gain, and you are guaranteed to see ice and mountain goats."

"Oohs" and "Ahs" filled the room.

"For those who want a shorter hike, you can go the other way on the Gunsight Pass Trail and climb to the top of Lincoln Peak, where you'll get a great view of Lake Ellen Wilson spilling into Lincoln Lake far below in the adjacent valley. Or you can continue further to get a better view of Lake Ellen Wilson. Some of you may be hiking all the way to the trailhead at Jackson Glacier Overlook. If you have any questions, ask any of us at coffee hour or in the morning."

The other server stepped forward next to Phillip. "Hi, my name is Claire. I'm sure you've heard black bears and grizzly bears roam the park. Whether you go hiking or not, take your bear spray with you wherever you go, even to the bathroom. Be alert. Make plenty of noise if you head down the trail. But you're much more likely to see mountain goats. Admire them from a distance; they can be aggressive if you get too close."

Another young lady stepped forward. "Hi. My name is Lisa." She paused to wave at everybody. "I clean the rooms and do other odd chores around here. Chet wasn't joking about the ear plugs. Quiet time begins at ten o'clock. Please keep your voices down so you can all get a good night of sleep. There are no secrets here." The room erupted in laughter. "And keep your lanterns within easy reach. It gets very dark up here."

Chet walked back to the center of the room. "OK, everybody. Any burning questions?"

"What time does breakfast start in the morning?"

"Good question. Seven o'clock. We'll serve a hearty traditional breakfast to fuel you on your hikes. One more thing, we'll have coffee hour in here from nine to ten tonight, where we'll serve coffee, tea, and hot chocolate. A few of us will be around to answer more questions then. Good night, everybody."

Liz leaned over to speak to Bob as the noise level rose again. "Is that trail to the glacier the one you're planning to hike tomorrow?

"Yes."

"Mind if I come along?"

"Not at all. In fact, I'd love the company–if you think you're up to it." Bob winked.

Liz smirked. "I'm up for almost anything."

8

Reflection

Bob settled in his tent after visiting with some of his neighbors on the way to his campsite. The skies were clear, and the temperature had plummeted since he left for dinner. Fortunately, his tent had retained some of the warmth from the afternoon sun. For now, he laid on top of his mummy-style sleeping bag. His bare feet were icebergs, but they needed to breathe after being confined in his sweaty shoes all day.

He thought of his campsite at Tuolumne Meadows the night before his JMT hike, where he had met Hannah, a young solo hiker who he hiked with for over 100 miles. She brought back memories of Mark, Linda, Brock, and Jessica, a family of four on their first backpacking trip. They had formed a trail family, or tramily, which helped each other through the low spots on the trail; not those filled with water, but those where their spirits, confidence, or energy lagged. Some finished their hike as planned; some did not.

During the spring, Jessica and Hannah had both lobbied Bob to help them hike the sections of the trail they missed the year before. Hannah was old enough to hike by herself, but Jessica was only thirteen. Though she was the most determined and thoughtful teenager he knew, she was too young to backpack alone. Her mother had vowed never to backpack again, and her father had started a new job and couldn't afford to get away. And Hannah was not ready to take on the responsibility of caring for Jessica on the trail by herself after her difficult hike last year.

Bob had been Jessica's last resort, but he let her down. It pained him to do so, but he knew she would understand. Perhaps they could arrange a hike on short notice in late August before school started, but Bob had to fulfill his vow to Cathy first. Jessica knew that. Hannah knew that.

He had let Cathy down in the worst possible way. He had backed out of their JMT hike a week before they were supposed to start together. At the time, he believed things would fall apart at work if he left for three weeks. In hindsight, he was foolish. As much as it hurt, he realized his team would have done just as well without him. If he hadn't abandoned Cathy, she would still be alive. Ridden with guilt, he could only make peace with himself and Cathy by helping her finish her bucket list of hiking trips. They couldn't hike together physically anymore, but he promised to help her finish in spirit. He tackled the most spectacular and difficult, the JMT, first. But backpacking in Glacier and staying at the Sperry Chalet were next on her list.

* * *

Dear Cathy,

I was just thinking of my trail friends from the JMT. I hope I meet others on this trip. The Gunsight Pass Trail is only twenty miles, versus the 200+ miles of the JMT, so it should be relatively easy. But we both know that unforeseen challenges await, where I may need their support. At least, I know you will be with me every step of the way.

Sperry Chalet was wonderful. I was surprised when they let me eat lunch there. At dinner, the atmosphere was warm and cozy, and the food was basic and hearty. You would have loved it. I wish I could have sat across from you, watching you smile as you basked in the rustic surroundings, savored your meal, and made new friends. Listening to Chet and his staff give tips for the guests rekindled the regret I feel for missing out on a reservation. Perhaps I should have been calling twice a day instead of once.

I had company at dinner, but it wasn't the same. Liz sat across from me. She was pleasant and seemed adventurous. Since she is also alone, she plans to hike with me to Sperry Glacier tomorrow. Perhaps she will be my first trail friend. Unfortunately, the rude guy I encountered on the trail sat with us and continued to be obnoxious. What a spoiled brat! Liz gave him a mouthful. I was so proud of her. But even he couldn't ruin a wonderful evening.

I'm staring at our hiking mascot, Marty, resting in a pocket on the ceiling of the tent. I didn't see any real marmots today, but I did meet a huge mountain goat who acts like the campground host, and I expect to see many others on the way to Sperry Glacier. I'll have to watch Marty closely tomorrow so he isn't kidnapped again.

Love, Bob

IV

Day Three

July 27, 2023
Glacier National Park

9

Blockade

Footsteps on the wooden porch of the dining room interrupted Bob's gaze at the fog resting on Lake McDonald.

"Hey Bob. What a beautiful morning."

Bob stood up and faced Liz. "Good morning. How was breakfast?"

"I was surprised you weren't there."

"I ate the oatmeal I brought with me. I woke up early and needed to get rid of some weight in my pack."

"Well, the food was great; the company, not so much."

Bob frowned. "Jason?"

Liz nodded.

"What was it this time?"

"He's trying to get out of here already."

"What?" Bob's head flinched back. "I thought they were staying three days?"

"Evidently, he can't live without electricity and showers that long."

"Didn't he know about those things before?"

Liz shrugged. "That's a source of contention between him and Crystal. I think Crystal was desperate to try anything to get them out in the wilderness as a family. He tried using his cell phone to call the pack horse company, but couldn't get a signal. Chet told him he might find better reception up on Lincoln Pass, but he wanted no part of that. Chet agreed to try to contact them, but only after breakfast was over."

Bob looked down and shook his head. "Oh boy. On one hand, I wish they'd pick him up this morning, but then Crystal and Thomas would be devastated. They're really looking forward to hiking."

Liz waved her hand toward the corner of the patio from which she came. "Let's go. At least we won't have to deal with Jason again until we return from our hike."

"Yes, ma'am."

Liz scowled at him and walked around the corner, nearly bumping into Philip. He grabbed her shoulders to steady her balance.

"Oops. Sorry, Phillip."

"I'm OK. Hey … I wanted to thank you for last night."

"We're the ones who are grateful," Bob said. "Dinner was wonderful."

"Yeah, but I was talking about standing up to Jason. I was biting my lip the whole time. You know, 'the customer is always right.'"

"That's bullshit!" Liz barked. Her head bobbed with each syllable. "I used to be in the restaurant business, so I understand how hard your job is, especially up here. No one deserves to be treated that way."

"Thanks. You're right. The limited supply runs, lack of electricity, and small crew make work up here difficult. Generally, the customers are delighted to be here and very grateful, but every once in a while …"

Bob patted him on the shoulder. "Hey, don't let him get you down and keep up the good work. You've treated me like a king."

Phillip smiled. "Are you two hiking together today?"

"Yep," said Liz. "We're taking your advice–Sperry Glacier. Hope you don't let us down."

"Great! Have a wonderful time and be careful."

* * *

A few minutes after they turned off the trail they had hiked up yesterday, they entered a natural amphitheater of multicolored rock, white ribbons of water falling a thousand feet, and greens of all shades. The trail clung to the side of a horseshoe-shaped wall of rock.

Bob was fascinated by the variety of rock on the mountainside. For most of JMT, he was surrounded by grayish white granite, which weathered mostly in rounded formations, like Half Dome in Yosemite. Here, the layers of different colored rocks indicated they were sedimentary in nature, mostly limestones and shales. He couldn't identify all the colors for certain, but he thought he saw lots of grays, blacks, greens, and reds, accented by a few whites and yellows.

He tried to imagine the geological forces that turned the layers of rock on their side and created the wavy patterns, but they were beyond his comprehension. He felt a sense of awe and respect for Mother Nature. Her power radiated from the trail, through his legs, to his soul. As a safety manager at a chemical plant, such power scared him and drove him to try to control it in every way possible. Here, he had no control; he could only be prepared. This must be why Cathy couldn't stay away. *I get it now!*

Bob led the way since Liz had not had a chance to research the trail like he had. He pointed at the top of the rock wall at the middle of the bend of the horseshoe. "There are only two ways out of this basin: the trail we just took and over that rock wall. Are you sure you're up to it?"

"If you can do it, so can I."

Liz smiled and walked around Bob to their first obstacle, a massive pile of talus stacked at a forty-five degree angle. The trail consisted of smaller rocks filling the gaps between the larger native rocks to create a more stable walking surface. Just like the cobbles he dreaded on the JMT, the rocks screeched as they ground against each other under their footsteps and caused a chill to rise up Bob's spine. At least they would be through this in a few minutes.

Near the middle of the horseshoe, one of the ribbons of water which appeared to be so thin moments ago splashed onto a thirty-foot section of trail. Bob held his breath as Liz jogged across a metal bridge lying on large, flat rocks at each end and anchored with steel cables. Bob suspected the park service removed it at the end of the hiking season to prevent avalanches and the spring snowmelt from carrying it away. Liz showed him the biggest smile he had seen since Jessica's on the JMT. She put her hands on her hips while Bob shuffled across, using both of his hiking poles.

Liz resumed walking, but Bob said, "Hold on just a minute, please." He took off his backpack, filled only with his snacks and bare essentials for the day, and removed Marty. "Can you hold him while I take his picture by the waterfall?"

Liz shrugged, grabbed the plush marmot, and posed as requested. "What's his story?"

"I'll explain when we get to the top. For now, let's just say that I've learned the hard way not to set him free next to running water."

Liz tossed Marty back to Bob. He panicked inside as he reached out to catch Marty, but tried to disguise it.

They continued to the end of the horseshoe, did a U-turn, and began climbing steeply. A flat rock shelf about midway up the rock wall was now visible. As they approached the shelf, Liz said, "I think we're almost there."

Bob, however, was well-conditioned to false summits and let her down easily.

"Not quite. That looks like an intermediate shelf, then we have one last push to the top."

Liz took one step forward then stopped suddenly.

"Look! Mountain goats. And a little baby. He's so cute."

She grabbed her phone and took pictures. Bob stepped up to her side and did the same. A snow white adult with short, but sharp, black horns stared at them from the rocks above the trail, while a kid walked nearby and nibbled on grass between the rocks.

"Cool. I saw an even bigger one at the campground last night, hanging out by the food preparation area. When you're done with your pictures, let's walk by slowly so we don't spook them. If they move suddenly, they could kick rocks down on us."

Bob followed on Liz's heels as they crept by. Gravel fell on the trail in front of them as the kid scampered closer to its mother. The mama goat peered at them as they passed, ready to defend her kid if needed.

The shelf was not only rock, but an oasis of small ponds and patches of grass mixed with boulders which had fallen from the rock wall above. The area reminded him of Evolution Basin along the JMT. Because of their sedimentary origin, boulders here broke into large cubes with sharp edges instead of the rounded shapes he observed in the Sierra last summer. Bob struggled to keep his balance as he spun his head around to soak in the views while walking along the trail.

Liz stared at the rock wall in front of them. "Are you sure we can get over that wall? I'm game for almost anything, but not rock climbing."

"Yes, there's a way, and you're going to love it. I can't see where it is yet, but I've seen it on hiking videos. No spoilers. You'll know it when you see it."

Liz allowed Bob to take the lead for a change. They walked along the base of a vertical wall of rock until the trail appeared to end abruptly. Bob looked to his right, and whispered, "Woowwww." His mouth remained fully open.

A four-foot-wide staircase blasted through the wall would take them up the final sixty feet to Comeau Pass. Bob was amazed by the feats the trail builders could accomplish in such remote areas at high elevation. He was winded just climbing the trail, much less carrying heavy tools and rocks. They had even been considerate enough to attach a steel cable to the side to provide a handrail.

Liz stepped beside him to see what had caused him to stop.

"Wow! This is so cool. I'm glad you didn't spoil the surprise. She put her arm around him briefly and squeezed until their sides touched. She pulled her arm back when Bob turned his attention from the chute above them to her face.

Liz stepped in front of him and started climbing the stairs. "Let's go. This will be fun."

"Uh … Liz … hold on a second."

She turned around, ready to pose for a picture, but Bob pointed to the top of the staircase where a large white face with black horns stared down at them.

"Uh-oh."

The goat descended the stairs, and another took its place at the top. Liz backed down the few steps she had climbed while Bob held her elbow to prevent her from tripping.

When the first goat was halfway down, it sat on one of the wider steps.

"Seems like a good time for a snack break," he said.

Not only was it a good time for a break but also a great place. Bob realized he hadn't looked behind him enough during the climb when he turned and saw the peaceful tarns in the foreground and the rugged mountain walls in the background. They retraced their steps out of the goat's view, sat down, and took snacks out of their packs. Bob opened a plastic bag of roasted and salted nuts, and Liz opened a granola bar.

10

Scramble

Thomas grabbed the door handle. "Dad, are you sure you don't want to come? It's a short hike."

"I'm sure. You two go ahead. I'm sore from riding that damn horse yesterday. I'll stay here and read."

Thomas left the room and shook his head as he walked toward his mother.

"Thanks for trying," she said.

His mom marched toward the trail just dozens of feet from the dormitory building and turned right. What a fantastic location. Last night, he had gone back to the dining room for coffee hour to escape from his bickering parents and have some hot chocolate. When he had asked Phillip about a good beginner trail, he recommended the hike to Lincoln Peak. Phillip told him that an easy one-mile hike would bring them to Lincoln Pass. From there, he could climb another 150 feet to the top of Lincoln Peak for a much better view of Lincoln Lake. Such a jaunt wouldn't be enough of a challenge for his mother, given her fitness and her hiking experience from her youth, but it would provide him a taste without regretting it tomorrow.

He stopped at the sign for the Sperry Campground. His mother sped ahead, so he didn't linger. This must be where Bob stayed last night. Maybe Bob would show him around later since his mother seemed to have no interest in such a detour.

Thomas occasionally lost sight of his mom as the trail weaved back and forth up to the pass. Now he understood why she insisted they each carry a can of bear spray. About thirty minutes later, he paused to see how much further he had to hike, and his mom was already standing on top of the pass. What a climbing machine. She must be taking out years of frustration of foregone hikes on this short trail. He almost felt sorry for the ground she pounded with her feet.

He breathed heavily as he reached the flat ground she was standing on. Her breathing was the same as when she walked from the dining room to the dormitory at the chalet. *And I'm thirty years younger! I need to do something about this.*

She patted him on the back. "Way to go! Welcome to Lincoln Pass." She pointed to the left. "The Gunsight Pass Trail continues along the side of the mountain there. Lake Ellen Wilson must be around the bend."

She stepped off the trail and walked down the steep slope to stand on a large boulder. She looked back at him and beckoned him with her arm. "Come on down. You can see Lincoln Lake from here."

"Um … that's OK. The view from here is nice."

"Come on. You can make it."

Thomas took small steps down the slope, slid the last couple of feet on loose rocks, and stopped himself by placing his hands on the boulder. "Whoa!"

His mom laughed. She scooted over to one side and pulled him up next to her. "Look, down there."

"Nice, but you can only see part of the lake from here. Phillip said we could climb a small peak to get a better view."

His mom surveyed the peak to their right. "I see a faint climber's trail over there."

"What? That?"

She nodded.

"That doesn't look like much of a trail. It goes straight up and is very rocky, like the rocks I just slid on."

"We'll be fine. Just follow me and take your time."

His mother jumped off the boulder and scrambled over to the climber's trail. When she waved him over, he reluctantly sat on the boulder, slid down until his feet were on the ground, and fought his way back to the main trail. As he tried to catch up with his mother, the tips of his shoes slid when he tried to push off, twice causing him to put his hands on the path in front of his face.

His mother reached out to help him up. "This is going to be so much fun. If it's too steep, weave back and forth like the main trail did on the way up here. You don't have to stay on the beaten path. Make your own switchbacks. That's what makes scrambling so much fun."

Despite her own advice, his mom marched straight up the trail no matter how much her feet slid. When she encountered a rockier section, she hopped from rock to rock to rock effortlessly.

She looked back after climbing about one hundred feet. "Come on. I'll wait for you here."

Thomas weaved through the slick section to lessen the grade. Instead of hopping on the rocks, he paused before each step to identify the most stable rock to step on next.

"There you go."

"That was fun. You can go ahead now. I'll be fine."

He sped up as he gained confidence. When the trail became faint, he looked up to spot his mother to ensure he was on the right track. However, the peak was so small he could hardly get lost. *If in doubt, just head up.*

About fifteen minutes later, he heard, "Whoa! Thomas. Wait until you see this view."

Thomas's heart pounded and his breathing was labored, so he couldn't alter his steady pace. When he arrived at the top, his mother wasn't alone. A girl not much older than himself sat with a straw hat on her head and a sketch pad on her lap.

"Thomas, come over here."

"Hold … on."

He put his hands on his hips. His entire torso bobbed as he struggled to catch his breath. He smiled and nodded at the girl. She grinned and said, "Hi."

Or is she holding back a giggle instead of grinning? Great, she must think I'm a wimp.

He was finally able to say, "Hi," then walked over to his mother. She still wasn't winded.

"Wow. Phillip knows his stuff," Thomas said.

Water fell down a cliff over 1000 feet from one lake to another.

"Look, we can see part of Lake Ellen Wilson from here," said his mom. "That must be where the water comes from. And there, you can see all of Lincoln Lake now."

Thomas turned toward the girl and pointed at the higher lake. "Is that Lake Ellen Wilson?"

"Sure is."

"Awesome."

She nodded and raised her sketch pad. "That's why I'm up here with this. I have the best job ever."

"I'm Thomas, and this is my mom, Crystal."

His mom waved, but then returned her attention to the view.

"My name is Eva. I'm a resident artist staying at the chalet."

Thomas turned back to admire the outstanding scenery. The rock wall down which the water fell reminded him of the massive dams built on the Colorado River. As he scanned the mountainside, he saw other waterfalls oozing out of snowfields high above Lake Ellen Wilson.

His mother wrapped her arm around him. "I've missed this so much. Thanks for coming with me. If we could just get your father interested."

"We'll try again tomorrow. A few great pictures might help."

Thomas took a few steps toward the artist. "Eva, would you mind taking a few pictures of us?"

"No problem." She closed her sketch pad, put a fist-sized rock on top of the cover, and stood up. Thomas handed her his phone.

After snapping several shots with both lakes in the background, Thomas took back his phone and snapped shots of the beautiful scene on its own.

"Thanks."

A few minutes later, they sat next to Eva and pulled the water bottles out of their backpacks.

"I didn't know Sperry had a resident artist," said his mom.

Eva nodded. "Yeah. I was surprised to hear about it as well and thrilled to be selected."

"What exactly do you do?" asked his mother.

She held her arms out. "This!"

"Who do you draw for?" Thomas asked.

"Sometimes for the organizations supporting the chalet, but also for guests. Would you like me to sketch you something real quick?" She picked up her sketchbook.

Thomas looked at his mom, then said, "Sure. You can do that?"

"Of course. That's what I do."

She opened the book to a blank page. Her pencil whisked about the paper in seemingly random directions for the next twenty minutes as they discussed what it was like to live at the chalet. Most of the guests were great to be around, but some required a lot of patience on her part. He and his mom glanced at each other and grinned.

"How long are you up here for?" he asked.

"A couple of weeks."

"And you don't have electricity or a cell signal. How do you manage without the internet, videos, staying in touch with family–"

Eva took a break from sketching. "Just fine. I wanted to get away from all that. It was mostly weighing me down. I have to admit, it's a little harder than I thought. We have a little power from the solar panels to keep our devices charged, and I have a weak cell signal at the chalet most of the time. And up here, the reception is pretty good. To be honest, I'm quite busy drawing and helping out at the chalet. And when I'm not, I get to do this."

"Wow. A part of me is jealous, but I don't think I could make it more than a week without all that stuff," said Thomas.

Eva snorted. "Sure you could. How long are you staying up here?"

"Three days."

Eva raised her eyebrows. "Oh, that's good. Most people only stay one night, a few stay two. Let me know how you feel after three." She grinned.

His mother left to explore the rest of the small peak and seek different views.

Shortly after she returned, Eva flipped the pad around so they could see the sketch. "All done!"

His mom brought her hand over her mouth. "Wow! It's beautiful. Now I see why they selected you. You're very talented."

Eva blushed. "Thank you. I've had a lot of practice with this scene, being so close to the chalet. Hey, why don't I leave this on the tablet until we get back to the chalet so it doesn't get wrinkled?"

"Good idea. Thanks again," said his mom.

On the way back to the main trail, Thomas now had two women monitoring his progress. Going down such a path was much trickier than going up, and he didn't want to embarrass himself in front of such a fascinating girl by sliding down on his butt. When they were back on the pass, his mother looked as if she was being beckoned to the east.

"Thomas, can we keep hiking down the trail until we can see all of Lake Ellen Wilson?"

Her eyes and lips pleaded with him. She had been waiting to explore areas like this for much too long.

He looked back at Eva. "I don't know, Mom. Climbing that peak took a lot out of me."

"Actually, the next mile or two isn't too hard," Eva said. "I need to head back to the chalet, but you should go."

He turned from his mom to Eva and back again. "OK, Mom. Let's go. But please slow down a little."

"You two have fun. Let me know when you return so I can give you the sketch."

11

Connecting

Bob sensed Liz staring at him as he ate his snack.

"What?" he asked. Did she expect him to read her mind after less than a day together?

"You owe me a story."

"A story?"

"Marty."

"Oh, yeah. Are you sure you want to hear it?" He stared at the vast valley below. "It's kind of a sad story."

"Oh, really? Sorry … but, yeah, I'd like to get to know you better."

"I bought Marty for my wife … my late wife … I'm a widower …"

Liz placed her hand on his knee. "I'm so sorry, Bob. I didn't know. That's something else we have in common. I'm a widow."

Bob looked into her eyes, but before he could say more, she said, "Go ahead. Please."

"Sorry to hear that. Well, she loved to hike and backpack in the mountains and always came back with dozens of photos of marmots."

Liz furrowed her eyebrows. "Came back? You weren't with her?"

"Sometimes. But most of the time, no. I found it hard to pull myself away from work. I was a safety manager at a chemical plant and was convinced someone would get hurt if I wasn't there to protect them. She finally started going without me. I'm retired now, but a couple of years too late."

"What do you mean—oops, sorry for interrupting."

"Two years ago, we planned to hike the John Muir Trail together. It's over two hundred miles, so no simple feat. We thought it would take us about three weeks."

Liz's eyes grew large. "Three weeks! Wow! That's ambitious, even for me."

"Yeah. We had the permit, we shipped our food ahead, and we were in the best shape of our lives. But there was a big problem at the plant, and I backed out of the trip the week before."

"No! You didn't." Liz covered her mouth with her hand.

Bob nodded and sniffled. "I know it wasn't much, but I bought her this plush marmot to keep her company on her hike." He wiped his eyes with his shirt sleeves. "Well, she never came back. She died on the trail."

He sobbed now and stared down the valley. When he mustered the courage to look at her, she put her arm around him instead of looking at him with shame or questioning his poor judgment.

"How terrible. You poor man."

"Don't feel sorry for me. I really could have gone. I could have saved her. We should still be hiking together."

Liz pulled him closer.

"Once she was gone, I committed to help her finish her bucket list of hikes. The JMT was on top of the list, but this hike, specifically Sperry Chalet, was second."

"What a great way to remember her. What was her name?" Liz raised her arm and patted him on the shoulder.

"Cathy."

Bob stood up and wiped his eyes again. "Let me check if the goats are still guarding the pass."

He returned to the chute. The goat on the landing seemed comfortable—too comfortable. Bob wondered whether he would be able to show Sperry Glacier to Cathy—and Liz—after all. He had already missed out on a night in the chalet. For Cathy, he would wait here for hours if he had to. But would that be fair to Liz?

As he walked back toward Liz, he heard someone yell, "Move, goat! Move. Damn it."

Bob turned around. The large goat emerged from the chute and headed straight for him. Bob sped up and grabbed Liz's arm when he reached her.

"Hurry. Get out of the way."

"What–Oh!"

He pulled her up and hurried further down the trail.

They stopped a hundred feet later. The goat had descended the steep slope below the trail, and a young male hiker jogged toward them.

"That damn goat was interrupting my run."

"You're running this?" asked Liz.

"Yep. Gotta go."

They stepped aside and allowed him to pass.

Liz jogged toward the chute. "Come on, before another goat blocks the way."

Bob's knees refused to jog. Liz built a gap between them and darted up the chute. By the time Bob arrived, she was halfway up.

"How cool!" Liz's voice echoed in the narrow chute.

Bob grabbed both hiking poles in his left hand and used the wire handrail to climb to the top. When he emerged from the chute, he whispered, "Wow," as he opened his mouth wide and admired the peaks, glaciers, and–more goats.

Liz's head swung like a pendulum from one horizon to another. "This is amazing."

She wrapped her arms around Bob. "Thanks for letting me come along. I can't believe I was so close and almost missed this place. I guess I should have done a little more research before this trip."

Though they hadn't finished their snacks earlier, they explored the area thoroughly. Patches of snow clung to the mountains on their right. Sperry Glacier had receded so much that Bob couldn't tell which were snowfields and which were remnants of the glacier. The cool breeze flowing over the ice and their sweaty shirts chilled them. A pointed triangular peak named Little Matterhorn blocked their view to the left. They walked over rock with grooves scoured into it over millennia by the moving ice and somehow crossed the small streams of meltwater without getting their feet wet. Three goats followed fifty feet behind, impatiently waiting for them to drop some food or leave some of their gear unattended. When they topped the ridge, he saw Avalanche Lake below.

"Oh my gosh! I was way down there a couple days ago," said Liz. "I can't believe I'm at the top of the mountains I saw from the beach. No wonder yesterday's hike was so hard."

"I haven't made it there yet. Is it worth the hike? It appeared to be too easy to be any good when I read the trail guide."

"Oh yeah. Do it. The trail follows a gorge through a rainforest. It's a wonderful hike."

"Hmm." Bob raised his eyebrows. "Maybe I'll do that on my way back to the airport at the end of the trip. But the first priority is this backpacking trip for Cathy."

Liz surveyed the rocky surface surrounding them. "Let's sit here and finish our snack."

Once they had resumed eating, Bob said, "OK. So I told my story. Do you feel comfortable sharing yours?"

"Mine is a little more typical, but tragic nonetheless. David and I both worked and had a son. Seems like all we did was work and raise Alan. Then one day, David didn't wake up. He was lying right next to me, and I had no idea he was gone. The coroner said he had a massive stroke. There was nothing I could have done."

"How awful! You poor thing." He began to reach around her, but placed his hand on her nearest shoulder instead.

"After Alan finished college, I buried myself in my work. Like I said earlier, I was in the restaurant business, so that wasn't hard to do."

Bob nodded in acknowledgment.

"I never thought I'd find another David, so I didn't bother trying."

"So, you've gotten out of the restaurant business?"

"Yeah. Sold it all. Retired. My mother was alone and ailing, so I wanted to spend more time with her. She's gone now as well."

Bob rubbed her back, just below the neck. "Wow, you've been through some tough times as well."

Liz's lips quivered. She paused. "She was all alone. I was the only one she had. I don't want to end up like that." She sniffled then took a deep breath.

How could she be so composed?

They sat in silence, both staring at the surrounding peaks, but he only saw a blurred landscape. No sharp peaks, no more layers in the rocks, no streams flowing down the mountainside. Just a gray blur.

Liz broke his spell. "Anyway, that's why I'm staying at the chalet alone. It must seem odd to some people, a single woman in the wilderness, but I had no one else to go with."

"Why's that so strange?" Bob pointed to his own chest. "I'm doing the same."

"Yeah, but you're a guy. It's different." She squeezed her empty wrapper into a ball. "But you know what? I don't care. I won't let them or anyone else stop me from enjoying myself."

"Good for you."

Liz put her snack wrapper in her pocket, so Bob ate the last bite of his sausage stick and put the wrapper back in his food bag. She stood up and offered to help him up.

"Come on. Let's lighten things up a bit." She began walking and waved her hand forward.

About halfway back to the pass, she veered toward a small snowfield.

"Can I have Marty please?"

Bob pulled Marty out of his pack and handed him to her.

"Be careful with him. He's only got a couple of lives left, at most."

"We're going glissading."

"What! Are you crazy?"

"Nope. Just living."

She climbed the rocks around the snowfield until she was 100 feet above him.

Bob didn't budge.

"Come on!"

"No way. It's too dangerous."

Liz waved him up. "Oh, come on, safety man. It's short and not very steep."

Bob shook his head.

Liz pouted, then walked to the middle of the snowfield, flattening the snow under each foot before putting her full weight on it. Bob held his breath. She sat down, gave herself a push, and screamed as she picked up speed. Bob edged forward toward the bottom of the snowfield. Halfway down, she reached back to dig her fingers in the snow, but they just slid over the surface. She slid off the ice into a small stream collecting the meltwater and yelled, "Whoa!"

Bob ran toward her, but slowed down when she started laughing while lying flat on her back in the stream.

Bob helped her up and watched the water drip from her arms, shirt, and pants.

"Are you OK?"

"Of course. Just a little wet."

"And a little crazy."

She shrugged.

Bob opened his pack and removed the sweatshirt he had worn early in the morning until the uphill hiking had warmed him up.

"Here, you can wear this so you don't get chilled on the way down. Sorry, not much I can do for your pants, unless you want to watch me hike down in boxer briefs."

Liz looked down at his dry pants and grinned. She pulled her shirt over her head without turning around. She tried to hand it to Bob, but he had turned away.

"Come on, Bob. It's nothing you haven't seen before. And I'm getting all wrinkled anyway."

Bob looked at her, grabbed her wet shirt, and gave her his sweatshirt. He told his eyes not to linger, but he didn't see many wrinkles.

Liz put the sweatshirt on, then reached down to remove Marty from the water. She squeezed a few ounces of water out of him.

"Sorry," Liz said with a wide grin. "Another of his lives gone. How many do marmots get anyway?"

"I don't know. He's already living on borrowed time."

She tossed him back to Bob, probably just to see him flinch again.

"Let's head back before you get too cold. Hopefully, the goats aren't blocking our way down the chute."

"Bob."

He turned around, and her arms surrounded him. She had squeezed the air out of him, so he was barely able to respond.

"Yes?"

"Thank you so much. I know you may have preferred to hike alone–to be with Cathy. But this is the most fun I've had in years."

<h1 style="text-align:center">12</h1>

<h1 style="text-align:center">Progress</h1>

Thomas and his mom found his dad eating lunch in the dining room. Thomas knew better than to ask if the food was any good. Food and drink, or the lack thereof, had become a trigger point for his dad. Once he and his mom had made their own lunch choices, Thomas showed Eva's sketch to his father.

"You won't believe this. The chalet has a resident artist. We met her on top of Lincoln Peak, and she drew this for us."

His dad raised his eyebrows, pursed his lips, and nodded. "A resident artist, huh! That's a nice drawing. How much did it cost?"

"Nothing. She drew it for us while we talked."

Thomas took his phone out of his pocket and found the pictures from the peak. "And here's what it looks like for real."

"Wow. That's nice, really nice." His dad scrolled through the pictures. "And you two look so happy. How hard was the hike?"

"It was pretty easy. Mom gave me some good tips along the way. She's a hiking machine."

His mom smiled.

His dad glanced at his mom. "That's what I'm afraid of. The hike must have been hard at some point. Weren't you climbing a mountain peak?"

"Yeah, but the peak was only about 150 feet above the pass," he said. "It was kind of steep, and I slipped here and there, but it wasn't hard. If I can do it, you can too."

His father tilted his head down and looked from him to his mom.

"What?" his mom said. "He's telling the truth. Anyone could do it. After Lincoln Peak, we hiked another mile and a half to get a good view of Lake Ellen Wilson, the bigger lake in the photos."

Claire brought their chicken noodle soup and ham and cheese sandwiches.

"Thanks," said his mom.

Claire pointed to the sketch. "You must have run into Eva. Isn't she great? We love having her here. She loves to draw, and she makes the guests so happy."

Thomas smiled wide then said, "She sure is!"

His mom smirked.

"What?" he asked.

"Oh, nothing. I agree." A smile replaced her smirk.

Claire gave a thumbs up and walked off.

"Dad—Mom and I were talking on the way back—"

His dad stopped chewing. "Uh-oh. That sounds like trouble."

His mom playfully slapped his dad's hand on the table, and Thomas continued. "Seriously. We'd like to hike to Sperry Glacier tomorrow. It's a little longer, but it's supposed to be even more beautiful. Will you please come with us? You just said how happy we looked. I think you would be happy as well."

Thomas almost mentioned the recommendation came from Phillip, but after the exchange at dinner last night, he thought it best not to. It would be difficult enough to convince his dad already.

"I don't know. Maybe I should try something easier for my first hike."

"The whole hike is supposed to be beautiful, so we can turn around at any point and still have fun."

"Come on, Jason. Please. Thomas had so much fun. What else are you going to do?"

His dad tossed his napkin on the table. "Well, you have a point. My phone will be dead soon, so I won't have much else to do." He glanced at the sketch again.

"OK. I'll give it a try." He pointed his finger at each of them. "But I'm warning you, if you guys leave me behind, I'm turning around. And I'm not getting anywhere near those goats. I don't like the way they look at me."

"You saw goats?" asked his mom.

"Yeah. They were hanging around the dining room when I came over for lunch. You didn't see them?"

He and his mom shook their heads.

"Don't worry, we'll make sure you have fun," said Thomas, who then devoured his sandwich.

13

Invitation

After Bob and Liz returned to the chalet, they sat on the massive rock steps outside the dormitory building.

"Looks like your pants are mostly dry. Were you cold?"

"A little bit, but I'd do it all over again, except I'd try not to drop Marty in the water." She leaned over and bumped her shoulder against his.

"That was a great hike. Much better than the steep slog through the trees yesterday. And the rest of the Gunsight Pass Trail should be just as good or better. We'll get to see Lake Ellen Wilson and Gunsight Lake. And there's a hut or shelter on Gunsight Pass."

"Um … Bob."

"Yeah?"

"You said you really wanted to stay in the chalet–"

"Yeah. I tried for months to get a reservation and even checked for a cancelation when I arrived yesterday. I'm eating dinner here again tonight; that's the best I can do. I think Cathy will understand."

"But you can stay at the chalet."

Bob squinted as he looked at Liz.

"My room has two double beds, and one will be empty, just like it was last night. You're welcome to stay in my room."

Bob squirmed and didn't reply right away. He glanced at Liz, then stared at the dining room.

"It's OK, Bob. I know it sounds strange. No expectations or obligations. We're two mature adults. Heck, some would even say old folks." She chuckled. "At our age, we may not get another chance at anything."

"I don't know …"

"Well, you said staying here was second on Cathy's bucket list. You can make it happen if you want to. It's your choice."

"Of course, I want to … are you sure it's OK? We just met."

"Hey, the walls are so thin that if you try any funny business, everyone will know."

Liz showed him another of the sarcastic grins he was beginning to enjoy.

"OK." He nodded slowly. "You talked me into it. That's so nice of you."

He wasn't convinced he had made the right decision, but he forced a smile anyway. He didn't mind spending another night at the campground. But Cathy really wanted to stay here. She had placed Sperry Chalet on her bucket list specifically, not just Glacier NP or the Gunsight Pass Trail. She was devastated when it burned to the ground. But would she want it this way?

Bob had been so distracted by Liz's proposal that he hadn't noticed she was now leaning against him. He stood up slowly so she wouldn't fall over, then helped her up. She groaned as she straightened her legs.

So, that's not just an old man thing.

"I'll go pack up camp and meet you back here in a couple of hours. By then, it should be close to dinner time again. Seems like all we do here is walk and eat. It will be nice not to pack up in the morning when everything is cold and wet. That's one of my least favorite parts of backpacking."

"OK. See you later. Room 10."

14

Tour

Thomas came out of the dormitory building as Liz reached for the door handle.

"Hi, Thomas."

He smiled at her briefly and said, "Hi," before yelling to Bob.

"Bob, are you going up to the campground now?"

"Yeah."

"Can I come with you? I'd like to see what it's like and what gear you have."

"Sure. Just get your bear spray and tell your parents where you'll be."

Thomas said, "OK," and walked through the door Liz was still holding open.

She looked at Bob and shrugged, then entered the dormitory herself.

When Thomas returned, Bob asked him about his hike.

"Great. My mom and I had a blast. We hiked up to Lincoln Peak, then continued on the Gunsight Pass Trail until we could see all of Lake Ellen Wilson."

"Liz and I are headed that way tomorrow. How was the lake?"

"I haven't seen a lot of mountain lakes, but my mom was pretty impressed. Deep blue. Waterfalls filling it from the mountainsides and falling out the other end into Lincoln Lake."

"Nice. Did your dad go with you?"

Thomas shook his head, then smiled. "No, but when he saw the photos, he agreed to go to Sperry Glacier with us tomorrow. I can't wait."

"That's fantastic, but let me give you some advice. That trail is more difficult. Go easy on him. You may need to turn around before the end if he gets frustrated. Baby steps!" Bob winked. "Liz and I hiked it today. It's beautiful the entire way, so you won't be too disappointed if you stop before the end. Heck, we almost had to turn around near the end when goats blocked the way up the pass."

His head lurched forward and eyes grew large. "Goats?"

"Lots of them. Just keep your distance and move slowly."

Thomas winced. "Uh-oh. My dad said he wasn't going anywhere near goats. Let's keep that as our little secret, OK?"

"I don't think it's much of a secret, but OK." Bob zipped his lips shut.

They arrived at a sign for the trail junction with a map of the campground attached. "See here. This campground has four designated spots, a pit toilet, and a food prep and storage area."

Bob pointed to the enclosed pit toilet off to the left. Thomas went over and opened the door. He pinched his nose as he walked back toward Bob.

"Hey, don't knock it. That's a luxury. On the John Muir Trail, there was no place to sit down and no walls. I had to squat behind a tree and go. Tough to do with sore thighs."

"Really?"

Bob nodded.

They passed one empty campsite, then Bob pointed to his tent at the next one. "Let me show you the food prep area before I show you my gear."

They passed one more occupied site and another empty site before arriving at an open area with four logs forming a square. A table made from rock slabs sat in the middle.

"This is also a luxury. Next best thing to a picnic table, but probably a lot more durable."

He pointed to the horizontal metal pole, fifteen feet off the ground, supported by two vertical poles. "And you can hang your food bag on that pole so the bears, goats, and marmots can't get to it. I have a bear canister at my campsite, so I don't need to use it."

"Wow, I didn't know you had to be so careful with food."

"It's mostly to protect the bears. If they associate food with people, they seek them out and become aggressive. Once that happens, the park service may have to put them down. Plus, it keeps the squirrels and marmots from chewing on everything."

Thomas frowned, then looked at the horizon toward Lake McDonald. "And what a view."

Bob led Thomas back down the path to his campsite. "Here is home, sweet home. Well, at least it was last night."

"What do you mean?"

Bob hesitated for a couple of seconds. "Uh, Liz offered to let me stay in her extra bed, so I'm staying at the chalet tonight."

Thomas tried to hide his grin, but it broke through his defenses.

Bob grinned back. "It's not what you think."

"OK, if you say so. It's none of my business anyway."

"Do you want to get in my tent, then help me take it down?"

"Yeah. That would be cool."

"Go ahead. Excuse the mess. Pretty much everything in my pack gets spread all over the floor of the tent. I like to keep all my gear in the tent, away from the critters."

Thomas got in and laid down on top of the sleeping bag, which rested on a two-inch-thick air pad.

"This isn't bad. I figured you'd be lying on the hard ground."

Bob chuckled. "Not these old bones. Plus, the ground is cold at night and sucks the heat out of you. The sleeping bag is warmer than it appears. I'm comfortable down to at least thirty-five degrees."

Thomas crawled out of the tent. "Where is that bear canister you talked about?"

Bob retrieved it from under a nearby bush and handed it to him.

Thomas nearly dropped it before setting it on the ground. "Wow. That's heavy. I wouldn't want to carry that around very long."

"The heaviest thing in my pack. Try to open it."

Thomas tried unscrewing the black lid from the blue, heavy duty plastic can, but it kept getting stuck.

"I give up."

Bob showed him how easily it unscrewed when pressing a couple of inconspicuous tabs.

"Ahhh."

"This is so cool, Bob. I wish I could camp like this. My mom would love it–but my dad thinks the only good vacations are on cruise ships. They're nice, but my mom and I get so bored." He paused. "I don't know if she'll put up with him much longer. This trip might be the final straw. She hiked a lot when she was young, and I think she's tired of waiting to get back to it."

"Sorry about that. Like I said, don't push it tomorrow. Take lots of breaks to enjoy the views. You'll see a magnificent waterfall in the first mile."

"He loved the photos from Lincoln Peak, so maybe that will work."

"And if he does well, try a little further the next day. Maybe over to Lake Ellen Wilson. There are so many wonderful sights around here. It's a great home base."

He paused to survey the entire campsite again.

"Thanks for the tour–and the advice. Do you need any help packing up?"

"Sure, you can help with the tent. Have a seat while I pack everything inside."

Bob picked up his backpack from inside the tent and pointed to a long pocket on the side. "The tent goes right here."

While Bob was packing, he poked his head out of the tent several times to show Thomas some of the more interesting pieces of gear, like his water filter, headlamp, patch kit for his sleeping pad, gas stove and fuel canister, and even a little rechargeable pump used to inflate the sleeping pad. The more Thomas learned, the more he wanted to try this for himself. But he couldn't imagine his father doing so. Based on his father's reaction when they had arrived yesterday, his father thought staying at the chalet was roughing it. One step at a time. Get him hiking, then go from there. He'd have to look after his dad carefully tomorrow–and protect him from his overzealous mother–and the goats.

15

Newlyweds

When Bob returned to the dormitory building, he found the door to room 10 cracked open. He knocked softly and heard no response, so he nudged the door open further and peeked inside.

"Liz?"

She was lying in bed under a blanket. Her eyes opened, and she sat up enough to lean on her elbows.

"Hi Bob. I thought that might happen. That's why I left the door open. I needed to warm up after hiking back in wet pants. I guess all the fun caught up with me."

"Sorry to wake you. You look so relaxed."

"Please come in."

He entered the room and set his pack down against the foot of the other bed.

"Maybe you're not so invincible after all."

He looked at her with an exaggerated smile, then ducked to dodge the pillow thrown his way.

Liz was quiet while he explored the room. It was beautiful in its simplicity. A couple of beds and chairs and a small table, just enough to rest up for the next day of exploration. Similar to the simplicity of hiking, where getting from A to B was all you had to worry about. No traffic, news alerts, or solicitors banging on the door.

However, with every thought about how lucky he was to stay here tonight came worry about what Cathy would think. He now understood why it was so high on her bucket list. But was the price of staying in the chalet too high? Or was she happy he was having fun? Happy to share him with someone else?

"Bob, are you OK? Why don't you sit down?"

She sat up and patted the bed next to her. Bob sat across from her on the other bed.

"Yeah. I can't believe I'm here. Thank you so much."

"It's no problem. Really. That bed was going to be empty, or actually, covered with dirty clothes. But you know what I mean."

Bob bounced softly on the edge of the bed. "But we hardly know each other."

"So what. We had a great time today and shared some heavy stuff with each other. Neither of us can afford to wait around for good things to happen."

He mumbled, "Yeah, I learned that lesson the hard way."

"Hey, let's go to the dining room before Jason cleans them out or chases everyone away," said Liz.

The splendid hike with Liz had enabled him to forget about Jason for hours. Bob's shoulders drooped momentarily, but then he perked up.

"Sure. We never really had lunch, did we?"

Liz shook her head, ran her fingers through her hair, and put on her shoes.

* * *

When they entered the dining room, Bob saw Crystal and Thomas sitting next to a young couple full of smiles, but no Jason.

Did he ride back to the trailhead alone? Did they lock him in their room? What was going on?

Liz sat across from Crystal and next to the young lady, and Bob sat next to Thomas.

Tony and Abbie introduced themselves. They were from Nashville and on their honeymoon. Except for their smiles, the couple's appearance was full of contrast. Tony had short, curly black hair and a pale complexion, whereas Abbie's light blond hair matched the white teeth surrounded by her golden face. They both wore Glacier National Park sweatshirts, his black and hers white.

"Congratulations!" Liz said. "What a great place for a honeymoon. No distractions from family, friends, and email, only the mountains, lakes, and wildlife. But remember, we can hear through the walls in the dormitory as if they aren't there."

Abbie looked at Tony and giggled.

"Where is Jason?" Bob asked Crystal.

"He talked the kitchen staff into taking his food on the patio. I think they were happy to get rid of him after last night."

Tony looked puzzled. "What?"

Crystal froze for a moment. "You don't want to know."

Bob didn't want to go there either. "Crystal, I understand you and Thomas enjoyed your hike to Lincoln Peak and Lake Ellen Wilson. I'm glad you ventured out from the chalet."

Crystal nodded and smiled at her son. "Thomas did great. He was a little tentative at first, but he really enjoyed himself."

"I was just trying to keep up with the hiking diva here."

Crystal scowled at Thomas, but everyone else laughed.

Phillip arrived with bread and lemonade. "Hi Bob, Liz. How was your hike?"

"Fantastic," said Liz. "Except for the goat traffic jam at the pass."

"Yeah, those guys can be aggressive. Well, good, let's get you fueled back up."

"What hike was that?" asked Crystal.

"Sperry Glacier," Bob said.

She looked at Thomas. "Isn't that the hike you wanted to do tomorrow?"

He nodded.

"How was it?" asked Crystal.

"Just wonderful," Liz said. "Probably a little tougher than what you did today, but I'm sure you can handle it. And we saw plenty of snow, so I did a little glissading. Bob was too chicken to try."

Bob felt something bump his knee, probably Liz's shoe.

"Yeah, but I didn't have to hike back in wet pants, did I?"

Liz and Abbie laughed.

"I hear Jason is going with you," added Bob. "Like I told Thomas earlier, take it easy on him."

Phillip brought their serving dishes. Tonight's meal had a Thanksgiving theme: turkey and gravy, dressing, and cranberry sauce.

"Bob, thanks for showing Thomas around your campground. Did you have any problems last night?" asked Crystal.

"Not at all. Nice and toasty in my sleeping bag. No bears. The sites are spread out, so I heard no snoring. A good night."

"Did you check if they had a last-minute cancelation here?"

Bob peeked at Liz, who grinned.

Crystal looked at him, then at Liz. "What?"

Bob glanced down at the table and squirmed in his chair. "Actually–Liz invited me to stay in her room tonight since she has an extra bed."

Crystal raised her eyebrows. "Ooh!"

"Remember what Liz said about the walls," remarked Tony.

Abbie reached across the table and slapped his hand, but then laughed.

Liz finally said, "Ha ha. I'm glad you all enjoyed that, but it's purely a thank you for a great hike. You'll be the first to know if he tries anything ungentlemanly."

Bob had enough of the insinuations and asked Tony, "So, what are you two doing tomorrow?"

"We're only spending one night here. We'll be camping at Lake Ellen Wilson Campground tomorrow night, then hiking to the trailhead at Jackson Glacier Overlook the following day."

"Liz and I are heading the same way. Maybe we can start out together, but I'm sure you'll drop us before long."

"Speak for yourself," said Liz.

"Sounds great," Tony said. "Let's leave together right after breakfast so we have plenty of time to enjoy the trail."

16

Escape

Bob changed into his sleep clothes while Liz went to the restroom building to use the bathroom and wash up. The chalet had no showers for guests, but the bathrooms had running water in the sinks. A rechargeable lantern lit the room. He pulled up his wool pajama bottoms then put on the sweatshirt he had loaned to Liz after she had slid in the stream. It might be overkill for tonight, but it kept him warm on the cold nights in the tent. Plus, it was his only choice since he minimized the clothes he packed to reduce the weight on his back.

The shirt felt familiar, but the aroma was different. His stomach rose slightly. Was that guilt or excitement–or something else?

Liz walked in as he was sniffing his shoulder.

Liz covered her mouth with her hand. "Oh no. I didn't make your shirt stinky that quick, did I?"

"No, no, it's just … different. OK, I'm going to the restroom so you can change too."

When Bob returned, Liz was tucked under two blankets and was looking at her phone. He slipped under the blankets on the other bed. He hoped they would be as warm as his sleeping bag normally was. They certainly wouldn't be as confining.

"These pictures are fantastic, but they don't do the hike justice," said Liz.

"They never do."

"And here's Marty. It's so sweet that you carry him around to remember Cathy."

Bob didn't reply and rolled over to face the other way.

"I'm sorry, Bob. I shouldn't have mentioned her. This must be difficult for you."

Bob replied after a long silence. "Yes, but it's been such a wonderful day. I can't believe how fortunate I've been this week–getting the walk-up backpacking permit and now a night at Sperry Chalet."

"Liz …"

"Yeah?"

"What about your son? You couldn't get him to come with you? This may be a once in a lifetime opportunity."

Liz snapped her head back as she replied. "Huh! He's busy with his own life now. Hectic job, new girlfriend. I get to see him every Christmas–maybe again during the summer. You know how it goes. I don't want to be that clingy parent."

"Actually, I don't. Cathy and I never had kids. She couldn't …"

Bob's response was interrupted by the conversation in the next room.

"My power bank is dead. Dad, did you use all my charge?"

Bob turned toward Liz. "Uh-oh. You didn't tell me we were next to Jason's room."

Liz shrugged. "They were quiet last night. I didn't notice."

"Yes. My phone ran out of juice while you guys were off hiking," admitted Jason.

"Now I can't charge my phone. I won't be able to watch my videos," yelled Thomas.

"Sorry, if this place had power like every other hotel in the world, I wouldn't have had to do that."

"Jason, we've been through this. You should have brought more power capacity," Crystal replied.

Bob sat up and shook his head. Liz winced at every inflection. He heard shuffling next door.

"Where are you going?" asked Jason.

"Anywhere but here," yelled Thomas.

Bob's bed shook as the door slammed.

"Uh-oh," Liz whispered.

"Now see what you've done," yelled Crystal.

Bob and Liz laid back down.

"Should we go help?" asked Bob.

"Give it some time. Where else is he going to go?"

Fifteen minutes later, Crystal pleaded, "Jason, do something!"

"I'm sure he's just sitting in the dining room or on the patio. He needs to grow up."

Bob's bed frame rattled as another door slammed.

Good, maybe Thomas has returned.

His hope was short-lived. Someone pounded on their door. Liz looked at him, but didn't budge. Crystal charged in when he opened the door and nearly knocked him over. Tears ran down her cheeks, and her chin trembled. She pounded on his shoulders.

"Thom-m-mas! He's g-g-gone! Help. Pleas-s-se!"

Bob put his arm around her and escorted her to Liz's bed, where Liz was now sitting up. She patted the bed next to her. "Sit here."

Liz put her arm around Crystal once she sat down.

"Jas-s-son–"

"We know," Liz said. "We heard everything."

Crystal cried even louder.

Bob put his shoes and jacket on and took his headlamp out of his backpack.

"Try to calm down, Crystal. I'll go look for him."

Crystal took a few deep breaths, and her wails subsided.

"Did he take a light?" asked Bob.

Crystal nodded.

"Liz, why don't you two check the bathrooms and the dining room, then wait here. He'll probably come back soon."

"Sure, but where are you going?" asked Liz.

"I have a hunch."

Bob walked out the door, headed to the trail, and turned right toward Lincoln Pass.

* * *

Bob turned right at the sign for the campground. He proceeded directly to the eating area beyond all the campsites. Two red lights shone on his face as he approached. Bob was grateful both people had both switched from the harsh white lights to the more friendly red lights. He realized he had not done the same and pushed the button on top of his headlamp. "Sorry."

"Thomas?"

"Bob? How did you know I was here?"

Bob sat on the log opposite from Thomas. He looked toward the other light. "Hi. I'm Bob. Thanks for keeping Thomas company."

"No problem. Sounds like his family is really messed up. Name is Jake, by the way." The red light on Jake's head bobbed up and down.

"Thomas, I didn't know for sure, but I had a hunch."

Thomas's headlamp lit up the rock table between the logs. "I guess my mom and dad are mad?"

"I'd say more worried than mad. You know you can't stay out here, right?"

The light on Thomas's head bobbed up and down.

Jake stood up. "I'm gonna hit the sack. You don't need me here anymore, do you?"

Bob shook his head. "Thanks."

"I know your dad's being a pain in the ass. Hell, I've been mad at him too. But think of how much fun you had hiking today. And how tomorrow will be even better."

"Yeah, but then I have to go home where I have nowhere to escape." Thomas's voice rose throughout his response. The other folks at the campground would not be happy campers.

Bob sat next to Thomas and put his hand on his shoulder. "You're a strong boy. You convinced your dad to go hiking tomorrow. That's no small feat. Let's go. OK?"

89

Thomas stood up suddenly and walked down the trail. Bob followed. One of the tents glowed as they headed back to the trail.

"Have a good night, Jake," said Bob, as he passed Thomas.

About halfway back to the chalet, Bob stopped suddenly, and Thomas ran into his back.

"Bob, what the–"

Bob yelled. "Bear! Stop. Bear. Go away, bear!"

He turned his headlamp back to white light and reached down to his waist. He patted his right hip, then his left hip.

His shoulders drooped. "Uh-oh!"

"What's wrong?"

"Do you have your bear spray?"

He reached his right hand behind him, like a relay sprinter waiting for the baton.

"No. I left in a hurry." Thomas stepped up to his side.

"Me too. Stay behind me."

"But I want to see the bear."

Bob swept Thomas behind him with his arm, then waved his arms high above his head.

"Get out of here, bear!" he yelled, but the darkness seemed to absorb the noise.

He stopped waving his arms. Wait, unless this was a polar bear, it wasn't a bear at all.

Bob aimed his light at the white creature, which was perfectly still and stared at him. Two ten-inch, black horns rose from the top of its head.

Thomas took a couple of steps back and imitated Bob's gestures and screams. "Run, bear, run."

"Calm down, Thomas. It's not a bear. It's the big goat that hangs around the campground."

Thomas stepped up to Bob's side again.

"But it's coming toward us." Thomas retreated behind Bob, and they crept backward.

Bob clapped his hands above his head and in front of him.

The goat kept walking toward them, faster. He acted as if he was guarding the campground or enforcing a curfew.

Thomas kicked a rock on the trail and lost his balance. He grabbed the back of Bob's jacket to stop his fall.

Lights approached on the other side of the goat.

"Watch out. Aggressive goat on the trail," Bob yelled.

"Got it. We've got spray."

"Hey goat, hey!" someone yelled. It sounded like Phillip.

The goat looked back to check his pursuers. Bob and Thomas stopped. The others continued to approach the goat, but it didn't budge. Bob heard an aerosol spray.

"Go goat. Take that. Get out of here."

The goat headed back toward Bob and Thomas, shaking its head. They walked backwards. When the goat was twenty feet away, it dashed off the trail. Branches snapped as the goat made its way through the brush.

Bob stood still and quiet. Phillip approached them, and Chet followed with another can of bear spray ready to discharge.

"Phillip, Chet. Just in time. That was scary!" said Bob.

"Are you guys OK?" asked Chet.

"Yeah," said Bob.

Thomas was frozen at his side and didn't respond.

"Let's go back to the chalet. I'll bring up the rear with the spray," said Chet. "Liz told us you went searching for Thomas. We didn't know if you had bear spray or not."

"I rushed away, so I forgot. Stupid, I know. I need to pay more attention out here. I guess I let my guard down while staying in the chalet."

Phillip shook his head and led them back toward the chalet. Bob pushed Thomas ahead of him to get him moving and followed. Chet brought up the rear with a full can of bear spray.

A few minutes later, Crystal yelled, "Thomas?"

Thomas ran around Phillip into his mother's outstretched arms. He tried to reassure her with a pained voice. "Mom, I'm OK. Stop squeezing so hard."

She backed off, but shook both of his shoulders. "I had no idea where you went. It's so dark–and the wild animals."

Jason ran up and put his arms around both of them. "Son, I'm sorry. I didn't mean to upset you. I guess I was being a jerk. Let's go back to the room."

Crystal and Thomas walked together, arms around each other. Jason grabbed Bob's shoulder with one hand and shook his hand with the other. "I have to admit, I feel like a coward. You barely know us, and you went out in the dark and found Thomas. Thanks. And sorry about last night. I shouldn't have spoiled dinner."

Jason jogged down the trail to catch up with Crystal and Thomas.

Bob shook Phillip's hand and nodded to Chet. "Thanks again, guys."

When Bob turned back around, Liz enveloped him in her arms. She stood on her toes and rested her chin on his shoulders. "I was so scared when I kept hearing you yell, 'Bear.'"

"Thanks for sending the cavalry. I was pretty scared myself. That goat was not backing down, kind of like the one at Comeau Pass. They don't seem to be afraid of anything."

Phillip walked by and grinned at Bob. Liz eased her grip, and Bob tried to catch his breath. She took his hand and led him back to the dormitory building.

* * *

Dear Cathy,

Oh, what a night–and day, for that matter!

I don't think I'll sleep well tonight with all the adrenaline in my bloodstream. I thought I was having my third grizzly encounter in three days. That might have been enough to chase me back down to Lake McDonald.

Poor Thomas. He's such a good kid, but he feels trapped by his father. I hope he doesn't spiral down like Brock did. The goat incident might have gotten through to Jason. Or perhaps Crystal let him have it while I was out searching for Thomas. I hope they take a step forward as a family tomorrow on their hike. I've seen the trail do much more.

I hope you enjoyed the Sperry Glacier trail as much as I did. So much to explore on such a short trail. I enjoyed Liz's company, but I'm worried that it cut into our time together. I usually think of you during my breaks or Marty's photo opportunities, but Liz distracted me most of the day. She was so eager and excited; I couldn't help it. What are you thinking? Are you happy I have a new trail friend? Or do you wish I was hiking alone, spending more time with you? I know I had trail friends last year, and a couple were female, but they're young enough to be my daughters. This felt different.

And now, I'm alone with her in a room in the chalet. Maybe I crossed the line. I'm so confused. Liz doesn't appear to have many lines. She's willing to try almost anything. She doesn't want to waste any opportunities. Kind of like you in some respects. You now get to stay in the chalet with me. But is the price too high? Liz is just a friend doing an injured soul a favor. It's nothing more than that. I hope you understand.

"Bob, what are you doing? Still looking at pictures?"

He flinched and dropped the phone on his chest. Right on his sternum. That hurt!

Since he was in a room with Liz, he was typing his nightly note to Cathy instead of using the voice recorder. Heck, even if he was alone, he'd probably still be typing, considering how easily noise traveled in this building.

"No. Just capturing notes from the hike. I like to jot down how I felt during my hikes before I forget. The pictures kind of capture what I saw, but not what I felt."

"What a great idea. So, what did you feel?"

Bob hesitated. "Awe, satisfaction, redemption. What about you?"

"Well, I'll steal awe from you and add gratitude, happiness, anticipation—"

"Yeah, the hike tomorrow should be even better."

"That's hard to believe, but it's not exactly what I meant."

"Anticipating what, then?"

Liz hesitated. "Oh ... just life."

Sorry, Cathy. Got interrupted. No, not another goat or bear, fortunately. Tomorrow, our adventure continues along Lake Ellen Wilson and Gunsight Lake. We'll be up high all day, so the views should be fantastic. And we'll be a foursome to start with. We met some newlyweds at dinner. They are so happy just being together. Made me regret abandoning you even more. We should be like them, staying here tonight, only focused on each other and the magnificent beauty around us.

Love, Bob

V

Interlude

August 17, 2017
Houston, Texas

17

Rejection

"Bob, guess what! I got a reservation. Someone must have canceled," Cathy yelled from the home office.

"What? Where?" He walked from the kitchen to the office.

"In Glacier."

"But Sperry Chalet burned down."

"Yes, but I got a reservation at Granite Park Chalet. I've been calling every day for two weeks."

Bob almost forgot he had suggested they could stay there instead of Sperry. At the time, he figured the chalet was booked for the summer, so they would try later to reserve a room for the following summer. After burning down, Sperry Chalet wouldn't be an option for several years, if ever. He didn't expect Cathy would pursue a stay at Granite Park this summer and snag a rare cancelation. He should have known better. She had looked forward to visiting Glacier for years. She didn't give up so easily.

Most people preferred Sperry Chalet because it had running water and served hot meals. Granite Park was just as beautiful, but guests had to provide their own meals and bring in or fetch their own water. However, it was in the heart of the park and easier to access via the relatively flat Highline Trail.

"Great, honey. When is it?"

She jotted something on the notepaper on her desk. "Two weeks from today. And it's for two nights. There are some great day hikes near the chalet, just like at Sperry. Maybe we can continue north on the Highline Trail on the day in between, then hike out to the east over Swiftcurrent Pass. It's similar to the Gunsight Pass Trail."

"Wow, I didn't realize there was so much to do there. What about all the other hikes we were planning to do?"

"I don't know." She turned her palms up. "I need to see where I can get hotel reservations on such short notice. Maybe I can snag canceled reservations at Many Glacier Hotel, Swiftcurrent Motor Inn, or the Rising Sun Inn. There are lots of places to stay. Heck, we could even get a campsite. Some of the campgrounds have first come / first serve campsites."

"That sounds like a lot of work. Shouldn't we just wait until next summer so we can plan everything better?"

"Not if we can pull it off now. Let me check." Cathy got out of her email and opened her browser.

"I'll check my work calendar to see if I have anything going on." Bob walked back to the kitchen to get his phone.

"Come on. You always have something going on at work."

Cathy's fingers pounded the keyboard while he checked the calendar on his phone. It wasn't bad. Besides the normal standing meetings, he had an all day meeting with the local industry safety committee. But that's not the kind of conflict he was concerned about. Instead, he worried about those events not on his calendar: the injuries, the spills, the air releases, the surprise inspections by the local regulator.

He walked back into the home office. "I don't know, Cathy. I have a trade association meeting that week, and who knows what else will happen between now and then."

"That doesn't sound like a conflict to me. Like I said, you always have something going on. I know your job is demanding and important, and I appreciate the nice paycheck, but you have a team. It's not all on your shoulders."

"But they might need me–"

She stopped typing and pounded the top of the desk. "Stop it, Bob. When are you going to retire? I'm tired of waiting for you and planning around your imaginary conflicts. We have enough money. We need to enjoy it before we get too old."

"Maybe next year."

Cathy crumbled up the paper she had written on earlier and threw it in the trash can. "OK. Fine. We'll go to Glacier next year. You're right about one thing; it will be much easier to plan further in advance. The good places to stay fill up quickly. But I'm going to Colorado instead, with or without you. There are plenty of great hikes and more places to stay. I miss the mountains."

"I'll send you some dates that would work best."

"Don't bother. I'll do the best I can, and you are welcome to come. In fact, I'd love for you to come. It's much harder to do this by myself. But whatever dates you give me, you'll back out when it gets close."

VI

Day Four

July 28, 2023
Glacier National Park

<h1 style="text-align:center">18</h1>

<h1 style="text-align:center">Goodbye</h1>

For breakfast, Bob and Liz sat in a similar arrangement with their dinner partners from last night, with minor adjustments to accommodate Jason. Phillip brought a bowl of scrambled eggs and a platter of bacon and sausage.

"Phillip, do you get any time off?" Liz asked. "Seems like you're always serving us."

"Not really. Only when guests get trapped on the trail by bears or goats."

Liz and Thomas laughed, Bob and Jason grinned, but Crystal did neither.

"I'll be right back with toast." Phillip started to walk away. Jason stood up and said, "Phillip, hold on a minute."

Crystal and Thomas clenched their jaws and glanced at each other.

Here we go again, Bob thought. *I guess the small sign of progress I observed last night didn't last long.*

"Bob, I want to thank you in front of everybody for what you did last night. You did what a good father should have done. I'm sorry I didn't have the courage to do so."

Bob raised his eyebrows in surprise, then exhaled when he realized Jason might have actually learned something.

"And Phillip, you're not much older than Thomas, but you knew exactly what to do and had the courage to scare the goat away. Thank you for that. And thank you for putting up with me for the last couple of days. You'll get a break today, because I'm going hiking with Crystal and Thomas."

Phillip peered at Jason with suspicion, then walked to the kitchen. Chet greeted him with a pat on the back and pinched the tip of his cap while looking at Jason.

"You're coming with us?" Crystal asked.

"Yeah. That's what I told you and Thomas yesterday."

"Great. I thought you might have changed your mind after last night."

"Don't know how far I'll make it, but I'll give it a try. Now, Bob, Liz, what can we expect?"

Bob was still too shocked to speak, so Liz responded. "The views are magnificent the entire way. But watch out for the goats and don't slide down the snow on your rear like I did. That made for a chilly descent."

Bob snorted.

"Goats. Did you say goats?" asked Jason.

Bob shrugged when Thomas looked at him and held his palms up.

"Yeah, we saw about six of them," said Liz.

"Ooh," Jason said.

"Don't worry, Dad. It'll be fine. We won't get too close. And Bob said we'll walk by a waterfall and climb through a chute to get over the pass. I can't wait to see the glacier."

"Ooh. That might be more than I bargained for, but I'll give it a try."

When they were all stuffed, Bob stood up first. "Well, the rest of us are heading east from here, so this will be goodbye. Have a great hike and an easy ride down in a couple of days."

Thomas stood up and shook Bob's hand. Crystal walked around the end of the table and hugged him almost as tightly as she had hugged Thomas last night. She whispered in his ear, "Thank you so much! I can't believe he's hiking with us."

Bob whispered back. "Thank Thomas, not me."

19

Theft

Bob slowed as they passed the site of the goat encounter. He looked in the brush on both sides of the trail, and his hand hovered over the bear spray on his belt. Last night, it was a goat; this morning, it could be worse.

Liz yelled, "Hey Bear," startling him.

He responded with, "Hey Goat," and heard her laugh. Laughing was good; the bears would hear that too.

Tony and Abbie opened up a gap, so Liz passed him and tried to close the distance between them. "Come on, Bob. If we fall behind, we may never catch up."

About thirty minutes later, Tony and Abbie stopped on the top of Lincoln Pass. Bob thought they had been dropped for the day, so he and Liz sped up to catch them before they bolted down the other side. Tony was looking at his phone when Bob arrived.

Bob pointed to the left with his hiking stick, which wobbled up and down as he tried to catch his breath. "The trail … goes … that way."

"Yeah, but I think this is the turnoff for Lincoln Peak." Tony pointed up the steep slope to the right. A faint trail went straight up the slope with no switchbacks to even out the effort.

Bob peeked over the edge and saw a sliver of an unexpected lake. "Look. I see another lake down there."

Tony looked from his phone to the lake, then the peak. "That's Lincoln

Lake, and up there is Lincoln Peak. The map shows a trail going to the top. I remember reading that you can see the entire lake from up there. Let's go."

"Right behind you," said Liz.

Tony and Abbie set their packs down and trudged up the steep slope.

"Hey, wait a minute," Bob said. "That's awfully steep. I have a long day ahead of me."

"Come on, Bob! I've seen you hike. You're in better shape than most twenty-year-olds, except for these two, of course," Liz said, pointing toward Tony and Abbie.

Abbie waved him uphill. "You can do it, Bob. It won't take long."

Bob looked from them to the three packs on the ground and back. "OK, hold on."

Bob removed his pack and caught up to them. He was pleasantly surprised he could keep up with the youngsters, and so could Liz. Maybe she was right after all.

When he reached the top, he thanked them for encouraging him up the spur trail. "Wow, what a view. A beautiful bonus lake down there."

Liz stood next to him. "You're not as old as you think you are, Bob. Live it up!"

She walked over to Abbie, and they both giggled after a few whispers.

After ten minutes of soaking in the views in all directions, Tony said, "Time to go down. I can't wait to get to camp by the lake."

He jogged down the trail without poles. Every few steps, one of his feet slid, but he was unfazed and took the next step. Unlike on the ascent, Bob couldn't keep up, even with Liz. He had become accustomed to using his poles extensively on downhills to protect his knees. He zigged and zagged, making his own switchbacks to reduce the stress further. When he arrived at the bottom, Liz, Tony, and Abbie were all drinking from their water bottles and exchanging laughs, probably about him. But when he looked beyond them, he became concerned.

"Liz, your pack!" Bob yelled.

They looked at where they had left their packs. A marmot was chewing on the waist belt on Liz's pack. Bob was the marmot expert among the group and knew they craved salt like mountain goats, who were known to destroy packs and hiking pole grips and even lick the soil on which people urinated.

Tony ran toward the packs. The marmot bit down on the belt and ran down the steep slope. When Tony continued chasing, the marmot let go, but the pack kept tumbling down the mountainside.

"Oh no!" Bob yelled.

"Don't worry. I can get it." Tony pointed 100 feet down the slope where the pack had been stopped by a tree trunk. A few feet to the right or left, and it might be splashing in the lake by now.

"Tony, be careful," Bob yelled. "It's so steep. Do you want to use my poles?"

"No, I'm good."

Bob put his arm around Liz to provide comfort, but she just smiled at him. She didn't appear to be worried at all. How could that be? If it were his pack, he'd be mulling over the scenarios of what else could go wrong, how he would get out of here safely, and why the trail was conspiring against him.

He started to pull his arm back, but stopped when she leaned her head on his shoulder.

Bob looked at Abbie. She appeared to be enjoying the tension. *What is with these two?*

"I think we'll keep our packs with us at all times from here on out," said Bob.

Tony got down to Liz's pack easily, but he struggled to climb back up with the heavy and bulky pack. He finally put it on his back and trudged uphill, grabbing the trunks of the small trees and bushes whenever his feet began to slide. Abbie inched forward to the ledge, grabbed his hand, and helped him up the last few feet.

Tony took off the pack. "There. No harm done, except for a tattered strap."

Liz immediately put the pack on her back. "Bob, can you ask your marmot friend to tell his buddies to behave themselves?"

"Marmot friend?" asked Abbie.

Bob took Marty out of his pack, showed Abbie, and held him up for Liz.

"Have at it."

"Marty, why are your buddies so mischievous? They almost ruined my trip."

While Marty was out, he handed him to Abbie and took his picture with Abbie and Tony in front of Lincoln Peak. Bob thought he saw Marty turn his head toward the top of the peak and say, *Why didn't you take me out up there?*

20

Sharing

As the adrenaline from the start of the hike and near disaster at Lincoln Pass wore off, Bob and Liz fell behind the energetic newlyweds. Watching Abbie skip along the trail and Tony race from photo op to photo op wore him out as much as the detour to Lincoln Peak. Liz opened up a gap in front of him, turned to check on him, then slowed down. They had yo-yoed like this for the last thirty minutes. Liz appeared to be torn between joining the enthusiastic couple and staying with the cautious old man. But Bob knew only one speed, and with views like they had now, he took a lot of photo breaks.

Ribbons of water, even longer than they had seen yesterday, wound down the steep mountain slopes on both sides of them into the blue-green Lake Ellen Wilson several hundred feet below. A large waterfall fed the lake at the far end, and at the near end, a natural dam held back the water from flooding the valley below.

That would be a fun ridge to explore.

Bear grass now surrounded them on both sides of the trail. Long stalks with large clumps of tiny white flowers waved back and forth in the breeze at eye level, occasionally striking him on the side of the head. The sound of the rustling leaves drowned out his footsteps and the distant waterfalls. Despite the name, the grass wasn't a part of a bear's diet. Nonetheless, Bob was more alert walking through such areas where visibility was limited.

In wide open areas, he could see potential bear threats for hundreds to thousands of feet. In areas like this, he could inadvertently pass ten feet away from a grizzly snacking in the high brush–a bit unnerving! He slowed even more and lost sight of Liz.

Shortly after he exited the sea of bear grass, he encountered a trail to the right, which dipped down toward the lake. Liz stood next to a trail sign waiting for him. The smile he had enjoyed all morning had vanished.

"Is this your campground already?" Bob asked.

He peeked at his phone. "It's only been three miles, plus the little detour to the peak."

"Yeah. It was either this or Gunsight Lake in another four miles, but most trail reviewers recommended this one."

She looked down at the small peninsula jutting out into the lake. "Now I understand why. Wonderful views and easy access to the shoreline."

"I have to admit; I'm a little jealous. I think the campsites at the Gunsight Lake Campground are tucked away in the woods."

Liz's eyes grew, and she opened her mouth. Bob recognized that look. What was coming this time?

"Why don't you stay here instead? I imagine the sites are big enough for two tents. Heck, my tent is even large enough for the two of us, if need be." She grinned and leaned forward.

Bob stared at the trail sign.

"How big was your site at Sperry Campground?" she asked.

"Big enough for two tents. I think they all were."

"Well?" Her face froze in anticipation.

"Is your permit for two people?"

"No. I gave up the extra spot when I picked up the permit."

"So I wouldn't have a permit to stay here, would I?"

Liz appeared to be nibbling on the inside of her lips.

"I guess not, but what's it going to hurt? We'll be in my designated spot. I'm sure Abbie and Tony won't mind."

Bob's eyes wandered from the campground below to the mountainside across the lake to the waterfall below Gunsight Pass. The views were magnificent, and the company would be wonderful. But it was against the rules. What if a ranger came by to check? No one had checked while he was at Sperry Campground, but they must patrol the area regularly.

"Bob, you're making it way too complicated." She tipped her head toward the lake. "Let's go."

Bob's throat clenched briefly. He had heard that line so many times at work. He was always accused of getting in the way and slowing things down. Many thought he was overly conservative and a stickler for following the rules, but he was just trying to save lives. They didn't seem to understand what was at stake and his true motivations.

Liz put her hand on his shoulder. "Are you OK? Did I upset you? Is it Cathy?"

"No, no. You reminded me of work for a minute. I've tried to leave all that behind." Bob looked up and down the trail. He saw no rangers. "OK. Thanks. I'd rather not be camping alone anyway."

Liz bounced on her toes, then headed down the trail. She glanced back after about a dozen steps, then continued toward the lake. The trail to the campground was about a half-mile long, making a total of four miles for the day. He almost felt guilty about stopping so soon. He would pay for it tomorrow with an eleven-mile day–but he wouldn't be alone.

21

Creature

Thomas's mother convinced his dad they should leave right after breakfast to beat the midday heat since they would be above the tree line for most of the hike. Thomas volunteered to walk behind his dad so he wouldn't feel left behind. Even if his mother opened a gap, Thomas could encourage his father and point out some of the surrounding beauty. He wouldn't be able to keep up with his mother anyway. He could barely do so yesterday, but today his calves, thighs, and butt were sore. Good thing they hadn't tried this hike yesterday, or he might still be lying in bed like his father did yesterday–just another reason to take it easy on his dad today.

When they broke out of the trees and saw the glacial cirque with waterfalls cascading down the face of the mountain, his dad stopped and surveyed his surroundings. "This is pretty nice."

His mother did the same a hundred feet ahead of them.

Thomas pointed to the trail winding around the cirque and under the big waterfall in the center. "That's where we're going. The trail is nice and flat for quite a while."

"But where are we going after that?"

Thomas bit the inside of his lip. He reluctantly pointed to a ledge midway up the rock wall.

"Way up there? And how do we get around that waterfall?"

"Don't worry. It'll be fun. So we might get a little wet."

His mom started walking again, trying to urge them on. His dad continued, then stopped to watch his mom cross the metal bridge over the water running across the trail. She stopped on the other side to wipe her face with her sleeve.

"How wet did you get?" asked his dad.

"Not bad. It feels great. We'll be in the sun soon, so we'll dry off quickly."

His dad looked back at him, so he held his hand out toward the bridge; not that his dad needed his permission. His dad walked across the bridge a bit slower than his mom, then he followed close behind.

"Woo hoo!" yelled his dad. "That woke me up." He wiped the water off his face and shook his hands at his side. "That was fun. What are you waiting for? Let's go."

When they arrived at the first switchback and the slope steepened, his dad slowed but didn't complain. Thomas continued to follow about ten feet behind. His mother increased the gap.

I wish she wouldn't do that. I guess she can't hold back her pent up frustration, but it must put pressure on my dad to catch up.

When they reached the rocky shelf he had pointed to earlier, his dad sat down on a boulder with a convenient flat top and grabbed his water bottle.

Thomas sat next to him. "Good idea. That was a tougher climb than yesterday. Nice job."

His dad nodded since his mouth was full of water.

His mom pointed down the valley through which they had hiked. "Beautiful! Thanks so much for coming, Jason. Isn't it great to enjoy this as a family?"

His dad was still short of breath, so he nodded again.

After a fifteen minute break, Thomas asked his dad, "Can you go further?"

"Where to next?"

His mom pointed to the meandering path. "Looks like we get a reprieve until we have to go up there." She raised her finger to the top of the next wall of rock.

His dad's shoulders drooped, but he said, "Okay. Let's stop and reassess before the trail gets steep again."

"Mom, why don't you go ahead? I'll stay with Dad."

"Are you sure?"

"Yeah. We're just slowing you down."

His mom responded as she walked away. "OK. See you in a bit."

She was out of sight within five minutes as he and his dad wove their way through the massive boulders, over the scoured rock, and across the small streams of meltwater. Thomas noticed his father taking numerous, quick breaks to enjoy the magnificent surroundings. There was so much to see, yet they had to be careful to check each footfall. It was a bit overwhelming.

As they approached the final climb to the pass, his father stopped suddenly.

"What's wrong? Did you hurt yourself?"

His dad shook his head and pointed to a small animal in a burrow on the side of the trail. Its head was pointed and had black and white stripes. The creature's lips quivered over its bared teeth. Thomas didn't know whether to call the noise it made a growl, spit, or a hiss, but clearly it meant, *Don't come any closer.*

No worries, buddy!

He tugged on the back of his dad's shirt. "Back up slowly with me."

They backed up about ten steps before they stopped.

"What in the hell is that?" asked his dad.

"I have no idea."

"With those teeth and that noise, I'm not getting anywhere close to it."

"Me neither. Phillip said we might see goats, and we know about the bears, but he didn't say anything about that creature, whatever it is."

"Goats are tame compared to this thing. How about we turn around here?"

The creature lurched out of the hole briefly and returned. His dad jumped back and stepped on his toe. The noise became louder and made him cringe.

"That's it. I'm out of here," his dad said, as he walked the other way.

Thomas looked up, trying to spot his mother, then stared at the black and white beast who hadn't retreated an inch.

"But Mom is up ahead. She'll be expecting us."

His dad stopped and looked back. "The way she was moving, I don't think she'll be looking back. She knows what she's doing. She'll be OK."

Thomas hesitated. He wanted to finish the hike, and at some point, his mom would notice they were missing and worry. But he couldn't abandon his father. If he had a terrible experience, they may never get him on the trail again.

"OK. It's been a great hike so far. Let's not ruin it. How about this? Why don't we take a break at one of the tarns we passed earlier, away from this monster, and wait for Mom? If she doesn't come back soon, we'll head back to the chalet."

"Sounds good to me." His dad continued walking back toward the chalet.

Thomas followed, looking back every few steps to check if the creature was following them down the trail.

22

Bath

Bob and Liz sat with Tony and Abbie on the gravel beach adjacent to the campground after setting up their tents. As with the Sperry Campground, the sites were spread out, so they each had some privacy. Liz selected the largest of the sites, but any would have accommodated their two tents. They were still full from the hearty breakfast at the chalet, but they nibbled on their lunches knowing they would need the calories tomorrow.

So far, they were the only two groups at the campground, but then again, it was quite early to be setting up camp. In fact, a middle-aged male hiker was leaving just as they arrived and heading toward the chalet.

An intermittent breeze cooled Bob's face and caused ripples from the lake to break on his bare feet. Waterfalls murmured from across the large lake.

"So, Abbie and Tony, we didn't get to talk much at dinner last night. What do you two do for a living?" asked Liz.

Tony and Abbie looked at each other and grinned.

"What?"

"We don't really work," said Abbie.

"What do you mean?" asked Bob.

Tony picked up a pebble and tossed it in the water. "We're traveling the country and enjoying life in our van."

"But you still have expenses," said Liz.

"Well—we told you this was our honeymoon—and it is—but we were actually married over a year ago. I am a book editor, and Tony is great with wood. After our wedding, we decided to work hard for six months, then hit the road. I can still do some editing here and there on the road, but basically, we plan to keep traveling until we run out of money. Then we'll work for a while to build up enough for the next trip."

Tony added, "We don't want to waste our youthful enthusiasm. Perhaps we'll settle down when we get older. It's kind of like retirement turned upside down."

Liz's feet sank into the rocks as she wiggled them from side to side. "I envy you so much. My husband died so young. If I had known that when we were married, we might have done the same. Now I have to explore alone. And I don't know how much longer I can do hikes like this. It's hard on a sixty-year-old body."

"Sixty! You're kidding, right?" said Tony.

Liz shook her head. "Sixty-one, actually."

Abbie looked Liz over from head to toe. "I hope I look that good when I'm sixty. I think you have quite a few years left in you, girl."

"And you're not alone; you have the three of us," said Tony.

"You guys are great company, but you know what I mean. I don't have a deep connection with anyone else. Like you two. When you can finish each other's sentences and be confident ordering a meal for them at a restaurant. David was taken from me way too soon. It could happen to me at any time."

Liz turned her attention back to her feet, which were completely buried now. Abbie put her arm around her. "But you'll find somebody. Just keep exploring."

Liz turned her gaze to the mountainside across the lake. "When I made my Sperry reservation back in January, I thought I would at least find a travel partner by now. But it's a lot harder than I thought."

Abbie patted her on the back. "Maybe Bob is the guy."

She leaned forward so Liz could see her grin.

Liz pushed her away playfully, looked at Bob, and smiled. "Maybe. You never know."

"No pressure, Bob," Tony added.

Bob didn't like where this discussion was headed. "Seriously, I have regrets too. I worked way too much. I should have retired when Cathy first asked me to. I'll never spend all the money I made, and I don't have Cathy anymore. I let her go off alone, and she didn't come back."

Tony stood up and stretched his back. "Whoa! You guys are killing the buzz. How about we talk about what we face tomorrow versus next month or next year?"

Bob looked to his left and followed the Gunsight Pass Trail with his eyes. From here, it appeared to pass right under a large waterfall splashing its way all the way from Gunsight Pass to the lake. He wondered if they would get a cold shower in the morning. He then fixed his gaze on the top of the pass.

"Do any of you see a shelter, or mountain hut, on the pass?"

Abbie was already facing the pass. Her head snapped around to face Bob. "There's a mountain hut?"

"Yeah, not like the chalet, but a small shelter for emergencies."

"No. I can't see it either," said Liz.

"Well, I guess it will be a surprise to explore tomorrow," said Bob.

Tony helped Abbie stand up. They picked up their food and trash and walked back to their campsite.

"Liz …"

"Yeah?"

"Thanks for pushing me out of my comfort zone. This is wonderful."

"You're welcome. And it's only noon. It could get even better!"

Bob placed his feet back in the water. He alternated between submerging them in the frigid water and resting them on the warm rocks, a technique he had perfected on the John Muir Trail. His feet weren't sore after such a short hike, but he maintained the habit.

Laughs and screams startled them from behind. Tony and Abbie ran by, dropping their clothes on the dry rocks, then slowing down as they entered the water. They were naked.

Bob looked at Liz as she giggled.

Abbie brought her arms against her chest to ward off the goosebumps.

Tony held his arms up from his side to keep them out of the frigid water as long as possible. Bob shivered just watching them. When they were about waist deep, they dipped down and submerged their heads. Abbie shrieked as her head shot back above the surface. Tony wrapped his arms around her. They walked further out until the water was right below Abbie's shoulders.

Liz looked at Bob.

"What?"

"Come on in, guys. It's not bad," yelled Abbie.

She and Tony bobbed up and down. The waves they created traveled toward the beach.

"Yeah, right. My feet are in the water, you know," said Bob.

Liz stood up. "You can sit here and be an old fart, but I'm going in."

She took off her pants, shirt, and sports bra and dropped them right beside Bob. He looked down at the discarded clothes, then back up to Liz as she offered to help him up. She shrugged when he didn't reach out and walked into the water.

"You go, girl!" yelled Abbie. "Come on, Bob. It won't kill you."

Liz wobbled as she walked on the rocky bottom. When the water rose to the middle of her thighs, she turned around, pouted, and waved Bob in.

He really could use a bath. It had been what–almost four days now–including lots of sweating on the Grinnell and Sperry Glacier trails. He felt guilty about stinking up Liz's room last night, but she hadn't complained. He lowered his chin and struggled to stand up on the loose rocks. He took off his pants, shirt, and hat and dropped them next to Liz's clothes.

The first few steps were not bad since his feet were already numb.

"Go, Bob, go," yelled Tony.

Liz clapped her hands softly in front of her chest.

He walked out slowly with his arms waving at his side as the mostly smooth rocks wobbled under his feet. When the water was about waist deep, he stepped on a sharp rock, lost his balance, and fell underwater. He immediately shot up and took a long, deep breath through his chattering teeth.

"Woooo!"

Liz reached out to grab his hand. "Are you OK?"

She giggled after he nodded, then pulled him into deeper water. It was her turn to inhale deeply as the water reached her chest for the first time. She let go and went underwater. She came back up, but went right back under–and again.

After the third time, she wiped the water from her face. "Oooh! I feel so alive!"

She splashed Bob, so he went under, this time rubbing his face and hair before coming up. When he came up for air, he rubbed the rest of his body, trying to remove days of grime and sweat. Liz bounced up and down with a huge smile on her face. The waves splashed Bob in the face, so he stood up.

Tony and Abbie walked by.

"See, Liz. Maybe he is the one," Abbie said.

Liz splashed her. She grabbed Bob's hand, and they followed in Tony and Abbie's wake.

Abbie and Tony grabbed their clothes and headed back to their tent. "See you later," said Abbie.

"You kids be good, OK," said Liz.

Liz swiped the larger water droplets off her body, then sat down on the beach. Bob shook like a dog instead and sat down next to her. The warm rocks brought instant relief to his cold bottom. Liz ran her fingers through her hair, then leaned back with her eyes closed, soaking up the warm sun. "Ahhh."

Bob looked at the goosebumps all over her well-toned body before doing the same. The gentle breeze brought on an occasional shiver.

"We'll be dry in no time," said Bob.

"I'm in no hurry. The warm sun on my face and chest. The warm rocks on my bottom. My senses haven't been this alive in years. Aren't you glad you came down here?"

Bob heard giggling from the campground behind them. He and Liz looked at each other and smiled. Bob looked at his pile of dirty clothes. They needed washing as well, but that could wait. Moments like this were rare.

23

Seed

When Thomas and his father reached the chalet, his dad went to their room to rest. Thomas was still full of energy and anxious for his mother to return, so he went back outside and sat on the steps to the dormitory. They had waited for his mom near the tarns for twenty minutes and took their time hiking back. She must have made it to the top and done some exploring. Good for her. She deserved it after waiting all those years. He thought he would be more disappointed by not reaching the glacier, but he was content. The variety and beauty of the scenery were fantastic, but more importantly, his father seemed to enjoy the walk and the scenery.

He turned around when the dormitory door opened. Eva walked through and sat next to him.

"I thought you were hiking to Sperry Glacier today?"

"Hi Eva. We just got back; at least, my dad and I did."

Eva furrowed her brows.

"My mom hiked ahead of us, then my dad and I ran into some black and white animal with a pointed face and a nasty attitude right before the final climb. We had no room to get past that beast, so we came back separately. But the hike was still beautiful, and I think my dad enjoyed it. My mom hasn't returned yet, so she must be having a blast."

"Sounds like a badger. They can be quite aggressive, so you made the right decision to turn around."

"A badger. No one told me about those. I hope it doesn't get my mom on the way down."

"I'm sure she'll be alright. But good news overall; sounds like you made progress. I imagine you must be a little disappointed. It's absolutely beautiful up at the top. When you take those last steps through the chute to Comeau Pass, you enter a whole new world."

He moved dirt back and forth with one of his shoes. "Just a little, but I told my dad we could turn around when he had enough. The badger forced the decision. I'm good."

"If you want to give it another shot, I'd be happy to guide you and your parents up there tomorrow. I could even draw another picture for you."

"Really? You would do that?"

"Sure, that's why I'm here."

Phillip came out of the restroom building and walked toward them.

"How was your hike?"

"Great. We didn't make it all the way, but Eva has volunteered to guide us to the top tomorrow."

"I bet she offered to draw something for you as well." Phillip winked at Eva, and she swatted at his leg.

Phillip sat on the other side of Thomas.

"So, what's it like living here? Don't you miss your laptop, TV, and friends?"

Phillip and Eva looked at each other, but she waved for Phillip to go first.

"We kind of have a second family up here. I see more of them than I saw of my real family back home. And yeah, I feel out of touch sometimes, but look where I get to work."

He waved his hand at the mountains surrounding them.

"But you also have to deal with problem customers, like my dad."

Phillip smiled, but not too long. "Yeah, but that's life everywhere."

Eva added, "Actually, I see a lot less of that here than back home. Nearly everyone is happy and polite up here. The beauty of the surroundings must be infectious."

"What kind of schedule do you work? One week on, one week off?"

Phillip and Eva laughed.

"No. Try all summer–eleven straight weeks," said Phillip.

"Eleven weeks! You don't get any days off?"

"Not really. We swap around duties to free up blocks of time to enjoy the area and relax, but we're expected to be here every night."

"And no showers?" Thomas grimaced. "How do you stay clean?"

"Ah! Eva, should we let him in on our little secret?"

She leaned forward and peered at Thomas. "I guess he looks trustworthy."

"We have showers for the employees–but don't tell your dad." Phillip put his hand over his mouth as if to stop the words before they reached Thomas's ear, but Thomas laughed.

"How many of you work here?"

"Usually nine, but ten right now, with Eva: Chet, a cook, a baker, a dishwasher, two waitstaff (me and Claire), two housekeepers, and a utility person."

"How old do you have to be to work here?"

"Eighteen," replied Phillip. "Why? Are you interested?"

"Maybe. I'll be eighteen in March."

"Well, if you're interested, I recommend you talk to Chet before you leave." Phillip nodded toward the dining room.

"Thanks. Good idea."

Phillip stood up. "Speaking of work. Time to get back to the dining room."

Thomas and Eva stood up.

"I'll talk to my mom and dad about tomorrow and let you know."

24

Move

Tony and Abbie had stayed in their tent after their swim to allegedly warm up and take a nap. Without them around, Liz and Bob had to create their own energy. Bob had been intrigued by what appeared to be an infinity edge at the west end of the lake, and he easily convinced Liz to attempt to scramble along the shoreline so they could explore the area. Their progress had been slow as they hopped on and around boulders and climbed up into the trees to get around the larger ones. About halfway there, a massive talus field entering the lake at a sixty-degree-angle abruptly ended their attempt. Even Liz could envision herself tumbling into the frigid water. While they didn't reach their target, Bob relished the mental and physical challenges of creating their own trail versus walking down a groomed path.

When they had returned to the campground, they met a middle-aged couple who were setting up their tent. They had begun their hike at the other end of the trail and stayed at the Gunsight Lake Campground the previous night. When asked to compare the two, they couldn't pick a favorite. The views from their tent at Gunsight Lake hadn't been as good as here, but sitting at the end of the long lake at sunset watching the waterfalls wind their way down the mountainside was mesmerizing. And just when they had thought it couldn't get any better, a moose lumbered out into the lake for an evening snack. Since they had brought their puffy jackets with them, they were able to watch the beautiful creature until it left, even as the temperature plummeted.

Since their hike today was short, they had taken a detour up the mountainside for a better view of Jackson Glacier, for which the pullout at the trailhead was named. The glacier was barely visible from the trailhead but much more impressive from the end of the spur trail, especially with the rising sun reflecting off the smooth ice. They hadn't enjoyed walking through the thick willow bushes along the lower portion of Gunsight Lake, but were relieved not to encounter a bear or moose along the way. They began to describe the mountain hut on Gunsight Pass, but Bob stopped them so they wouldn't spoil the surprise.

The couple went to the rocky beach to clean up and attempt to replicate the wonderful evening they had the night before. Now he and Liz sat with Tony and Abbie in the designated eating area. They sipped red wine, courtesy of Tony and Abbie, and rummaged through their bear canister and food bags to select their dinners. The added weight of the wine in Tony's pack was yet another sign of the couple's boundless energy. Bob spent hours trying to figure out which foods packed the most calories per ounce. Wine wasn't close to making the list. Instead, he chose calorie-dense foods such as nuts, peanut butter, corn chips, cheese crisps, oatmeal, snack bars, and a couple of freeze-dried backpacking meals.

Bob pulled out a Mountain House spaghetti and meat sauce dinner to pair with his dry red wine. Liz held up a package of ramen and a packet of cooked chicken and pouted.

"Not the best pairing, huh? How about we share some of each?" Bob offered.

Abbie whispered to Tony, probably louder than she intended, "Aw, isn't that sweet?"

Liz tossed a pebble at her, which almost bounced into their open bag of dehydrated lasagna.

With three stoves roaring, Bob didn't hear the approaching stranger in a green and gray uniform until he said, "Hi, backpackers."

Bob almost kicked his cooking pot off the small gas stove as he flinched.

"Sorry, I didn't mean to startle you."

"Hi Ranger, what can we do for you?" asked Liz.

'Bart P' was embroidered on a patch on the ranger's shirt.

"Just came by for the usual—to warn you about the goats, check your food storage, and verify your permits."

Bob's stomach rose toward his heart, which now pounded his chest.

"Goats?" asked Abbie. "How can they be trouble? They're so cute."

"Yes, but they can be pretty aggressive trying to steal your food, and even your backpacks and hiking poles. They crave salt and will try to lick anything with sweat on it."

Bob said, "I saw a huge one at Sperry Campground last night acting like the campground host."

"Yeah, he's a fixture up there. The ones here are even more rambunctious. Don't be surprised if they bang into your tents tonight."

The ranger pointed at Bob's bear canister. "I see you're set for food storage."

"Yeah. I used that on the JMT last year. It's kind of bulky, but convenient. Just close it up and set it aside."

"How about the rest of you? Did you see the food pole?"

Abbie said, "Oh, is that–" Tony banged her knee with his.

"Yes, Ranger. We'll hang up our food bag when we're done." He raised their food bag off the ground for the ranger.

"Great. Don't forget to put your toiletries and trash in there too."

Tony nodded.

"And I need to check your permits."

None of them had their permits with them, so he, Tony, and Liz left to retrieve them from their tents.

They all returned together, and Tony handed his permit to the ranger.

"Looks good, Tony."

Liz did the same.

"Same for you, Liz."

Bob tried to step around her, but she put her arm out. "Actually, he's staying with me," Liz said.

The ranger took her permit back and examined it more closely. "But this is only good for one person."

Bart looked at Bob again. "Sir, do you have your own?"

Bob handed him his permit. The ranger squinted as he looked over the permit, then at Bob and Liz, and back at the permit.

"This says you should be camping at Gunsight Lake tonight."

"Yeah, but my spot is plenty big enough, so I told him he could camp here with me," said Liz.

The ranger rubbed his chin with his fingers. "I'm sorry, ma'am. That's not the way it works. Sir, I'm afraid you have to move."

Liz continued. "But there's only six of us here, and only one campsite remains."

The ranger shook his head.

"I'm sorry, Ranger," Bob said. "I get it. But if I leave now, I'll be hiking into dusk, maybe even dark. Is that such a good idea in grizzly country?"

"Sorry, sir. That's what you signed up for. You should know better."

Bob shook his head and clenched his teeth.

Liz continued his defense. "What's the harm in him staying here? As a solo hiker, I wanted some company with all the wild animals around here. Don't you tell everyone not to backpack alone?"

"Yes, but …"

Liz stormed back to her tent. Bob followed. The ranger appeared to be following him, but then walked toward the other couple on the beach.

Liz wrapped her arms around him when he arrived at their campsite. Her body trembled. "Bob, I'm so sorry. I guess you were right after all. It's been such a great day–two days, for that matter."

She let go and stepped back. "Hey, why don't I come with you?"

"Liz, it has been a wonderful two days, but if you come with me, that just pushes the problem to the next campsite."

Liz folded her arms against her chest. "So what. This is ridiculous."

Bob brought his finger to his chin and paused. "Hey, how about this? I'll hike on to Gunsight Lake tonight, and hike back to the pass with just a day pack in the morning. We can enjoy the view and explore the hut together, then hike all the way out."

"I don't know. I don't want to be alone tonight. I really enjoy being with you. The last couple of days remind me of what I've been missing. So do Tony and Abbie."

They were both silent for a minute.

"Liz, I like being with you too, but … I need some time. You understand–right?"

Liz shrugged.

"Let's go finish dinner, then I'll pack up and leave."

Bob grabbed her hand. She glared at the ranger on the beach. "Don't worry. You got your way, but we're eating dinner first."

When they arrived back at the eating area, Abbie came over and sat next to Liz while her dinner rehydrated. When it was ready to eat, she moved back next to Tony and watched him and Liz exchange spoonfuls of spaghetti and ramen while sipping wine in between bites.

25

Sold

Thomas lay on his bed looking at photos on his phone while his dad slept in the other bed. His spirits were high, but nearly every muscle in his legs hurt, even worse than yesterday. If it hadn't been so important to get his dad on the trail, perhaps he would have taken the day off. His dad woke up when his mother opened the door.

"There you are. I was worried about you two," she said.

"We're fine," his dad said. "If you were so worried, you shouldn't have gone so far ahead."

"Sorry, I didn't want you to feel rushed. What happened?"

Thomas sat up. "We ran into a badger on the trail. We couldn't pass, so we came back to the chalet after waiting for you a while."

"Oh, my gosh. I didn't notice it either time I passed. I must have walked right by it. But aside from that, did you enjoy the hike?"

His dad groaned as he sat up. "A badger? Is that what it was? Who told you that?"

"Eva–the artist. She hikes up here a lot, so she should know. Other than that, the hike was great, and Dad did so well."

"I have to admit, the hike was beautiful the entire way, except for that nasty creature on the trail. Actually, he was kind of cute, but sure could use a better temperament."

Thomas thought, so could you, Dad!

"How was the glacier?" he asked his mother.

She handed him her phone. "Here. The pictures tell the story much better than I can."

Thomas sat next to his dad with the phone. "Wow! A rock staircase. And you saw goats, too."

"Look at all the ice and rock. There's not a single tree up there. It's like another planet," said his dad.

"I didn't get to explore as much as I wanted. I got worried when you didn't show up."

"Huh," muttered his dad.

"Mom, what do you have planned for tomorrow?" he asked.

She shrugged and looked at his dad.

"I talked to Eva this afternoon, and she offered to guide us up to the glacier. Maybe we can all make it to the top tomorrow. What do you think?"

"What's she going to charge us for that?" asked his dad.

"Does it really matter? Let's do it. If you and Thomas enjoyed the first part of the trail, you'll love it up there. And it wasn't much more work."

"Come on, Dad. This is Glacier National Park, and I haven't seen a single glacier yet?"

Thomas stopped bouncing his leg when he noticed it was shaking the bed.

"OK. OK. It's our last day, so let's go for it. But she has to deal with the animals if they get in our way."

Thomas jumped off the bed and stood up. His dad nearly fell forward.

"I'm sure she can manage that."

26

Tumble

Bob struggled on the steep climb back to the Gunsight Pass Trail, but now he could recover on the flatter trail before the final push to Gunsight Pass. Following the pass, the trail was all downhill to the Gunsight Lake Campground. Bob's apprehension rose as he approached the waterfall crossing the trail. When he was still a few hundred feet away, he heard someone yelling. He looked back down at the campground and saw Liz waving her hands above her head. He did the same and continued.

She really was going to miss him. Why was she so interested in him? She seemed to be getting fed up with his rigid ways, yet she still wanted to be together. He realized he would miss her too.

Bob stopped again when he faced water rushing over the rocky trail. He had also struggled with water crossings on the JMT. He preferred to cross streams with someone nearby, just in case he slipped or fell and needed help, but he saw no one else on the trail and darkness loomed. Since the surrounding mountainside was sedimentary, the rocks in the stream resembled garden stepping stones. Perhaps this crossing wouldn't be so difficult after all. Plus, the water was only about ankle-deep.

He imagined Marty in his pack screaming, *Let me out! Take my picture.*

No way, Marty. Not after the stunts you pulled on the JMT. You can get some fresh air when we get to the pass.

Bob unbuckled the straps on his backpack. Before putting his full weight on each rock, he tested its stability with his foot while his poles were firmly planted. The rocks weren't covered with slick algae, but the surface of the wet shale was still slippery.

About halfway across, he looked up to check if Liz was still watching him. She appeared to be taking a photo. As he raised his poles to pose, his left foot slid off a small flat rock. He tried to hop back to regain his balance, but his right foot slipped as well.

He fell backwards, and his poles flew out of his hands when his arms flailed. He landed on his backpack, knocking his breath away. The shallow but raging water grabbed his legs and pulled him out of his backpack.

"Help!" he screamed. "Help me!"

His arms continued to flail as the water carried him faster and faster down the slick, steep slope. He regained control of his arms and grabbed at rocks to stop his slide, but the water washed his hands away.

His slide slowed as the slope lessened, and he was finally able to stop. When he tried to stand back up, his shaking legs gave way, and he resumed his slide. He sped up as he hit the steepest part of the waterfall.

He began to freefall, so he closed his eyes and took a deep breath. But instead of landing on the soft water, pain shot up his back as his butt landed on a large, flat rock. Once again, he lost his breath.

He opened his eyes. He now teetered on the edge of the rock, his legs dangling and useless. There was nothing but water in front of him. He waved his arms as water pushed him forward. He slipped over the edge and fell through the air again, this time toward the lake.

The frigid water made him gasp for air. Fortunately, he was able to close his mouth before his head went underwater. He sank–and sank–and sank. The water couldn't be very deep this close to shore. Could it? Where is the bottom?

Finally, his feet landed on the rocky bottom. His last breath had been cut short. He needed air. Now. He pushed himself back to the surface with his legs. If his backpack hadn't come off, he'd still be underwater, trying to breathe water instead of air.

He attempted to tread water. What was nearly effortless in the swimming pool at the gym was nearly impossible as his drenched clothes and shoes became anchors. Fortunately, the shore was only feet away. His muscles would seize up soon in the icy water. He let himself sink to the bottom again, then pushed himself up at an angle toward the bank. One more push and he was back to the large block of rock he had fallen from.

The face of the rock was nearly vertical and slick, so he couldn't climb out of the water there. He scooted along the shoreline until he found dry rocks and bushes. Using the trunks of the bushes, he pulled himself out of the water and sat on a dry rock to catch his breath and gather his wits.

He began to shiver. As exhausted as he was, he had to move up to the trail where others might find him. Otherwise, he would die down here. He zigzagged up the steep slope by pulling on and stepping against the trunks of the bushes and rocks. He yanked several of the smaller bushes out of the loose soil and lost hard-earned progress. When he finally returned to the trail, he collapsed, shivering more violently now.

My pack! Where is my pack? Without it, his hike was over. Maybe even his life. His satellite communication device was clipped to the outside. If no one passed in the next few minutes, he could press the SOS button to summon help. That's why he lugged around the extra six ounces–just in case.

He took a couple of deep breaths and mustered the strength to sit up and look toward the water-covered trail. There it was! Still sitting in the stream where he'd fallen. But he had to retrieve it before the water carried it into the lake. The surprising sight motivated him to stand up and walk back onto the slick stones that had sent him sliding minutes ago.

He didn't hesitate this time. Too much was at stake. He tried to pick up the pack, but it slipped out of his hand. The pack was much heavier than before. He lost his balance and almost fell again. The pack started tumbling down the slope, so he grabbed it by one of the trailing straps and dragged it to the dry trail on the other side of the stream. He collapsed on top of the drenched pack and closed his eyes while he caught his breath. He had to get dry and warm. But how?

He took stock of his injuries. They must not be too serious since he was able to climb up the steep slope to the trail. His butt and hips were sore. Some of his fingers were bleeding. But he didn't remember hitting his head. He ran his hands through his hair to make sure and felt a twinge in his left shoulder. He must have strained that while trying to slow himself. He breathed deeply, concentrating on his ribs. They weren't sore–at least, not yet. He couldn't believe it. How could he have been so lucky? Cathy hadn't been so fortunate.

If Liz hadn't distracted him, he never would have slipped.

No! He couldn't blame this on Liz. It was his decision to stop, not hers. She had been nothing but wonderful to him.

If the damn ranger hadn't made him move … No, it wasn't his fault either. He was just doing his job.

I can only blame myself, my own careless self.

He continued to shiver as the adrenaline released during the fall wore off. He opened his pack. The inside was wet. *Oh no! My sleeping bag–and clothes!* Normally, he placed them in a plastic garbage bag and crammed it into the bottom of his pack. But in his haste to leave the campsite, he hadn't done so. When he reached the bottom of the pack, sure enough, his sleeping bag and sleeping clothes were drenched.

He fell on top of his pack and yelled, "Noooo!"

He sat back up and looked for a savior on the trail in both directions. No one.

"Help! Please help!"

He unclipped the satellite device from his pack. The screen had been cracked and had dark blotches underneath. Pressing the power button did nothing. No sound. No message on the screen. Nothing. It must have taken a direct blow when he fell. Only luck would save him now. What an awful feeling.

He called out for help again, but his voice was weakening, and he barely heard himself over the rushing water. He laid in a ball, hugging his drenched backpack to minimize heat loss. His teeth chattered and his eyes closed.

He pictured Cathy walking toward him on the trail. She saw him and ran. "Bob!"

He thought, Cathy, don't run! You'll hurt yourself. I need you!

Someone shook his shoulder.

"Cathy?"

"Bob?"

"Oh, Cathy. I need help. Sorry I got so far ahead of you."

"Bob! It's me. Liz."

He looked up. "Liz. Thank goodness you came."

"I saw you fall and heard you scream. It was awful. I thought you had drowned at first. But then I saw you climb out of the water and ran over here as fast as I could."

His body was frozen in a fetal position surrounding his pack. She sat down next to him and put her arm around him. "Are you hurt? I mean, really hurt?"

He shook his head. He'd have to explain later when he could talk.

She took off her puffy jacket. She peeled Bob's arms away from his pack, then straightened his legs. He started to bring his arms back to his chest, but she stopped them and unbuttoned his wet shirt. Once it was off, she helped him put on her jacket. Next, she stood up and took off her pants. She helped him do the same and put hers on him over his wet underwear.

"Sorry about the fit, but it will do until Tony gets here. He's bringing more of our stuff. I just grabbed the first aid kit and ran."

"Thanks-s-s!"

She looked at his feet. "Sorry, I don't think my socks will fit you."

She sat behind him, wrapped her legs around him, and hugged against his back. Neither said a word. Bob's teeth stopped chattering, but he still shivered occasionally. Whenever he did, Liz tried to adjust her position and squeeze tighter, but she couldn't cover all his body's surface area.

Tony arrived a few minutes later.

"He's OK," Liz said. "But shivering."

Tony flung things out of his backpack. When he got to Liz's sleeping pants, he tossed them to her. Liz stood up and put them on quickly. She grabbed her sleeping bag off the ground and unzipped it. She removed Bob's drenched shoes and socks and asked him to put his legs in the bottom half of the bag. Tony lifted him while Liz slid the upper half over the rest of his body, then zipped it up. She put the hood of the mummy bag over his head and cinched the cord.

"That should warm you up. Do you feel better?" she asked.

"Yes-s. Thank you s-so m-much. And y-you t-too, Tony."

They both stared at him with concern.

Tony handed Liz her wool hat and fleece jacket. He picked up the first aid kit. "Do we need this?"

Liz nodded, but Bob said, "My fingers are a little b-banged up, b-but that can w-wait."

Tony threw the first aid kit into his mostly empty backpack.

He pulled out his water bottle and held it to Bob's lips. Here, drink a little water."

Bob sipped from the bottle.

"We'll fix you something warm soon. Liz, how can I help now? I told Abbie to stay at camp until we knew more. Should we take him back to camp?"

"Either that or take him up to the shelter on top of the pass." She looked up toward the pass. "Either way, I'm staying with him."

"Bob, what do you think is best?"

He still couldn't concentrate, so he shrugged and leaned his head against hers.

"I think it's best to take him back down to camp," Liz said. "It's downhill, my tent is already set up, and it will probably be warmer than that old, exposed hut."

Bob nodded his head inside the mummy bag.

Liz smiled. "You like that idea?"

Bob continued to nod.

"I think you're right," said Tony.

"But let's warm him up a little more in the sleeping bag first."

Tony sat on the other side of Bob. Liz rubbed her hand up and down Bob's back.

"My hiking poles! Where are my hiking poles?"

Bob tried to get out of the sleeping bag.

"Hold on, Bob. You can't get out now."

She put her arm around him and squeezed.

He hadn't seen his poles while retrieving his pack. The black poles would be hard to spot against the gray rocks, darkened by the water. The water must have carried the light poles into the lake. He would normally grieve the loss of his beloved poles, but the loss seemed inconsequential now.

Tony stood up and scanned the waterfall.

"Sorry, Bob. I don't see them. We'll try again tomorrow when the light is better."

Ten minutes later, Abbie arrived. "Sorry, I couldn't wait any longer. Is he OK?"

Tony said, "We think so."

"I brought our cook kit, water, and hot chocolate mix."

Bob raised his eyebrows.

"You like the sound of that?" said Abbie, as she began heating water.

When the hot chocolate was ready, Liz helped him drink so he could keep his arms in the mummy bag. He was afraid he would burn his mouth with someone else guiding the cup to his lips, but Liz was so gentle. He had only seen her adventurous side so far. What a wonderful lady. She reminded him so much of Cathy.

When the hot chocolate was gone, Liz helped Bob out of the mummy bag. Tony stuffed it in his pack and gave it to Abbie. Bob winced as he put on his cold socks and shoes. They stung his feet, but the bruises and cuts on his stiff hands hurt as well.

Liz and Abbie helped him stand up, and each held an elbow. Bob winced, and his legs gave way. Liz and Abbie stopped him from falling again.

"Are you OK?" Liz asked.

"My butt and lower back really hurt."

His earlier self assessment had been done while they weren't bearing any weight. On the second try, he was able to stand up, now that he was prepared for the pain.

Tony grimaced as he put on Bob's wet backpack. He had given Abbie his puffy jacket so it wouldn't get wet.

After they crossed back over the stream, Abbie let go of Bob's elbow and followed Tony down the trail. Liz held Bob's elbow for the first few dozen steps.

"I think I'm OK now. You can let go."

Liz let go of his elbow, but slid her hand down his arm and held his hand the rest of the way to camp.

* * *

When they arrived at camp, Liz helped Bob get settled in her tent. She told him to get in her sleeping bag and lay on her inflatable sleep pad. Bob took off the awkwardly fitting hiking pants and his wet socks and slipped into the mummy bag.

"But what about you?"

"Don't worry about me. I'll talk to Tony and Abbie, and we'll figure something out."

It felt so good to lie down. What had begun as a fun day with his new trail friends had become a nerve-wracking, exhausting near-nightmare. It would have been a nightmare had it not been for Liz. He heard voices, but they were too far away to understand. They had taken great care of him so far. He knew they would continue. He didn't deserve this. If only Cathy had received such wonderful help while she was on the trail. He would have done so, but he wasn't with her when she needed him most.

Liz, Tony, and Abbie returned about fifteen minutes later. Liz slid another inflatable sleeping pad into the tent.

"Whose is this?"

"It's mine," Tony said, "but one of the other campers carries a foam pad as a backup to his inflatable pad. He's letting me use that."

Tony handed him dry socks. "These are my sleeping socks. They're not too dirty–I promise." He grinned. "I'll sleep in my hiking socks tonight."

Liz turned to Tony and Abbie. "Thank you so much. I think we'll get through this."

"If you need anything else, just come get us," Tony said. "I don't think any of us will sleep much tonight."

"At least we'll be warm," said Liz.

Abbie stepped around Liz and threw a Snickers bar in the tent. "Here, Bob. I don't think you ever had dessert. You'll need the calories to warm up."

"Thanks, Abbie. You're so sweet." He raised his voice further. "And Tony, thank you as well. I can't believe how quickly you and Liz got to me. You saved my life."

"You'd do the same for me. Good night."

"Good night. Don't let the bears bite."

"Well, I think he's starting to warm up," Liz said. "That's my Bob."

Abbie hugged Liz, and she and Tony walked away.

Liz crawled into the tent. "Aren't they great?"

"The best."

"And they're not done. We discussed starting a fire, but that's not allowed, so they're going to wring out your clothes and sleeping bag and hang them in the trees. We're already in enough trouble with the ranger. They won't dry overnight, but it will be a start. We can lay them out to dry on a break tomorrow. Maybe at Gunsight Pass."

Liz reached back outside the tent, then held Marty in front of his face.

"I'm surprised you haven't asked about this guy."

"Marty!"

Liz partly unzipped his bag when he struggled to get his arms out. He grabbed the wet marmot and gave him a little kiss.

"I think he's upset that you were more worried about your poles than him."

"Actually, he wanted to pose for a picture at the waterfall, but fortunately, I refused."

Liz grabbed Marty and put him in the mesh pocket near the tent ceiling. "Well, at least he got a bath today, like the rest of us. But it's going to be a while before he dries out."

Liz closed the tent zipper. The twilight from the late setting sun bathed the tent in soft light. She replaced her hiking socks with her thicker sleeping socks, then unzipped the sleeping bag.

"We don't have an extra sleeping bag, so we'll use it like a quilt and share."

She took off her wool cap and put it on Bob's now exposed head. She took off her hiking shirt and bra and looked at Bob. Bob's eyes wandered from hers. When they found her face again, he saw a grin. She pulled her fleece mid-layer over her head and covered her chest. She laid down, dragged half of the mummy bag over her, then reached over her head to grab the candy bar Abbie had tossed on the tent floor. It was as hard as a rock, but it would soften in no time under the warm sleeping bag. She pulled the quilt over both of their heads.

After a few minutes, she tore part of the wrapper off the candy bar and held it to his lips. He took a small bite and savored every peanut, the chocolate shell, and the now gooey caramel. "Mmmm."

Liz took a bite. "Mmmm."

He smiled and rubbed her cheek. It felt like she was smiling as well.

When they were done, Liz unzipped his puffy jacket, actually, her puffy jacket, and encouraged him out of it. He mumbled, "But–"

"Roll over on your side." He furrowed his brow while his eyes penetrated hers.

"Trust me."

He rolled over. After she squirmed around a bit, he felt fire on his back as the sleeping bag was dragged over them again. His back felt like his chest did earlier in the day on the beach. Her hand slid under his arm and rested against his chest. He covered it with hers and thought for the first time in hours that this trip might not end in disaster after all.

About thirty minutes later, she slid her arm out from under his and laid on her back. Bob did the same. He had not fallen asleep, and he knew Liz hadn't either. She hadn't spoken to him, but every few minutes her hand would rub or squeeze his chest, or she would twirl his chest hair with her finger. *What now? What does she expect? Is she getting cold? Is she a back sleeper?*

Liz rolled on her other side and reached back to grab his hand. She tugged on it until he was lying on his side.

"Time to warm up the other side. Plus, my back is getting cold."

When she lifted her arm, Bob reached through hesitantly. She grabbed his hand and placed it on her right breast, then covered it with hers. She scooted back until their skin was touching again. She was right; her back was cold, but his chest was now warm and would fix that in no time.

Liz breathed more deeply, but he couldn't sleep. Somehow, she still maintained a tight grip on his hand. He thought of Cathy. He always left her a message from his tent before he went to sleep. Usually, he recorded his voice on his phone app; sometimes he typed a message as he did while sharing a room with Liz at the chalet. He could do neither now. He would do so in the morning, but what would he say? He had no chance of sleeping until he figured that out–and it wouldn't be easy.

Tomorrow would be a difficult day: a lot of miles, a sore body, and wet and heavy gear. He didn't even know if he'd be able to walk. But that was tomorrow's problem. What about Cathy? Bob rolled onto his back. Liz tried to grab his hand, almost reflexively, but let it slide through her arm. She continued to lie on her side.

* * *

Dear Cathy,

I'm so sorry, Cathy. You must be wondering what in the heck is going on. Or you may be furious. 'Does he really miss me as much as he tells me every night?'

The trip was going so well, but one lapse, just a quick wave back to Liz from the trail, changed everything. As I slid down the waterfall toward the lake, all I thought about was not being able to speak to you again, even if you can't really hear me. But I can feel you. You helped me overcome my panic and get back to the shoreline. You helped me get back to the trail. But then I had other help, Liz, then Tony, then Abbie. I have a wonderful trail family once again. A family you didn't have on your last hike. You told me you needed help, and I ignored you. I tried to convince you that you could manage. But sometimes you need real help, not just encouragement. Without Liz, my hike would be over; perhaps my life would be over. But without you, Liz may have found me floating in the lake. Thanks for your help. The rest of our hike won't be the same as we imagined, but we will finish. My trail family will make sure of that. Even if they have to carry me out of here.

And what about me and Liz? I'm as confused as you must be. She reminds me a lot of you. Strong, adventurous, impatient—maybe that's not the right word—perhaps determined—determined not to let life slip by. She's fit and attractive. And she cares. I know I let you down many times, but I also know you cared. Otherwise, you wouldn't have tolerated my obsession with work.

Liz seems to want more … and quicker … quicker than I can move. You know how cautious I am—at work, at home, and on the trail. I've had to suppress some of that to help you finish your bucket list. That was my commitment to you. But I don't know how you feel about Liz, so I don't either. I don't know if you are jealous, resentful, angry—or perhaps happy. Please send me a sign. I won't know until you do.

Tomorrow—

Liz rolled over and raised her head by resting it on her hand. She stared down at him.

"Bob, are you OK? You were talking? Were you having a nightmare?" She smeared tears around his cheeks with her finger.

"What's wrong? You had a rough evening, but you'll be OK. I'll make sure of that."

Bob sniffled. "I don't know. Yeah, I guess I was talking to myself. Sorry. I can't get to sleep."

"I imagine so, after what you've been through. Or am I keeping you up?"

Bob stared at the top of the tent for a few seconds. "No, no. I don't know. So much is going through my mind. Nearly drowning, what tomorrow will bring, helping Cathy finish the hike, your generosity, Tony and Abbie, us … together … so close …"

"Oh, Bob, don't worry about that. Yes, I'm getting close to you. I love spending time with you, but we'll have time to sort that out later. Try to rest–get some sleep. You're right about one thing. Tomorrow may be difficult, but not as difficult as this evening. We'll figure it out between the four of us."

Liz grabbed her puffy jacket. "Here, put this on."

Bob shook his head, rolled on his side, and placed his arm over her chest.

VII

Day Five

July 29, 2023
Glacier National Park

27

Stiff

"Good morning, love birds. Are you ready for hot coffee?"

Liz grinned at Bob. He didn't know whether to react to the surprise room service or the insinuating remark. Liz rolled over and unzipped the mesh screen. Abbie unzipped the rainfly and handed Liz a coffee cup. Bob lifted himself up on his elbow. Abbie's smile matched her daring salutation. Liz wrapped both her hands around the cup before handing it to him, then reached back for the second cup. Bob wrapped the cup in his hands and held it close to his face in order to breathe in the steam rising from the cup.

"Abbie, you're an angel. We'll be out in a bit," said Liz.

"Take your time." Abbie winked and zipped up the rainfly.

Bob was glad they had gotten dressed a few hours ago in order to stay warm during their pee breaks, as it had prevented an awkward delay when Abbie arrived with the coffee. Bob must have gotten dehydrated during the chaos last night because he only had to go once versus the usual two or three times. They had both laughed while playing a game of Twister to get out of the tent in the dark. Perhaps that was the inspiration for Abbie's greeting. Oh well, he had bigger things to worry about.

Bob left the tent still dressed in Liz's puffy jacket and hiking pants. He grimaced, but tried not to groan any more than normal for an old man so Liz wouldn't pepper him with questions. He was still confident he hadn't been seriously injured, but the pain was worse than yesterday evening. His lower back, hips, and butt were severely bruised and a lot more tender this morning. Several of his fingers were swollen, and his shoulder was still sore. How would he carry a backpack today? He probably couldn't even get it on his back without help.

Bob's first order of business was to find his hiking pants. His gear was scattered everywhere, like a mini-tornado had entered his pack and thrown everything out. But when he looked closer, he saw order. His tent was set up near Liz's, and his sleeping bag was draped over a large boulder. His clothes hung on branches of the surrounding fir trees like ornaments on a Christmas tree. Tony and Abbie must have gone to bed much later than he and Liz. He regretted interrupting their honeymoon. They were supposed to be doting on each other, not an old man.

Tony walked toward him. "Sorry about the mess. I did the best I could."

"You and Abbie are too much." Bob's voice trembled. "Thank you. Thank you so much."

Liz approached them. "Yard sale! Hey Bob, how much do you want for the sleeping bag?"

Bob didn't laugh. He spotted his hiking pants and grabbed them off a small tree. "Ooh. Still damp, but sorry, Liz, your pants don't fit me well."

Tony looked at the horizon to the east. "The sun won't reach here for hours. How about we eat breakfast, pack up, and start hiking? The sun should be hitting the pass by the time we arrive. Right before we leave, you can swap pants. That way, they'll warm up and dry out quickly. If you put them on now, you'll just get chilled."

"OK." Bob hung the pants back on the tree.

Abbie joined them. "Bob, how are you feeling this morning?"

"Sore. Really sore. Fortunately, I slid down the wet rocks on my butt. If I had tumbled down, it wouldn't have mattered when y'all got to me."

Tony looked at Liz, then back at Abbie. "We'll split up some of your stuff to lighten your load. It will be heavier than normal since it's wet, especially the sleeping bag and your clothes. We'll dry all that stuff out as soon as we can."

"Thanks. To tell you the truth, I don't believe I could even put on a full backpack, much less carry it for eleven miles. Are you sure you can manage the extra weight?"

"We insist," Abbie said. "But let's eat first. We'll meet you at the food preparation area."

Tony pointed to the boulder over which Bob's sleeping bag was strewn. "Your bear canister and what's left of your pack are behind that rock."

"Thanks."

Bob surveyed the scattered gear. "Have you seen my hiking poles?"

"No," Tony said. "Remember, I looked for them last night, but couldn't find them."

Bob rolled his eyes upward. "Oh, that's right. The water must have carried them into the lake." He lowered his head and shook it slowly. "I'll make do, but those poles really help. Oh well, I'll be moving very slow today anyway."

"We'll look again when we get to the waterfall," Liz said. "You can use one of mine in the meantime."

"No thanks. I'm sure you need them as well. I'll manage."

Liz shrugged and went down to the lake to filter water while Bob grabbed a plastic bag containing his homemade oatmeal mix from his bear can. He found his stove, cook pot, and gas canister in his backpack.

Bob looked over his scattered gear again before heading to the food preparation area. He couldn't believe the goats and marmots hadn't further scattered or destroyed it. He wondered what else might be missing.

* * *

Liz, Tony, and Abbie could finally enjoy the mountains and waterfalls surrounding the trail now that Bob was out of immediate danger. Bob dreaded the march to the waterfall crossing on which he had fallen. In order to finish the hike for himself and Cathy–and with Liz–he had to cross that water yet again.

When they arrived at the crossing, Tony turned to face him. "Bob, you got this?"

Bob's eyes followed the water as it splashed on the trail, then continued down the steep slope to the lake. How had he survived that fall? It must have been magic–trail magic. That's how. Cathy had been looking after him, perhaps Jessica and Hannah as well. Then Liz, Tony, and Abbie did the rest.

He looked for his missing poles. Tony pointed. "There! I see one. The strap is hung up on a rock."

Bob breathed in sharply. "Yeah! That's one of mine. Good eye."

He started down the slope, but Abbie grabbed his arm, and Tony scrambled down to retrieve it. They continued to search for a few more minutes, then gave up. One pole was better than none.

Bob stepped cautiously onto the wet rocks. The water flow was lower this morning since the snow melt had slowed overnight with the cooler temperature.

"I'm right behind you if you need any help," Liz yelled over the rushing water.

Bob was determined not to stop this time, since that led to his trouble last night. His eyes focused solely on the next couple of foot placements. He didn't even notice Tony and Abbie anxiously waiting for him on the dry trail ahead. He tested the stability of the rocks ahead with his pole, but his legs wobbled without the other to provide a third point of contact. However, he wouldn't endanger Liz by asking for one of her poles. He'd just go a little slower.

When he reached the other side, Abbie grabbed his arm and pulled him to dry ground. Liz patted his backpack. "Nice job, Bob. I knew you could do it."

Tony patted him on the shoulder. "I've been looking for your other hiking pole from this side and didn't see it. It must be at the bottom of the lake."

Bob shrugged. "Yeah, I think you're right. Thanks for trying. I'm glad you found one. I can manage with that."

They looked back at Lake Ellen Wilson before climbing the switchbacks to Gunsight Pass. He spotted the peninsula on which they had slept last night, then admired the flat horizon at the other end of the lake. To their left, the long waterfalls they saw from the beach at the campground yesterday came to life. They now resembled rivers roaring down the mountainside versus white ribbons draped on the rock. It could have been worse; I could have slid down one of those!

The pain in Bob's lower back intensified as they climbed to Gunsight Pass. Not only did the bottom of his pack press harder on his back as they climbed uphill, but his mind was no longer preoccupied with the water crossing. That was behind him. Now his back screamed for attention. He tried to relieve the agony by moving his shoulders up and down and adjusting the straps, but nothing helped. His efforts only made his sore shoulder hurt more.

Behind him, Liz asked, "Bob, are you OK? Do we need to take more of your gear?"

"I don't know. My pack really hurts my back. It rests right where my worst bruises are."

Tony came back down to meet him. "Unbuckle your straps."

"What? Why?"

"Just unbuckle your straps, Bob," said Liz, resting her hands on her hips.

Bob did as he was told. Tony stepped around him and lifted the pack off of his shoulders. The relief was immediate. How could he be so helpless?

Tony headed back up toward the pass, hugging Bob's pack in front of him.

"Tony!" Bob yelled, but Tony continued marching up the steepening trail.

"Is that better?" Liz asked.

Bob nodded and began walking. His back felt better, but his pride had taken a beating.

28

Staircase

"Eva!" yelled his dad. "We found the badger right there."

Eva and his mom stopped. Thomas and his dad had fallen behind, so they kept walking until they caught up. His dad's pace was slower today as he complained about sore calves, thighs, feet, and hips all morning. Thomas knew how he felt and didn't have the heart to tell him they would hurt worse tomorrow. But he was still hiking, so Thomas stayed with him and tried to distract him with commentary on the wildflowers, colorful rocks, and a couple of marmots.

His mom stepped ahead of Eva and poked in the bushes on both sides of the trail. Eva crept forward, turning her head from side to side. Thomas and his dad stayed back, just in case Eva and his mom flushed out the ferocious badger. Once they were through the area, he and his dad rushed through.

They all walked together up the next rise and along the final obstacle between them and Sperry Glacier. Eva stopped on the trail right before Comeau Pass and pointed up the gap in the wall.

Thomas stepped in front of Eva. "Dad, you've got to see this."

His dad joined him and peeked up the chute blasted from the rock.

"Neat. A staircase. This shouldn't be too bad. And this brings us to the top, right?"

"Yep," Eva said. "You can explore forever up there, but the top of the pass is just up those steps."

"Good, that's about all I can handle–uh-oh!" He pointed up the chute.

"Cool. A goat," yelled Thomas.

Eva started up the stairs. "No worries. I'll take care of him. They're always waiting up top."

The goat moved away as Eva approached, but when Thomas reached the top, three of them stared at him from thirty feet away. He stood between the goats and the top of the chute so his father wouldn't be intimidated. When they were all up top, Eva led them away from the goats to a scenic viewpoint where they could eat in peace and she could draw.

"Jason, well done." Eva held up a hand, and Jason slapped it in between his deep breaths. "What do you think?"

"I'm having trouble speaking now, but words can't really describe it anyway. Thanks for helping us get up here. Where's the glacier?"

Eva pointed up and to the right. "That's what's left of it."

Thomas had been expecting a bright white field of ice, but with all the snow from last winter melted, the old ice was filthy with embedded rock debris.

Thomas pointed below the glacier. "Wow, see those blue pools of water over there? They look like swimming pools from here."

"That's because of the glacial flour in the meltwater from the glacier," said Eva. "What do you want me to draw?"

His mom suggested the glacier, the surrounding mountains, and the bright blue tarns Thomas had just pointed out.

"That sounds good," said his dad. "But can you sketch Thomas in the foreground?"

"Sure. Thomas, you sit facing me, and I'll start sketching while you three eat lunch."

After his mom distributed their sandwiches, she raised her water bottle and looked at the other bottles, indicating he and his dad should do the same.

"Thanks, Jason, Thomas. It's been a magnificent day and a wonderful trip."

They banged their water bottles together, and each took a sip.

Thomas and his mother scarfed down their sandwiches, itching to explore more of the area after all the hard work to get up there.

Thomas asked Eva, "Do you still need me to sit here?"

"No, you can go explore, but let me take your picture first."

His mom looked at his dad. After an awkward pause, his dad nodded toward the glacier. "Go ahead, but I'll stay here with Eva. I'm so sore from yesterday, I don't know if I can stand up, much less make it back to the chalet. Just be careful, OK?"

"Of course."

Thirty minutes later, he and his mom returned. His dad's gaze switched from the sketch to the surrounding ice and rock and back again.

"Look at this. Isn't Eva a fabulous artist?"

His mom covered her mouth with her hand. "Oh my gosh. It's beautiful, Eva. I don't know how you captured this place so well. I can't do so with my camera."

"And doesn't Thomas look so happy?" asked his dad.

Eva looked at Thomas and grinned. "That's because he is."

29

Drying

Two more switchbacks. Tony and Abbie must have reached the top of the pass, but he couldn't see them. Liz refused to pass him, no matter how slowly he walked or how much he pleaded. He despised that his suffering dulled her enthusiasm. When he awoke this morning, he thought he had recovered well overnight, but he had no energy ever since the grade of the trail increased. With only one hiking pole, he couldn't effectively utilize his arms to help propel him up the trail. The adrenaline rush and deep chill must have taken a much larger toll than the bruises alone. And he hadn't slept well while trying to decipher Liz's intentions and how Cathy felt about them—how he felt about them. But her tender care was the only reason he was even on the trail today.

As he climbed the last switchback, Bob sensed Liz getting closer and closer. When he finally reached the top, he bent over and put his hands on his knees. When he stood up again, she placed her hands on both of his shoulders and pecked him on the cheek. But she deserved more than a peck after all he put her through. He tilted his head and kissed her lips. Her look of pity was replaced by a wide smile. Abbie must be enjoying this. Sure enough, when he looked over Liz's shoulder, she was standing next to the shelter and nudging Tony with her elbow.

Tony pointed to the side of the shelter. "More goats. A mama and her kid. They ran to greet us when we arrived and have hovered ever since."

155

"I didn't see a single mountain goat on the JMT, but here, they're everywhere."

"They sure are cute," Abbie said.

"I'm surprised they didn't mess with all my stuff last night," Bob said.

Bob entered the shelter to examine the rugged structure. He sat on a bench along the wall. The hard wood hurt the bruises on his butt, but allowed his back to rest after struggling up to the pass. The air was damp and musty. He tried not to breathe too deeply.

When he looked around the interior, his mind wandered back to the long night he had spent in the Muir Hut on the JMT. That night was the second most traumatic of his life. The first, of course, was the night after he learned Cathy had died on the trail. Last night paled in comparison.

This shelter differed from the Muir Hut in several ways. It was rectangular versus circular and had a more traditional corrugated metal roof supported by logs running its length. The roof of the Muir Hut was constructed entirely of rock, similar to the way igloos were built. The interior space was about the same, about twelve feet by twenty feet. A window on one side brightened the room, but the window opening on the other side was boarded. Rocks and mortar covered the area where a hearth once stood. The rock walls reminded him of the ones he had slept next to two nights ago.

"You love this place, don't you?" asked Liz.

She must have been watching his slack jaw instead of admiring the hut herself.

He nodded. "I'm thinking of all the blood, sweat, and tears that went into building such a beautiful structure in this isolated location. And we think it's hard just hiking up the trail to the pass!"

"Why don't you come out in the sun so you can warm up? The morning chill will linger awhile in here."

"Exactly what I was thinking."

He followed her out of the hut, stopping to pick up his pack on the way out.

"Liz, can we take an extended break here to dry out my stuff? I don't know how long the sun will be out."

"Of course."

Tony walked over. "We'll get your stuff out of our packs and spread it out. But someone needs to guard it against the goats. Maybe even two of us."

Before long, the top of the pass resembled their campsite earlier. They kept everything as close together as possible so they could defend it from the goats. A marmot had also appeared in search of a salty snack. When Bob saw it, he grabbed a still damp Marty and stuffed him inside one of the cargo pockets on his pants.

"Tony, Abbie, you can go ahead of us. I'm tired of being an anchor."

"Yeah, Bob and I can handle it from here. You've done more than enough already."

"No way. We're sticking with you until the end. Don't worry about us," said Abbie.

A solo, middle-aged male hiker arrived from the other side of the pass.

"Whoa! What happened here?"

"Just drying everything out," Bob said.

He turned his palms up. "But it didn't rain last night."

"It's a long story, but I took an unplanned bath in the lake last night." He pointed down at Lake Ellen Wilson. "You're up early this morning."

"Yeah, a bear paid us a visit at Gunsight Lake Campground last night. Couldn't get back to sleep, so I started hiking early. I have a long way to go today anyway."

Liz opened her eyes wide. "A bear! Are you kidding?"

"Nope. Grizzly, best I could tell."

Liz shook her head. "Bob was supposed to be camping there last night, but he stayed with us at Lake Ellen Wilson instead."

"Good move."

Liz's head lurched forward. "Exactly, but the ranger didn't agree when he checked our permits."

They all ate snacks while they took turns shooing the goats and marmots away. The first marmot must have snuck off to recruit his buddies so they could gang up on them. Bob wondered who would prevail if they all went inside the hut, the marmots or the goats?

"How was the hike up here?" asked Liz.

"Beautiful. Thin waterfalls meander down the mountains from the snowfields. The sun lit up the pass in front of me, but I guess you guys will be hiking into it. The trail gets pretty narrow for a while and hugs the mountain wall–and you walk through a waterfall at one point."

Bob's shoulders drooped. "Oh boy. Here we go again."

Their visitor looked confused, then continued. "And I had a surprise while hiking through the thick willows along the lake. They were so tall I couldn't see around the corner. The bear who came into camp could have gone up the trail ahead of me. I rounded a corner and saw nothing but brown fur. I took a couple of steps back, yelling 'Hey Bear' before I realized it had antlers. Tall and wide antlers. It was a moose nibbling on the bushes. I would have been here sooner, but I had to wait him out. I was probably standing way too close, but if I had backed away too much, I might still be down there."

"Wow. You saw a moose too," Liz said. "We talked to a couple who camped at Gunsight Lake two nights ago, and they watched one feeding in the water. I wonder if it was the same one."

"Don't know, but don't let their cool demeanor fool you. They can move a lot faster than their spindly legs might lead you to believe."

Liz's smile faded, but Bob sensed she was still looking forward to seeing the moose on the way down, maybe not on the trail, but perhaps in the water at the end of Gunsight Lake.

The visitor departed about ten minutes later.

Bob groaned as he leaned against a large boulder facing the sun. He rested his head against the hard rock and unzipped the puffy jacket that Liz had loaned him. He had put on his damp hiking pants right before leaving camp so Liz could have hers back, but couldn't bring himself to put on his wet hiking shirt in the cool shade. His shirt would be dry in no time in the morning sun and dry mountain air. He dozed off for a few minutes, but was jarred awake by a shrill scream from Abbie.

"What? What?" Bob asked, trying to clear away the haze from the much too brief nap.

Tony ran around the side of the hut chasing after the kid goat carrying a hiking pole, his hiking pole, his only hiking pole.

"Tony, don't run. It's not worth it," Liz yelled.

Abbie joined her. "Tony! Stop. You're going to hurt yourself."

He reappeared up the slope, above the roof of the hut. The kid was heading toward the east now, where Gunsight Lake lay far below. As Tony continued to approach the kid, the kid's mother bounded straight up the slope to intercept him.

"Tony. Watch out. The mama goat," yelled Abbie.

Tony must have seen the white blur coming because he stopped abruptly and stepped backwards. When the mother goat was convinced Tony had abandoned the chase, she trotted across to her kid, now resting on the rocks above and chewing on the hand grip. Tony raised his palms in resignation and hopped down the slope. Abbie greeted him with a long embrace about halfway up, and they strolled down together holding hands.

Bob sat up. "Thanks for trying. I'm glad you didn't hurt yourself. I've learned that chasing wildlife on their home terrain is hopeless. I chased a marmot on the JMT for about ten yards before I gave up."

"That mama goat seemed pretty angry. Thanks for the heads up, Abbie." Abbie hugged him from the side.

30

Turnaround

Bob had to be woken again as the ranger approached. He must have been utterly exhausted to fall asleep again after the exciting chase of the thieving goat.

"Bob, wake up. Ranger."

He opened his eyes, then squinted in the bright sun. Liz was shaking his shoulder.

"I'm so tired. Can't we stay a little longer? What? Ranger?"

"Yeah, the ranger from yesterday is almost here. Bart."

Bob was overheating in Liz's jacket, so he took it off and replaced it with his now dry hiking shirt. He hung the puffy in a tree to let it air out. Liz would have a lasting reminder of him until it was cleaned properly.

Sorry, Liz.

Bob and Tony checked the rest of his gear for wetness. All but the sleeping bag was dry. Good enough; he wouldn't need it tonight anyway, since they were hiking out to the trailhead.

They packed up Bob's stuff, putting even less in Bob's pack than before.

"Come on, Tony. It will be lighter now that it's dry. I can manage."

"You'll probably get more sore as the day goes on."

Bob shook his head. He despised imposing on such a wonderful couple and his new friend. Bob hesitated when he thought about that. Friend? Was that what Liz was? He still hadn't figured that out. He hoped he could sort everything out once this backpacking trip was over. Too much was rattling around in his head right now.

"Hi folks. It's me again."

"Hello Ranger," said Abbie.

"I'm afraid I have—wait a minute."

The ranger peered at Bob, then pointed his finger at him. "Didn't I tell you to hike to Gunsight Lake last night?"

"Yes, Ranger."

"What did you do, camp in the hut last night? I should have hiked out with you. I'll be following up on you when I get back to the office."

"Let me explain—"

Liz interrupted. "Following up! What do you mean, following up? I told you it wasn't safe to hike out so late in the day."

She stepped toward the ranger and pointed an index finger at him. "Do you know what happened? He almost died! That's what happened. And now you want to FOLLOW UP!"

"Almost died?"

Bob put his hand on Liz's shoulder, but she pushed it away.

"Yeah. He slipped and fell on the wet rocks on the way up to the pass, and slid all the way into the lake. He could have drowned. If I hadn't been watching from the campground and helped him back to camp, he would have frozen on the trail. Thanks to you."

She took another step and jabbed her finger toward his face. The ranger backed up.

Bob felt like saying those things, but he never would have. It wasn't his style. But Liz's forceful defense reinforced how much her feelings for him were growing. At this moment, his feelings for her were clearer. Unfortunately, he feared they would get muddy again on the hike out.

Thank you, Liz! I don't deserve this. You're too good for me. I let Cathy down; I don't want to let you down too.

"OK. Calm down, Miss—"

"My name is Liz, not Miss."

"Sorry, Liz. I understand. I was just doing my job last night, but after what happened, I would have taken him back to your camp as well. You did the right thing."

Liz stepped back and allowed Bob to put his arm around her. She was shaking, so he escorted her to the rock he had been leaning against, and they both sat down. Tony and Abbie grinned with pride as she passed.

"Well, folks, that's not even what I came up here for. I'm afraid I have more bad news. We have closed the trail from the trailhead to the campground at Gunsight Lake. Two bear encounters were reported last night, one at the campground and one near the Florence Falls Trail junction."

"But aren't bears pretty common all over the park?" Tony asked.

"Yeah, but these two bears hung around too long. They aren't shying away from people. That has us worried. So, to be safe, we've closed the trail. We do the same thing when bears are feeding on ripe berries along a trail."

"Oh, I see," said Tony.

"You need to turn around and hike out to Lake McDonald Lodge. You're about halfway through the trail, so you should be able to make it with no problem. If you left your car at the other trailhead, the shuttle bus can take you there."

Liz sighed. "Here we go again. But at least this time, you're making a little more sense."

"I'm going to hike ahead to notify others who left the chalet early or stayed at the Sperry Campground.

"Bob is pretty banged up. What if he can't make it out? Can we stay at Lake Ellen Wilson or Sperry Campground?" asked Tony.

The ranger hesitated. He looked at Bob, then Liz, and back at Tony.

"I suppose … under the circumstances."

"Thanks, Ranger," said Abbie.

"OK, can I trust you guys to turn around?"

They all nodded as the ranger looked each of them in the eye. His eyes fixed on Liz longer than the others.

"Thanks. Be careful out there." He hiked on.

"So much for seeing my moose. I guess we should finish packing up," Liz said.

She stood up, but Bob remained sitting, staring at Gunsight Lake. Liz held out a hand to help him up, but he just stared at it. His sight became blurry. Liz sat back down.

"Are you OK? Is your back getting worse?"

Bob shook his head.

"What's wrong then?"

"Thanks for defending me."

"I enjoyed that. He had no business sending you on your way last night."

"Now I can't finish the hike. I promised Cathy. I'm letting her down again."

Liz let out a deep breath and lowered her head. "Bob, it's OK. She'll understand. You don't think she wants you to get molested by a bear, do you? Just to finish this trail?"

"No, of course not. But it's just one more time. I can't keep disappointing her. She'll leave me for good."

"Hey, it's not under your control. You know that better than all of us. You showed her the best parts of the trail: the chalet, Sperry Glacier, Lake Ellen Wilson, the top of Lincoln Peak, the mountain hut here on the pass. She'll be proud of you. I promise."

He looked up at her with hope. "You think so? How do you know?"

"I just know, Bob. Call it female intuition."

Bob paused to regain his composure. "You've gotten to know me so well, so quickly."

"You're worth it."

31

Doubt

Thomas was sauntering through the rocky meadow with Eva when he heard footsteps. He stepped to the side to let the faster hiker through, and his jaw dropped when he saw who it was.

"Mom, I thought you were staying with Dad?"

"He was going so slow. I couldn't stand it."

"But we promised him someone would stay with him."

"Why can't he walk like the rest of us?"

He looked back at Eva, who was staring down the valley. "Eva, you can go ahead with my mom. I imagine you need to get back to the chalet."

"Where are you going?" asked his mother.

"To check on Dad."

She shrugged and said, "OK," then started walking again. Eva looked from him to his mother and back.

"Go ahead, please."

Thomas backtracked, but he dreaded the thought of more climbing. His legs were sore from yesterday, and he may have overdone his exploring on the other side of the pass. Fortunately, he found his father before the trail rose again, sitting down and rubbing his knees and thighs.

"I thought one of you was going to stay with me? Your mom didn't even wait for me to get down the first descent. She was out of sight when I got here."

"Yeah, I know. She passed me too. It's like she's venting all her pent-up hiking energy in three days."

"My legs are getting more sore every hour, and these descents kill my knees. I should have stayed at the chalet today. Yesterday's hike must be my limit."

He sat on another rock across the trail.

"My legs are hurting too. It takes some getting used to, like anything else."

"I don't have time for that. I can't wait to get back home."

"Just remember how pretty it was up there and how much fun you had hiking yesterday. You'll probably be itching to hike again by the morning. And some new gear would help. We need to buy hiking poles like Bob and Liz use. They would help a lot on the downhills and rocky sections."

"Are you going to stay with me?"

"Yes."

"OK. Let me take a quick break, then we can hobble down the trail together."

32

Warning

Bob started down the short but steep trail from Gunsight Pass that had depleted him on the way up. He hadn't said anything, but he was grateful Tony had asked the ranger about camping along the way. When he woke up this morning, he had no doubt he could make it to the trailhead. But now, he wasn't so sure. And he'd have to do so with one hiking pole after Liz insisted he take one of hers. While one pole didn't help as much as two, he was able to take a little stress off his knees. But would it be enough on the long descent following Sperry Chalet? At least his pack was much lighter now that his gear was dry and his trail friends had taken even more.

Liz offered to hike behind Bob, but he insisted she go ahead. Going downhill, his pack didn't rest so heavily on his bruises, but if he walked too fast, it pounded them with each step. His pace would be agonizingly slow. She told him she would wait for him at the waterfall, but he noticed her peeking back at him after each switchback. Tony and Abbie hiked ahead at a more comfortable pace for themselves, but had promised to take extended breaks to wait for him. That way, every step wouldn't remind them of the helpless old man behind them.

At the waterfall, Liz waved him ahead of her. The wet trail still terrified him, but he walked straight across so as not to show more weakness. The slope was now gradual enough that he could hike at a pace where Liz could follow comfortably. When he reached the spur trail to the campground, he

166

stopped. "You know, that was a great campground. We had a great time by the beach, a chance to clean up, a nice dinner, and even a soothing night."

"Indeed, it was. I haven't seen Gunsight Lake Campground, but this would be hard to beat."

"Yeah. Part of me wants to go down there and set up the tent again."

"Really?"

Bob pinched his lips together in regret. "Just wishful thinking, I guess. We're going to run out of food soon. I'm so tired. Last night took so much out of me."

"I can't even imagine. I'm not sure I could have even gotten out of the lake."

"Sure you could."

"I'm confident you can make it out of here." She pointed to Lincoln Pass ahead of them with her pole. "Only one more modest climb, then it's all downhill."

"That's what I'm afraid of. The downhills kill my knees, one of the few parts of my body that doesn't hurt right now."

"Ready to go?"

Bob waved her in front of him. The climb would begin shortly.

Two young male hikers appeared out of nowhere, almost running down the trail. Since Bob and Liz were blocking their way, they stopped abruptly.

"Excuse us."

"Walter?"

One of the hikers squinted as if trying to recall a distant memory. "Bob, right? From the permit office?"

"That's right. What are you doing here?"

As big as some of the national parks were, Bob was surprised how often he ran into the same people in different parts of the park. Probably because only a small fraction of the visitors ventured more than a mile from the road.

Walter pointed to his hiking partner. "I met Jude here on the Dawson-Pitamakan loop, and what do you know, he had an extra spot on his permit for this trail. Got back the spot you took away from me."

Bob bit his lower lip while Jude nodded.

Liz grabbed Bob's elbow. "Liz, this is the guy I met at the backcountry office while picking up my permit. Small world, or perhaps I should say, small park."

Liz grinned. "Hi."

"Why are you heading back toward Sperry?" asked Walter. "I thought you were going the other way."

"Well, I was, but wait, didn't you hear?"

"Hear what?"

"You didn't see a ranger up the trail?"

Walter and Jude looked at each other. "Ranger? What ranger?"

"The trail is closed up ahead due to bears. A ranger met us up on Gunsight Pass and told us to turn around. Said he was heading this way to notify everyone else."

"No. We didn't see him. We stayed at Sperry Campground last night."

Jude chimed in. "Oh, you know what. He must have passed while we were climbing Lincoln Peak."

"Oh. OK," said Bob. "Could be."

"So the trail's closed? What a bummer," said Jude.

"From Gunsight Lake Campground to the trailhead. You should turn around here."

Walter and Jude looked at each other again and shrugged.

"We'll take our chances. Our car is parked at Jackson Glacier Overlook," said Walter.

Walter patted the canister hanging from his belt. "Got my bear spray this time. We'll be fine."

"Bad idea. But I can't stop you."

"Alright, have a good hike out."

When Bob and Liz didn't step aside, they walked around them.

Liz raised her eyebrows. "Nice try. I hope they get out safely."

"Did you smell the smoke? They must have been smoking in their tent last night or something. Not a good idea either. Seems like they have a death wish."

"Alright Bob, enough playing safety manager. You have your own safety to worry about. Put them out of your mind. They're big boys and make their own choices."

"Yes, ma'am."

Bob regretted it as soon as it came out of his mouth. Liz glowered at him. Bob raised his shoulders. "Sorry."

She pecked him on the lips.

* * *

Bob labored up the trail to Lincoln Pass even more than the one to Gunsight Pass. He stopped every twenty to thirty steps. He hadn't even needed to do that on the 13,000-foot passes on the JMT where the air was much thinner. Liz crept further and further ahead. He wondered if she was tired of nursing the old man up the trail or didn't want to be overbearing. Their intimate moments in the tent last night seemed like weeks ago. Were they even real? Was he reading too much into them?

On the climb to Gunsight Pass, Bob had remained standing during his breaks to catch his breath and readjust his pack, but now he sat down on a boulder and took his pack off. He faced the lake so he wouldn't be reminded of the suffering in front of him. He drank the last of his water, raised his arms to stretch out his back, and rubbed his sore lower back gently. Footsteps grew louder on the trail behind him. And they were quick as well.

I thought the ranger was turning everyone around?

"There you are! We were beginning to worry."

Bob snapped his head around and barely recognized Tony without his pack.

"Are you OK?"

"Yeah, I'll make it, but I'm fading fast."

"You've been through a lot." He picked up Bob's pack.

"Come on, Tony–"

Tony held up his palm a foot from Bob's face. "I've got this. Abbie and I had a refreshing break at the pass."

Bob had planned to rest longer, but he stood up and followed Tony. Without the fifteen pounds on his back, he could keep up with the moderate pace Tony set. It seemed like Tony was pulling him up the trail like a tired dog on a leash at the end of a long walk.

As he approached the pass, Liz and Abbie clapped and said, "Yay," but not too loudly. They must have realized that even their muted encouragement might make him uncomfortable. But he was surprised. It helped. It really did. He hugged them both, one in each arm.

Tony put Bob's pack next to the others and held out his arms. "Hey, don't I get one? I did all the hard work."

Bob grabbed his hand, pulled their opposite shoulders together, and patted him on the back three times. "That's as close as you're gonna get."

Tony swatted him on the arm as he backed away.

"Less than a mile to the chalet. You got this," Tony said.

Bob sat down. Liz sat next to him and put her arm around him.

"Sorry about leaving you behind, but I figured you were getting tired of me hovering. I know I would if I were in your shoes."

"Thanks. I had to get up that hill by myself, though Tony sure made the last part much easier."

Liz looked at Bob's pack. "Are you out of water too?"

"Yeah. I guess we should have stopped to filter water at the waterfall, but I was preoccupied with the crossing—and I guess you were preoccupied with me."

Liz nodded.

"The chalet has plenty of treated water, so we can camel up there and fill our bottles for the descent," Tony said.

"Even better. Phillip might treat us to cold lemonade and snacks?" Bob said.

Liz sat up straighter. "Now that sounds like a good reason to get hiking."

33

Smoke

For the first time all day, the four of them hiked together on the slightly downhill trail. They passed the pond which supplied water to the chalet. Tony slowed his pace, then stopped and raised his nose.

"Do any of you smell smoke?"

They all raised their noses and spun their heads around.

Liz and Abbie nodded.

"Yeah, I do," said Bob.

"Me too," Abbie said. "I wonder if the chalet has their stove burning?"

Bob gazed at the sky over Lake McDonald. "You know what. It is a little hazy out here. Maybe smoke is blowing in from a new forest fire?"

"Could be. But it smells kind of strong." Liz scrunched her nose, then coughed.

Bob pointed to the other side of the pond with his hiking pole. "Oh, no! Looks like smoke is coming from the campground."

Bob darted down the trail, trying to ignore the pain during the burst of effort. He took a left off the main trail and jogged down the tortuous path through the campground. Seeing no tents and no fire, he continued to the food prep area, the most logical location to build a fire.

"Some idiots built a fire," Bob yelled.

Someone had built a fire right outside the logs surrounding the large rock table. Plenty of dry wood remained in and near the fire, and one of the log benches burned.

His eyes and nose burned. His face felt like he was checking on a pizza in his oven. He started coughing and couldn't stop, so he backed up and moved to the upwind side.

The others saw his reaction and joined him.

"Are you OK?" asked Tony.

"Yeah … Yeah … I will be." He sneezed and coughed.

"But no one is here," Tony said.

"They must have tried to put it out and failed. Idiots."

Bob's emergency response training from the plant kicked in.

"Liz?" He waited until she looked him in the eyes. "Can you go to the chalet and alert Chet? Tell him to bring help."

"OK." She set her pack down and jogged up the trail.

"Be careful," Bob yelled. She raised one of her hands and kept jogging.

"We have no water," said Tony.

What an awful time to be out of water. Bob pulled the empty water bag out of one pocket of his pack and his poop kit out of another. He gave the bag to Tony.

"Here, take this and your bags and bottles and fetch some water at the pond."

He and Abbie took another large bag and two bottles from their packs and were gone within seconds.

Bob kicked dirt on the pile of burning wood. When the loose dirt was gone, he used his trowel to gather more and throw it on the fire.

He yelled, "Fire. Help. Fire!" just in case others were passing by.

Tony came back a few minutes later and handed Bob a bag of water. They both dumped water on the edges of the fire. Bob lifted his shirt over his nose and mouth and walked around the fire. As Tony grabbed the empty bag and left, Abbie arrived with two full bottles. She handed Bob one of the bottles and held the other.

"Pour it around the edges. We just need to keep it from spreading until help from the chalet arrives."

They both poured out their water, and Abbie left for the pond. Bob continued to throw dirt onto the fire while they were gone.

Despite their efforts, the fire grew. The idiots had left too much fuel on the still smoldering fire. What were they thinking? Flames approached a ten-foot-tall dead fir tree. Tony and Abbie returned.

"Pour it over here. We can't let it spread that way."

The dead tree burst into flames. Tony and Abbie jumped back. Similar trees were nearby. The fire was getting out of control. They would have to retreat soon. The small amounts of dirt he kicked and shoveled into the flames were not helping. And the water source was too far away.

He sensed motion off to his right. Why is Tony coming from that direction? It's much longer. We can't afford to waste any time. But it wasn't Tony; it was Phillip, and he was carrying something red. A fire extinguisher! That might do it! And behind him was Chet, with another fire extinguisher. And Liz, with yet another. The fire brigade had arrived. He knew the chalet workers would be prepared with the memory of the devastating fire of 2017 fresh in their minds.

"Thank goodness! Phillip, can you spray that tree? It just caught fire, and the flames could spread to others around it."

Phillip blasted the ground a few feet from the tree.

"Phillip. What are you doing?"

"Marty! He's about to catch on fire." Phillip turned his face to the side as he stepped toward the burning tree and kicked the white marmot to the side. He backed away and began spraying the tree. He swiped the nozzle up and down as he circled the tree and disappeared in a cloud of white powder. He emerged quickly, coughing.

Chet stepped around him and discharged his extinguisher on the original site of the fire. Bob backed out of the way. Grit from the extinguishing agent crunched as he clenched his teeth. He spit toward the fire, but it didn't reach.

Tony and Abbie returned and put their water down. Phillip dropped his empty extinguisher and grabbed the one Liz held. He discharged it on the log adjacent to the main fire, where Chet had left off. Claire handed Chet another extinguisher. Instead of discharging it, he scanned the area for more flames.

The dead tree was no longer in flames. When flames reappeared in the pile of wood, Chet blasted them with a short burst from the extinguisher. He didn't take his eyes off the smoldering wood.

"Phillip?" yelled Chet.

Phillip approached Chet.

"Go back and get a couple of buckets and shovels."

"Yes, sir." Phillip trotted off.

Claire told Chet she had another extinguisher ready if he needed it. Chet nodded to acknowledge her remark.

"What happened here?" asked Chet.

Bob walked up to Chet so he wouldn't have to take his eye off the smoldering pile.

"We smelled smoke from the trail and came down to check it out. Some idiots must have tried to put it out before they left, but obviously, they didn't know what they were doing–or didn't care."

"Oh man! We can't thank you enough. This is so close to the chalet. And we have extra people there because of the trail closure. I guess that's why you're headed back this way."

"Yep."

"Should I dump this water on the pile?" Tony asked.

Chet shook his head. "Not right now. Let the powder do its job. I'll keep hitting any flare-ups. We'll dowse it once we've used the shovel to move around the embers."

"What else can we do to help?" asked Bob.

"Nothing for now. Let's wait until the buckets and shovels arrive.

They didn't have to wait long. Phillip arrived with a couple of shovels and a couple of five-gallon food buckets. He gave the buckets to Tony and Claire, who immediately marched toward the pond. He handed a shovel to Bob, but Abbie took it from him.

"Toss the embers and leftover wood, but back away if you see any flare-ups," Chet said,

Abbie and Phillip did as instructed, standing on opposite sides of the smoldering pile. They backed up almost immediately, and Chet blasted the new flames with his extinguisher. It sputtered toward the end of the blast, so he set it down, grabbed the fresh one, and pulled the pin.

Abbie and Phillip resumed when Chet gave them a nod. Phillip scraped the surface of the wood which had flared up. Abbie dug out ashes and put them on top.

When Tony and Claire returned, Chet asked Abbie and Phillip to back away.

"Thanks," Chet said. "Pour water on the embers and ash slowly, one at a time. Give it time to soak in."

The pile sizzled and popped as Claire poured the first bit of water on the pile. She jumped back, spilling precious water. She then walked around the pile, trying to cool as much of it as possible. When the last drops fell from the bucket, she headed back toward the pond, and Tony picked up where she left off.

When Tony was out of water, he also departed.

"Abbie, Phillip, now you can stir up the pile."

Smoke and steam rose from the embers. Chet nodded, looking pleased. After six buckets of water, he set the extinguisher down and took the shovel from Phillip.

"Great work. Let me give you a break."

Phillip took a seat next to the fully charged extinguisher, breathing heavily.

Claire took the shovel from Abbie, who coughed as she walked away from the fire.

Bob grabbed a bucket and went to the pond. He set the bucket down when he returned and sat next to Liz.

She reached around and patted him on the back. "I felt helpless sitting here, but you all had it under control."

"You got help. Without that, this fire would be out of control by now. Thanks for being quick. You didn't hurt yourself, did you?"

Liz shook her head, then handed Marty to Bob.

Bob grimaced. He shook the little marmot, and a small cloud of white drifted away.

"Poor guy! He must have fallen out of my pack when I pulled out my water bag and trowel."

Bob ruffled his fur with his thumb and found a small black spot.

"Ooh. Looks like he got singed."

"I guess he needs a little haircut," said Liz. She squeezed Bob closer.

"You know," she said. "I don't believe that was cigarette smoke we smelled on those two guys. I think they lit the fire this morning to warm up and didn't fully extinguish it."

Bob nodded. "Yeah, I bet you're right. Walter was kind of a jerk the other day. He tried to get the permit I wanted even though I was ahead of him in line."

"Ooh. And they didn't seem the type to follow instructions very well. Did they?"

Bob shook his head. "Or too worried about the risks out here. I wonder if they even knew the chalet burned down a few years ago. Lightning started that fire, but nonetheless, there is no room for carelessness out here. Look at what happened to me last night during a momentary lapse."

Liz pulled him tight with her arm. "Well, I'm glad neither one turned into a disaster."

* * *

Twenty minutes later, Chet said, "Let's go back to the chalet. We have extra guests to take care of because of the trail closure. Claire, can you stay here to keep an eye on the pile of ashes to make sure the fire is really out?"

"Yes."

Tony stood with his arm around Abbie. "Chet, Abbie and I will stay. Sounds like you need Claire's help back at the chalet."

"Yeah, you're right. Thanks folks. I'll send someone else to relieve you in an hour or so."

Phillip and Claire started down the trail. Before Chet did the same, he said, "I can't thank you two enough."

He shook Bob's hand with a firm grip and gave Liz a loose hug, putting their faces side by side.

"It would have been so easy to write off the smell as smoke from a distant fire and keep walking. If you had done so, the fire could have been at the chalet in no time. And we're packed with extra people. A real disaster in the making."

"No need to thank us. We were only doing the right thing. We might know who was behind this–"

Chet interrupted him. "Really? How?"

"When we were hiking back, we ran into a couple of guys heading the other way. The ranger must have missed them because they didn't know about the trail closure. They ended up continuing anyway, but they smelled smoky. I thought they might be cigarette smokers at the time, but I bet they were huddled around this fire last night or this morning instead."

Liz added, "They had no respect for the trail closure or the bear risk. They said they would 'take their chances.' Maybe they felt the same about the 'no campfire' rule?"

Chet clenched his jaw, then said, "Good lead. A ranger is at the chalet to help with the evacuees from the trail closure. Please share your story with him when you get back and let me know if you see them come back to the chalet tonight."

"What do you mean tonight?" Liz asked. "We need to get to the trailhead before dark."

"Well, you can do that if you wish. But you've had a long day, and we owe you a big favor, so you can stay at the chalet tonight if you want."

Liz opened her eyes wide. "Really?"

"I thought you said you were packed?" Bob said, quietly hoping Chet could accommodate them. He was dreading the descent to the Sperry Trailhead. And with the extra time spent here and a second adrenaline rush in two days, he would find it even harder to make it by sunset.

"Yeah, but we'll work something out."

Bob looked at Liz. Her teeth and eyes sparkled. He smiled and grabbed her hand. "Oh, we'd love that. You have no idea what the last twenty-four hours have been like."

"Alright, let's go. We still have some work to do."

34

Return

When Chet, Bob, and Liz arrived at the chalet, Chet said, "Why don't you come in the dining room while we sort out who is going where? We'll get you some lemonade and a snack. You must be parched."

"Sounds great," Liz said. "With all the confusion this morning, we never stopped for lunch and ran out of water on the climb to Lincoln Peak."

Liz pointed to a table next to the window by the patio. Bob removed his pack and groaned while he sat down.

Liz grimaced. "Ooh. Are you sure you're OK?"

She reached across the table and laid her hand on top of his.

"Nothing serious, but I expect I'll feel worse before getting better. My backpack pounded some of my bruises every single step."

"Poor guy."

Bob shook his head. "I'll be OK. Y'all have done so much. I'll never be able to repay you."

"I'm sure you'll pay back somebody on the trail in your travels."

Bob recalled his JMT hike. While he was the recipient of some special trail magic, he doled out more than he received. It wasn't *magic* to him. He was only doing what felt right, but the recipients probably felt otherwise.

"Enough about me. How are you doing? You had a rough night as well and a much heavier pack today?"

"I'm tired, but OK. That may change once the adrenaline wears off tonight.

I hope Chet can find a place for us."

"He will. And if not, we can camp right outside. At least we won't have to worry about running out of food here."

As if on cue, Phillip brought them cold lemonade and peanut butter and jelly sandwiches. "I hope this will do for now. We'll be serving dinner before too long, so I don't want to spoil your appetite."

"This is perfect, Phillip. Thank you," said Liz.

"What's for dinner tonight?" asked Bob.

"Tonight is usually roast beef night, but with our extra guests, we may need to fix something else, in addition. I better get back to the kitchen to help them get ready."

"I feel guilty staying here with all the commotion," Bob said. "But you know what? I don't believe I would have made it down to the trailhead."

"Just imagine. You came up here expecting you wouldn't be able to stay in Cathy's bucket list location, and now you may end up with two nights here. You've had a rough night and day, but you've been fortunate as well."

"You're right. The trail usually gives more than it takes. And it brought us together, too."

They gazed into each other's eyes as they chewed their sandwiches, not looking down while taking their next bites.

Thirty minutes later, Chet stopped by their table. "Did that hit the spot?"

"Yes indeed," Liz said. "We both could have eaten two more, but we're looking forward to another hearty dinner."

"Good call. Dinner will be a little different tonight, but I think we've figured it out."

"Chet, do you want us to go rescue Tony and Abbie from fire duty?" asked Bob.

"Thanks for the offer, but I was just going to check on them and the fire. I need to see and touch it for myself. I'm sure you understand."

"Fully," Bob said.

"You might as well hang out here. My team is trying to round up everybody for a four o'clock meeting so we can figure out where everyone is going to sleep."

Bob glanced at his watch; it was a few minutes past three o'clock. "OK, we'll be here."

The ranger who Bob and Liz had met twice already entered the dining room.

Chet greeted him. "Hi Bart. Good timing. Did you hear about the fire at the campground?"

"No. Sperry Campground?"

"Yeah." Chet pointed to Bob and Liz. "They found it and came here to get help. We managed to put it out, and someone is watching over it now."

Bob and Liz lifted their hands in an attempt to wave. Their energy reserves were depleted.

"You. Again."

"Do you know them?" asked Chet.

"Getting that way. We had a couple of, let's say, energetic discussions last night and this morning."

Chet tilted his head. "They may have spotted the culprits, so you need to talk to them, but why don't you come with me now, and I'll show you what we found. I want to make damn sure the fire is out. Whoever started it sure didn't do that."

Bart tipped his hat at Bob and Liz, then followed Chet out of the door.

Liz shook her head. "At least now he has a real problem to work on, instead of harassing us over sharing a campsite."

"It's OK, Liz. He was just doing his job. Hopefully, he can help those two idiots meet justice."

Bob and Liz patted their hands together above the table.

* * *

Forty-five minutes later, Bart walked around the corner of the patio. "There you are."

"Hi Bart," said Bob. "We needed some fresh air, so we came out here."

"Is the fire still out?" asked Liz.

"Yeah. You all did a damn good job. Thanks for being so attentive and calling for help. That fire could have put a lot of people in jeopardy, not to mention the chalet and the forest and its wildlife. Tell me more about the guys you ran into on the trail. I'm not sure how I missed them."

Bob said, "They said they climbed Lincoln Peak–"

Bart tilted his head back. "Oh–I see. I must have passed while they were on top."

"Their names are Walter and Jude. I met Walter four days ago when I was picking up my permit. Sorry, I didn't catch his last name, but the permit office should have it. They're in their mid-twenties, both wearing shorts and long-sleeve hoodies. One was blue, the other yellow."

Liz interrupted. "That would be one purple and one yellow. Are you color blind, Bob?"

Bob smiled. "Oops, I should know better by now. Thanks, Liz."

"And why were you suspicious?"

"Well, we weren't at the time; at least I wasn't." He looked at Liz, who nodded in agreement. "They smelled like smoke, but I just figured they were smokers. Plus, they were being jerks. We told them about the trail closure, but they kept heading east."

"OK. It's beginning to fit together. We have another ranger or two on the trail, so they will either turn them around or meet them at the trailhead. I'll call them on the radio and give them a heads up. If you see them here, please point them out to me."

"Will do. Thanks, Bart."

Bart almost collided with Tony as he turned to leave.

"Hey Tony, Abbie," said Liz. "I hear you've been relieved of fire watch duty. That was considerate of you to volunteer after such a long day. Chet has his hands full here."

"Oh, it was nothing," said Abbie. "We finally got a little time to ourselves." She grinned at Tony, then Liz.

"Good. It hasn't been the honeymoon you expected, huh?" said Liz.

"No, but that's why we enjoy traveling so much. The surprises make it interesting. I don't think anyone else has experienced a honeymoon quite like this. We won't forget it for the rest of our lives," said Abbie as she put her arm around Tony.

"Are you staying here tonight or hiking down to the trailhead?" Liz asked.

"We were planning to hike down, but Chet talked us into staying," Tony said. "'What's two more?' he said."

Liz stood up. "That's great. Hey, we better go back into the dining room for Chet's meeting."

"Yeah, he told us about that on the way back," said Abbie.

Bob tried to get up, but fell back in the chair. Tony walked over and offered his hand. "Here, old man. Looks like you need help. You were a real trooper out there today."

Bob slapped at the offered hand, but then grabbed it so Tony could help him stand.

35

Improvising

Chet walked into the buzzing dining room from the kitchen.

"Thank you all for coming and thanks in advance for your cooperation in adjusting to these unique circumstances. Usually, we hold a meeting after dinner to share tips about having a safe and enjoyable evening, but we need to cover a few other things before dinner tonight. Due to the trail closure, at least twelve additional people are staying here tonight. I want them to feel as welcome as those who reserved a room back in January. Please try to put yourself in their shoes."

Chet wandered around the tables, causing many to turn their heads.

"First, dinner. We normally have one sitting and one meal for dinner. Tonight, we'll have two sittings, at 5:00 and 6:30. We usually let folks linger to enjoy the company, but the early crowd will need to make room for the next sitting, and the late crew will need to allow time for us to prepare the dining room for those sleeping here."

"Sleeping here?"

"I'll cover that in just a minute. Please be patient with me. One more thing about dinner. This is normally roast beef night. We'll have that, but we'll also serve chicken to make sure everyone has plenty to eat. After the meeting, I'll post a list of the people in each sitting. Any questions on dinner?"

"Can we change our assigned time?"

"Sure, but please find someone to swap with. My staff will be busy preparing extra meals, so they won't be able to help with that."

Chet paused and surveyed the room. Seeing no hands go up and hearing no more questions, he continued.

"Now, for sleeping arrangements. We were fully booked before the trail was closed. For those spending the night here unexpectedly, you should already have your camping gear, so we will make space here in the dining room for you to sleep in your sleeping bags. If you'd prefer, you can camp on the grounds nearby for a little more privacy. The park ranger has given us permission to allow that. There might also be space available at the Sperry Campground."

The crowd had been still and quiet at the beginning of Chet's address, but the mumbling and squirming increased as he went on.

Bob overheard one of the louder voices at the table next to them. "We've had this reservation for eight months. Now we're being crowded out by these other people. We'll get no sleep tonight."

Bob felt like glaring at them in disgust, but Liz did it for him. She even went a step further and shushed them.

Chet couldn't miss the growing tension. "Hey folks. I know some of you have looked forward to staying here for months, even years. But let me remind you, this is the wilderness, not a five-star hotel. As some of you know, the dormitory burned down in 2017. Heck, we even had a fire to put out at the campground this afternoon."

The mumbling grew louder.

"Fire? What fire?"

"Are we still in danger?"

"Why didn't you tell us earlier?"

"The fire is out. No one here is in danger from that. But that's my point. There are risks up here that we need to manage. The goats, the bears, the weather. Please put yourself in the shoes of our new guests."

The mumbling continued, but many were nodding their heads and trying to calm their travel partners or family members."

"Are there any questions?"

The man next to Bob, who had been complaining earlier, raised his hand

and asked, "What time is breakfast tomorrow?"

Chet glanced at the floor and took a deep breath. "We'll serve breakfast here tomorrow morning, an hour later than normal, after we prepare the room for dining again."

The man shook his head, then looked around the room to pick out the extra guests, perhaps those who appeared to be more haggard than the rest.

"Anything else?"

Bob stood up. Liz looked up at him, surprised.

"Chet, I have a request for the guests staying here. My partner and I had the pleasure of staying here a couple of nights ago. It was a wonderful experience, thanks to Chet and his dedicated team. I had a rough night last night further down the trail, and Liz here, and Tony and Abbie, saved my life." Bob looked down at Tony and Abbie. "And then they helped put out the fire we found while returning to the chalet. The thing is, they're on their honeymoon. And they've spent the entire time helping others. If any of you have an extra bed in your room to share with another guest or couple to give Tony and Abbie the honeymoon they deserve, please let me know. I'd be happy to reimburse you for your room charge. Thank you."

Bob sat down. Tony shook his head. "Bob, we're OK. Really."

Abbie grabbed Tony's arm and rested her face on his shoulder. Liz's eyes were glossy. She was speechless.

The murmuring reached a pitch. A middle-aged man stood up. "Our room has two double beds. If another couple wants to share, we're happy to do so."

A single man, about the same age, raised his hand. "I'm alone in my room with two beds. I'm happy to share. Tony, Abbie, congratulations on your wedding."

The mumbling transformed into the warm gaiety that normally accompanied dinner. Eyebrows raised. Smiles abounded. Liz's cheeks were wet. Tony and Abbie stared at Bob. Chet winked at him.

"OK, folks, we'll see half of you back here in an hour for dinner. Thanks again for your cooperation."

People wandered out. A few patted Bob on the shoulder as they passed.

Some shook his hand. Others congratulated Tony and Abbie.

When most of the crowd had departed, Tony said, "Bob, you shouldn't have, but thanks. Our honeymoon has been fantastic, even if it turned out different from what we imagined. But like Chet said, that's being in the wilderness. You never know what obstacles you'll face and what magic will appear."

Liz's eyes became misty. "Magic. I like it. That's exactly what it is. Thanks, Bob."

Tony stood up. "Bob, we need to get all your gear back together. It's scattered in four packs right now. No matter where we're sleeping tonight, we'll be separating in the morning."

Abbie frowned.

"OK, let's meet up in your new room once you get settled," Bob said.

Tony nodded, and he and Abbie walked toward the door.

Jason, Crystal, and Thomas stopped by on their way out.

"Hi. You're still here!" said Bob.

"Yeah, the horses are meeting us tomorrow morning," Crystal said.

Liz looked at Thomas. "Did you make it up to Sperry Glacier?"

Thomas glowed. "Yeah. We tried to hike up there yesterday, but a badger scared us away–"

"A badger! What is that?" Liz said.

"Believe me, you don't want to know. We tried again today and made it all the way to the top. Including my dad!"

Bob looked up at Jason. He raised his hand, and Jason patted it. "Well done. What's next? The Grand Canyon?"

Crystal faced Jason. "Not yet. We're going to ease into this."

"We've been talking," Jason said. "Our room has two double beds, and Thomas has offered to sleep on the floor, or maybe they have a cot he can use. You or Liz are welcome to use the extra bed?"

Bob and Liz looked at each other, then Liz giggled.

"What's so funny?" asked Crystal.

"Oh, nothing," said Liz. "We'd love to take you up on your generous offer. Both of us."

"Oh!" Crystal replied. "How wonderful!"

"And Thomas," Bob said, "you can tell us all about the badger and the glacier–and how slow your dad was."

Jason slapped Bob on the shoulder. His exaggerated response knocked him against Liz, who held him against her for a moment.

"But it sounds like you have a more exciting story to tell," Jason said.

Liz stood up. "Let's go check what dinner seating we're in."

The roster showed they were all in the second seating.

"Why don't you come by and get settled before dinner?" said Crystal.

"OK, I need to get my gear back from Tony and Abbie, but we'll be there soon."

* * *

Bob tapped Jason and Crystal's door with his shoe since he and Liz had their arms full of gear retrieved from Tony and Abbie. Bob had hung his sleeping bag on the railing along the dormitory building before going inside so it could continue to dry out. Jason took a step back when he opened the door.

"Didn't know what you were getting into when you invited us in, did you?" Liz said.

"Whoa, what happened to all your gear?" asked Crystal.

"Long story," Bob said. "But don't worry. We'll pack up most of this stuff so it is out of the way."

They walked in and placed the gear on the floor at the foot of the bed Thomas was lying on.

Thomas hopped up. "Cool. You carry all that stuff on your back?"

"Yep, all forty pounds of it, maybe thirty now that my bear canister is almost empty," said Bob.

"Mom, Dad, when can we go backpacking like Bob and Liz?"

"Easy, Thomas. We just got your dad on the trail. You don't want to scare him away already."

Liz sat on the bed Thomas had vacated. "Yeah, backpacking allows you to experience some wonderful places, but it's a lot harder than day hiking.

The extra weight wears you down. But you get used to it after a while."

Thomas lifted Bob's wadded up tent. "Whose tent is this?"

Bob raised his hand. "I need to roll it up more neatly. We put everything away in a hurry this morning."

"Would you mind if I used it tonight?"

Bob looked at Jason and Crystal and shrugged.

Crystal stood up. "You want to camp? Tonight?"

"Why not? I'll be sleeping on the ground anyway. And they have all the stuff right here."

"I don't know, son," said Jason. "Bob, are you sure it's OK with you?"

"Sure. I won't be using it, thanks to your generosity. It's the least I can do. The only problem is that my sleeping bag is still kind of wet."

Liz interrupted. "But he can use mine."

"OK, Thomas, if you really want to," said Crystal.

Thomas jumped up. "Great. Let's go up to the campground and set it up."

"Campground?" asked Crystal.

"Yeah, Mom. The campground we passed on the way to Lincoln Peak."

"Oh, I was thinking of right outside the dormitory, where help would be close. Remember what happened the other night when you ran off."

Liz patted Thomas on the back. "That's probably best. You can ease into it, and if you have any problems with the gear, we're right here."

"OK, I guess that's a good idea."

"Great," said Bob. "Let's go set up your tent and sleeping gear before dinner. Liz, you can lie down and tell Jason and Crystal all about my misadventures last night and the fire we found this afternoon. I don't want to relive all that."

"OK. Now I can tell them what really happened out there." She smiled, and Bob lowered his chin and shook his head as he walked out the door.

He mumbled to Thomas. "You better watch out for women, Thomas." He turned around, smiled at Liz and Crystal, and closed the door.

36

Busted

Bob and Liz walked to the dining room with Jason, Crystal, and Thomas. Tony and Abbie were leaving and held the door open for them. They glowed with full bellies and anticipation of their unexpected private room of comfort.

"So you were in the early seating?" asked Liz.

"Yeah, we tried to save enough for you, but I don't know …" said Tony.

"Y'all behave tonight, OK?" said Bob.

Abbie slapped him on the shoulder as she passed.

Bob saw an empty table for six, so he rushed over and pulled a chair out for Liz.

"Wow, how quickly your town manners come back," Liz said, then looked at Crystal. "That all goes out the window when you're backpacking."

Thomas smiled. His interest in backpacking had blossomed as he learned more about it. Bob was curious to hear what he said tomorrow morning after a frosty night alone in a tent in bear country.

As soon as they were settled, a young lady who didn't appear much older than Thomas asked if she could take the open chair across from Thomas. She introduced herself as Anna. She was petite, with short and straight black hair and a pale complexion, except for the small tattoo of a mountain on each forearm. Jason introduced her to everyone.

Claire brought them six glasses and a couple of pitchers of lemonade. "Hi

190

again. I remember you two from the fire. Thanks for coming to get help so quickly."

"Just doing the right thing," Bob said. "Thanks for doing your part. I figured y'all would be well prepared."

"Yes sir. Chet trains us well when we arrive and conducts drills every week so we don't forget and can practice thinking in stressful situations."

"This is the first time Phillip hasn't waited on us. We were here a couple of days ago," said Bob.

"We'll try to be easy on you, but watch out for the guy over there." Liz nodded toward Jason.

Crystal giggled. Jason didn't, but he smiled. Thomas was too distracted by Anna to notice.

"I'll be right back with bread." She began to leave, but Phillip handed her a basket of bread and smiled at them all. "You're in good hands. Enjoy."

"Anna, what brings you to Sperry Chalet?" asked Jason.

"I graduated from high school in May in Florida and wanted to see the West before I start college. I read about the history of this place and the fire, so I called a week ago to check if anyone had canceled. Someone had just done so. It's been a wonderful summer."

"Wow, you don't know how lucky you were to grab a canceled reservation. I tried that for months and never got one. Good for you," said Bob.

"Come on, Bob," said Crystal. "I'd say you've been pretty fortunate yourself."

Bob looked at Liz and nodded.

"Anna, where else have you been?" asked Liz.

"Let's see." She looked up as if reading a map held in front of her. "I stopped in Colorado first, Rocky Mountain National Park, then on to Wyoming. Spent a few days backpacking in the Tetons, then almost a week in Yellowstone. So many things I've never seen before: the geysers, buffalo, bears. I almost didn't make it out of there. But I'm glad I did because Glacier is amazing. If you haven't hiked the Dawson-Pitamakan loop, and you have the time and energy, you gotta do that. Best day hike I've ever done. Then tomorrow I head to Utah for my last week. I'll only be able to scratch the surface with all the great hikes in that state."

"Have you been traveling alone all this time?" asked Thomas.

"Yeah, my mom and dad's idea of a vacation is sitting on a beach or gambling in Vegas or something like that. This was my first chance to finally get outdoors."

Crystal peeked over at Jason, but he didn't seem to notice.

"Wow!" was all Thomas could say. He must have been thinking she was living his dream.

"Thomas, tell us about your hike to Sperry Glacier," said Liz.

Claire appeared and placed a couple of platters on the table. "As Chet said, we have a mix of chicken and roast beef here. I'll be back with the potatoes and green beans." She picked up the empty bread basket. "Would you like more bread? I think we have a few pieces left in the kitchen."

Jason and Thomas nodded.

"It took us two attempts to get up there. Yesterday, my dad and I had to turn around because a badger wouldn't budge from the trail."

Claire turned around when she heard that. "You saw a badger? They're not common around here. That's special."

Jason said, "It was special alright. I was scared to death when it flashed its teeth and started spitting at us."

"My mom had already passed by, so she didn't know until she returned to the chalet."

"Sorry. I feel so bad about that. I shouldn't have hiked so far ahead."

"Then Eva volunteered to guide us up there today to sketch for us and run interference with the animals."

"Eva?" Liz asked.

"Yeah, she's the resident artist. Can you believe that?" said Crystal.

Crystal grabbed her phone and showed a picture of the sketch to Liz. Liz held it out so Bob could see.

"Awww. How nice. Thomas, you look so happy," said Liz.

Claire returned with the potatoes and green beans. She waved at the food on the table. "Dig in, folks."

"And then some goats hung out with us the whole time we were there. I wasn't too happy about them either," said Jason.

"They were probably waiting for you to pee," said Bob.

Crystal and Anna scrunched their noses.

Bob chuckled. "I'm serious. They crave salt. When we were on Gunsight Pass, a kid goat ran off with one of my hiking poles and chewed on the hand grip. I hear they will lick the ground wherever someone pees."

"Gross," said Anna.

Crystal puckered her face.

"Jason, how do you feel after your first big hike?" asked Bob.

"If you had asked me on the way down, I would have said, 'Never again.' My legs were so sore from the day before, and my knees were killing me on the downhill. Then Crystal left me all alone."

Crystal winced and mouthed, "Sorry."

"But Thomas came back to encourage me. It took us forever to get down, but we made it."

"The hike back is always tough, especially the last mile or two," Liz said. "But you always make it back."

"I feel much better now after taking a nap and lying down for a couple of hours. I don't know how you and Bob carry those heavy packs and hike day after day, all day long."

"You have to build up to it. Well, congratulations. Was the view worth it?" Liz asked.

Jason shrugged. "I guess so. Looking at the sketch helps. I need to get in better shape if I'm going to continue hiking. And get some of those hiking poles you and Bob use."

"You did good, Dad. I was struggling at the end too."

"I'm glad y'all had a great time," Bob said.

Crystal said, "It was so wonderful. Bob, thanks for telling us about the hike and encouraging us to go together as a family. I can't wait to start planning the next trip."

"Thanks y'all," said Anna. "Now I know what I'm doing tomorrow morning. I was planning to hike straight down, but I think I'll explore that area myself."

Claire arrived with a large plate of cookies for dessert. With all the discussion, their plates were still half full.

"Oops, I forgot. We're supposed to be eating quickly tonight," said Bob.

Claire winked at him. "You're fine. Chet was being a bit dramatic. He just didn't want people lingering too long and getting in the way. Keep enjoying yourselves. But I have to explain this dessert. The cookies are delicious, but we usually serve cake. We just ran a little short on time."

Liz reached out and put her hand on Claire's elbow. "No worries, dear. You and the rest of the staff are doing a brilliant job taking care of us rowdy guests."

"Rowdy. Who's being rowdy?" Jason said.

"Dad. Not now."

Jason and Crystal smiled.

But Bob wasn't smiling. In fact, he no longer heard what they were saying. He stared at the open door. The two guys he suspected of starting the fire had just walked in. They surveyed the room and stopped at the counter.

Bob tugged at Claire's arm and whispered, "Those are the guys who started the fire. Invite them to find a seat, and I'll go find Chet."

She nodded and walked toward the strangers. Bob followed her, but continued toward the kitchen, looking at the floor as he passed.

"Chet, the guys I was talking about earlier are here. Walter and Jude, the ones who might have started the fire. I asked Claire to find them a seat."

Chet laid the dishes he was washing in the sink and took off his apron. "Thanks. I'll get Bart. Go back to your table. Best to let him take care of it, since he is trained for these situations."

Bob returned to his table. All but Liz appeared to be puzzled.

"What's going on, Bob? Are you OK?" asked Crystal.

"Yeah. I'll tell you later. Just carry on."

Bob took a cookie from the plate and set it on his napkin. He glared at Walter and Jude.

A few minutes later, Bart and Chet approached the two late-arriving guests. They appeared to be quietly urging Walter and Jude to go outside.

Walter protested loudly instead. "What? Why us? We're starving."

Jude sighed and lowered his head. "Another ranger met us at Gunsight Lake and told us to turn around. Do you know how far that is?"

Bart raised his hands, turning his palms to Walter and Jude. "Calm down, sir. Of course, I do. This won't take long. There's a lot going on here at the chalet with the trail closure."

"OK, but make it quick." Walter looked at Chet. "Do you have any food left?"

Chet grabbed Phillip's arm as he passed. "Can you prepare a couple of plates of whatever we have left?"

"Sure."

Bart and Chet followed the two guys outside.

Bob stood up, but Liz pulled on his arm until he sat back down. "They got this, Bob. You've done your part."

Bart and Chet walked in behind the two guys about ten minutes later. Walter and Jude sat at one of the empty tables, glaring at Bob and Liz as they passed.

Chet walked among the other tables. "OK, folks. Dinner time is over. If you are sleeping here tonight, you're welcome to stay and help us get the room ready. If not, please go back to your rooms or enjoy the stars from the patio. We'll see you at breakfast tomorrow. Good night."

As Bob and the others filed out, Phillip left the kitchen with two plates.

Bob and Liz hung around outside the dining room for a few minutes, hoping for an update from Chet or Bart.

Chet noticed them through the window, waved Bart to the door, and opened it for him.

"So, what did they say?" asked Bob.

"They denied starting a campfire, of course," said Bart.

Bob shook his head. Liz put her arm around him. "Bob, don't worry. They'll get to the bottom of this."

"Already have, ma'am. This afternoon, I got the list of campers at Sperry last night and cross checked against Chet's list of extra guests. I found a match, so I tracked the couple down and talked to them separately. They stayed at the campground last night and both confirmed those guys started the fire. In fact, they had quite an argument about it."

Bob relaxed and put his arm around Liz. "What's next?"

"I told them they could stay in the dining room or outside in their tent, but either way, I would escort them out tomorrow and take them to the ranger station."

"Well done, Ranger. See Bob, all turned out well."

"Where are you two staying tonight?" asked Bart.

"Another couple invited us to share their room. Their son is camping by himself using our gear. He's the one who was sitting with us at dinner. He's so excited."

"Great."

"If you are up and about tonight, please check in on him, if you don't mind. His mother is a little worried. It's the green and gray tent by the dormitory building." Bob pointed up the hill.

"Will do. Have a good night. I need to get back in there."

Bob shook his hand, then Bart walked back into the dining room.

Liz pulled herself around him, hugged him, and kissed him.

37

Wonder

"Thomas, let's make sure you have everything you need for the night," said Bob.

"Thanks." Thomas jogged toward Bob's tent outside the dormitory.

"Jason, why don't you go along with the boys? Liz and I will go to the bathroom and get ready for bed. We've all had a long day."

Jason nodded. Liz flashed Bob a quick smile, then told Thomas, "Have a great night."

When they arrived at the tent, Bob said, "First, the most important thing–you don't have any food in your pockets, do you?"

"No, sir."

"Good, that would make you bear bait. And call me Bob, not sir. When you're done with your toothpaste, bring it to the room. No toiletries in your tent, either."

"Really? Bears are interested in that stuff?"

"That's what they say. Anything with a smell."

Jason and Thomas looked surprised.

Crystal arrived with another jacket, a fleece cap, and gloves.

"I thought you were getting ready for bed?" asked Jason.

"I don't want Thomas to get cold."

"Mom, I'll be OK. I'm less than a hundred feet from the room. Really. Stop worrying."

"Do you have bear spray?"

Jason held up the canister attached to his belt and handed it to Thomas.

"See? Now please go," said Thomas.

Crystal sulked back to the dormitory. Thomas rolled his eyes. "OK, where were we?"

Bob reached inside the tent and grabbed a headlamp from one of the mesh pockets on the wall. "I think you know how to use this, right?"

Thomas nodded.

"What should he do if an animal tries to tear down his tent?" asked Jason.

Thomas lowered his head. "Come on, Dad!"

"Just do like we did on the trail the other night. Make a lot of noise. Not only will it run away, but you'll wake up lots of people in the dormitory to help–so don't overdo it."

Bob looked around the tent. "I think that's it. Do you have any other questions?"

"No, I don't think so, and like my mom and dad said, you're not far away. I'm sure Mom will be peeking through the window at me anyway. Thanks for giving me the chance to try this out. Sure beats sleeping on the floor."

Jason stepped next to Thomas and put his arm around him. "OK. Good night, Son."

* * *

When Bob returned to their room, Liz and Crystal sat on one bed, sharing photos. Marty sat on a pillow on the other bed.

"Marty!"

He sat on the bed and grabbed his marmot friend. He wasn't white anymore, but his brown fur was still grizzled with remnants of the white fire extinguishing agent, like a grizzly bear. Someone had placed a bandage over the fur that had been singed. He peeked under the bandage and saw that the hard, black residue had been removed. Only one person could have done this. He looked across to the other bed, holding Marty to his chest. How could someone look so beautiful after four days of hiking, backpacking, water rescue, and fire fighting? Then again, the beauty on the inside wasn't tarnished by any of that.

"Liz, you're so sweet."

They both leaned forward and kissed.

Crystal stood up. "Jason, perhaps we should go hang out in the dining room for a while."

"Don't be silly," said Liz. "This is your room, after all. Plus, I think Bob's had enough strenuous exercise for today."

* * *

Bob walked toward his tent, or actually, Thomas's tent, tonight. When he started unzipping the rainfly, he heard, "Come on, Mom! It hasn't even been thirty minutes."

Thomas unzipped the mesh door on the tent body.

"Oh, Bob. I thought my mother was coming to check on me already."

"Don't worry. She's checking on you from the window." Bob winked. Thomas sighed.

Bob held out Marty. "Here, I forgot this. He prefers to sleep outside, so I figured he could keep you company."

Thomas grabbed Marty and set him in the tent. "Thanks."

Bob started to stand back up.

"Hey Bob, can I ask you a question?"

"Sure. Hold on." Bob groaned as he sat on the ground.

"OK. What's up?"

"I talked to Phillip and Eva yesterday and asked them what it's like to work here. Sounds pretty cool to me. What do you think? I'm afraid to even bring it up with my parents right now?"

"Why?"

"I don't know. They've been fighting a bunch the last few months, and you saw how Dad acted at dinner the first night. They're doing so much better the last couple of days. I don't want to mess it up."

"I understand. Well, it could be a great experience. You would learn a lot about people and being flexible and self-sufficient. Good life skills, overall. But make sure you think through all the inconveniences too. You don't want to be miserable all summer."

"Yeah. They told me about some of those. But they do have showers–oops, I wasn't supposed to tell you."

Bob zipped his lips with his fingers. "Maybe you should contact Phillip after the summer for more information. Then you can approach your parents when you're ready. You'll be going off on your own soon anyway."

"Thanks, Bob."

* * *

When Bob returned to the room, Liz and Crystal looked comfortable with blankets up to their chins. Jason sat in the chair. He looked like he might not have enough energy left to change into his pajamas.

Bob rummaged through his pile of gear on the floor for his sleeping clothes. Since they were now dry, he wouldn't have to wear a puffy jacket to bed. He headed toward the door. "I'm going to get ready for bed."

Jason managed to get up and pull his pajamas out of his duffel bag.

Liz said, "Don't be silly. You can both change here. Bob, I've already seen most of you on the trail." She grinned. "We'll peek out the window while you're doing so."

She and Crystal hopped out of bed and pulled aside the curtains. Bob heard giggles, and when he turned around, Liz was peeking at him with her hand over her mouth.

As he finished up, Crystal said, "Jason, when you're done, come over here."

Jason hobbled over to the window and took Liz's place.

Crystal said, "Awww. Look. Thomas and Anna are gazing at the stars."

"Oh boy. I bet you she's putting all kinds of ideas in his head about road tripping."

Bob peeked over Crystal's shoulder. "Good for him. But I have to pee and brush my teeth. I'll try to keep my distance."

"I'll go with you. It might seem less obtrusive that way."

Bob and Jason walked in a large arc around the tent to the bathrooms. He couldn't resist peeking at Thomas and Anna. They waved, then returned their attention to the sky.

When he and Jason returned to the dormitory building, Bob said, "I'm going to sit out here and enjoy the stars for a while. I need a little time alone."

"OK, see you in a bit."

Bob walked to a log up the hill from the building and out of sight of his tent. He pulled out his phone and started the voice recorder.

* * *

Dear Cathy,

Hi Honey. I'm sorry I neglected you so much today. I'm glad you didn't have to endure it all, but your care and support would have made it less difficult. Liz, Tony, and Abbie did way more than I could have expected from people I just met. They were wonderful. But they aren't you!

I just saw Thomas watching the stars with his new friend. It reminded me of one of the few camping trips we took together. Sitting on a large rock on the edge of a deep canyon, hip to hip, with a warm blanket covering our legs and puffy jackets zipped high. We could have done that on the JMT if I had gone with you. Maybe not every night, but when we camped at special places like Marie Lake.

And guess what; we get to spend another night at Sperry Chalet. After all I've been through, I wouldn't have made it to the trailhead tonight. Too far, too steep, too sore. Jason and Crystal were so generous in sharing their room with us. It appears they have grown much closer in the brief time we were away. I'm glad Jason is giving nature a chance to mend their fences.

But of course, you'll be sharing me with Liz again. I wonder how you feel about that; I wonder how I feel about that. I love these opportunities to talk to you and will always love you. But I can't touch you, hold you, and see your reactions. I've needed those things the past couple of days, but will I need it when I get home, when I'm not in crisis mode? Liz seems to need the companionship even more. I don't know if I can keep up with her–give her what she wants. I wonder how long she will wait. How long I have to figure things out. How you feel. I wonder and worry–

Sticks snapped. Rocks tumbled across the ground. The hair on the back of his neck rose. He stopped talking and turned around.

"Bob, are you OK?"

Liz stepped in front of him and held out his puffy jacket. Bob exhaled the breath he had been holding.

"Why are you sitting out here in the cold? Alone."

Bob put on his jacket. He hadn't realized he was shivering. Liz sat next to him, ensuring their hips touched. She rubbed his back to help him warm up.

Liz looked at the phone in his hand. "Cathy?"

Bob nodded. She stopped rubbing, reached to grab his far arm, and squeezed.

"Why didn't you tell me? Jason said something about the stars. I was worried about you. You're still weak. Good thing Thomas saw you come this way, or I'd be forming a search party."

His shivering got worse, but it wasn't just due to the cold.

"I don't know. It's awkward."

"I'm sorry, Bob. I don't mean to make you uncomfortable."

"How do you feel, Liz?"

"Mostly, I'm excited. Excited about the possibilities. I really like you. I'll always love my husband, but I'm still living. I can't wait around. I go after what I want."

Bob peered into her eyes.

"But you're not there yet with Cathy. I understand. I realize I need to be a little more patient. It's hard, but I believe I can manage."

"How long?"

"I don't know, Bob. Come on, let's go inside."

Bob stood up and grabbed Liz's hand. He pulled her up into a tight embrace. He didn't let go for a full minute. "You're too good for me."

"No. We're just what each other needs."

They held hands as they ambled back to their room.

Bob got into the bed first. When Liz did the same, they pulled up the covers.

"Bob, are you OK?" Crystal asked.

"Yeah. It's been a long and difficult twenty-four hours. I needed a little time alone. I haven't been alone since Liz found me after my fall."

"She told us more about that. I'm glad you're OK," said Jason.

"Now I understand why you spoke up at the meeting earlier. You had lots of help," said Crystal.

"I wouldn't have made it without them."

Liz rolled over and put her hand on his chest. "You would have found a way. You're stronger than you think."

"How is Thomas doing out there?" Crystal asked.

"Come on, Crystal. You know the answer to that. You've been peeking out the window every fifteen minutes." Crystal slapped Jason's chest.

"He's fine," Liz said. "Anna was just leaving when I stopped to ask if they had seen Bob. Can I turn off the lantern now? I'm exhausted from taking care of this old man all day."

"Yep," said Bob. Crystal and Jason grinned.

Bob lay on his back. When Liz got back in bed, she kissed him on the forehead and laid on her side facing the other way. After a few minutes, Bob rolled on his side and put his arm around Liz under the covers. She grabbed his hand instantly, dragged it toward the bed, and squeezed as if her life depended on it.

VIII

Interlude

September 30, 2017
Houston, Texas

<h1 style="text-align:center">38</h1>

<h1 style="text-align:center">Bucket</h1>

Bob worked on his laptop on the dining room table. Cathy pulled out the chair next to him, holding a sheet of paper in her other hand.

"Are you working again? It's Saturday. You need to rest. You worked late every day this week."

"I know. Still trying to catch up from our trip to Colorado."

"But that was two weeks ago."

"Someone fell and broke their hip while I was gone. I don't know if I'll ever catch up."

Cathy pulled his hands away from the keyboard.

"Bob, that wasn't your fault. The plant will keep running long after you leave."

Bob stared at the screen, seeing only a gray blur, no words.

She squeezed his hand. "Well, thank you for coming with me. I had a wonderful time. And it was so much better than going alone. Talking about the beautiful mountains, lakes, wildflowers, and wildlife with each other. Encouraging each other during the last few miles each day. Adjusting the itinerary due to the weather. I could have managed alone, but I loved having you with me. Even if I lost you to your phone for an hour or two each day."

Bob finally turned to look at her. "I had fun too. You picked some great hikes."

"We need to do more of that."

He looked away.

"Look. I want to show you something."

She placed the sheet of paper on the keyboard.

"What's this?"

"The beginning of our bucket list–hikes we need to do while we can, before we get too old. We won't be able to do some of these forever, you know."

Bob read the bulleted list that filled half the page.

"Wow, that's a long list."

"It's only the beginning. I want you to add to the list."

Bob pointed to the top of the list. "Is this in priority order?"

"Not yet."

"If we could do only one next year, which would it be?"

He thought he knew the answer, but he asked anyway. She had been trying to convince him to take three weeks off to hike the John Muir Trail for a few years now. She hadn't been able to secure a permit in the very competitive lottery, so he had wiggled off the hook every year.

"That's easy. The John Muir Trail. It's the hardest and perhaps the most beautiful, so we need to hike it soon."

"OK, let's hike it next summer if you can get a permit."

"Great. What else?"

"Isn't three weeks enough? We'll be worn out for a month or two after that."

She pointed to the list. "Bob, look at it. We'll never finish by knocking one hike off per year. You can fix that by retiring. You keep putting it off, one year after another. It's time to go."

Bob stared at the paper. He had to admit the hikes Cathy selected for the Colorado trip were spectacular. The hike to Sky Pond in Rocky Mountain National Park was fantastic, but the hike to Lone Eagle Peak jutting up over Mirror and Crater Lakes in Indian Peaks Wilderness was the best he had ever done. They had even summited one of Colorado's 14ers (14,000-foot peaks), La Plata Peak. He remembered his pride as much as the beauty. He felt like he was on top of the world.

He had dreaded the return to work, but soon became comfortable working long days again. Cathy kept looking through the photos and telling him about her favorite moments. She must have also been working on this bucket list. Her appetite for the outdoors was insatiable. He knew he needed to retire, but work had been a huge part of his life for so long. And what he did was so important–saving lives.

"Maybe next year, right before the JMT hike."

"Good. I'll believe it when I see it."

He tried to hand the paper back to her, but she pushed it away. "Keep it. I want you to pick your favorites and add any I missed. Maybe you can do that instead of working all weekend."

He searched her face for clues to her emotions. How serious was she? Deep down, he knew, but he searched for a sign that she may be joking or making small talk. But that wasn't her. She knew what she wanted, and she went after it. No messing around. He closed the laptop, took the list, grabbed a pencil, and laid down on the couch.

IX

Day Six

July 30, 2023
Glacier National Park

39

Missing

Someone banged on the door.

Bob threw the blankets off of him. "Hold on, Hannah. I'm coming," he muttered.

Liz shook his shoulder. "Bob. Are you OK? Who's Hannah?"

"What's going on? Am I still in Bishop?

"You must have been dreaming," Liz whispered.

"Mom, Dad."

Crystal jumped out of bed and opened the door. "Thomas!" Crystal stepped forward and hugged him. "Are you OK?"

"Mom, please, I'm fine."

He squirmed out of her embrace so he could step inside.

"I've been awake for a while, but I didn't want to wake everyone up too early."

Bob glanced at his watch: 7:05 AM. "Wow. I haven't slept so late in months."

Liz patted him on the shoulder. "Good. We both had some catching up to do."

Thomas and Crystal sat on the bed next to Jason.

"How was it? Did you get scared?" asked Crystal.

"No. It was great. That sleeping bag is amazing. My face was a little cold, but nothing else."

"No bears or goats?" Jason asked.

"Nope, but lots of people going to the bathroom."

Jason raised his hand. "Guilty."

Bob raised his hand too.

"Hey Bob, I believe those guys who started the fire left before everyone woke up. Chet and Bart were talking loudly down by the dining room. I heard Bart saying something about trying to track them down."

Bob jumped out of bed and searched for his camp shoes. Once he had them on over his socks, he grabbed his puffy jacket and left the room. He marched straight to the dining room.

Chet stood at the counter. "I think I know why you're here."

Chet walked toward the kitchen. Bob waved to the campers who were picking up their gear, then followed Chet.

"What happened?"

"First, have some coffee to help you calm down." Chet poured him a cup. "Milk, sugar?"

"Milk, please." Chet opened the commercial-scale refrigerator and poured milk in the cup.

"Here."

Bob held the cup with both hands and breathed in the hot, humid air above it. "Thanks."

"Walter and Jude chose to sleep in the dining room last night. When I got here around 5:30, they were gone. They must have snuck out early to avoid being taken into custody at the trailhead."

Bob put his cup on the counter and coffee sloshed over the top. "Sorry."

Chet tossed a hand towel to him.

"Bob, you're taking this too personal. You did your part. You found the fire and helped put it out. You helped us identify the culprits. Let the rangers do their job. There are only a couple of ways out of here."

"I know. I can't help it. Years of conditioning as a safety manager at a chemical plant. My wife used to tell me the same thing."

"Anyway, we searched for them outside and in the bathrooms. They were gone. Bart called someone on his radio to ask them to watch the trailhead, packed his things, and took off. Either he'll catch them from behind or another ranger will meet them at the trailhead."

"But what if they go off trail?"

"You hiked the trail. It's steep. That would be slow going. And then they have to get to their car, which is probably at the Jackson Glacier Overlook parking lot. The rangers have this covered."

"OK, thanks for the update." Bob raised his cup. "And the coffee. What time does breakfast start?"

Chet looked toward the dining room. "I see everyone is up now, so in about an hour or so."

"Hey, can I take some coffee for my roommates?"

Chet smiled. "Sure. Who are you trying to impress?"

"Oh, come on, Chet." Bob tossed the towel at Chet. "Not you too."

* * *

Bob walked back to the room with a tray full of five cups of coffee, a cup of milk, and some sugar packets. He knocked on the door with his foot when he got to the room.

Bob heard, "Just a minute," and the door opened moments later.

"Sorry, I didn't know you were bringing room service. Crystal and I were dressing while Jason and Thomas went to the bathroom."

Crystal sniffed the air and relaxed. "Coffee. You're so sweet."

"You have Chet to thank for this. I'm just the delivery boy. Does Thomas drink coffee?"

"Not really, but now is a good time to try. So many firsts for him on this trip. He's growing up so fast. Hard to believe he'll be off on his own soon. This trip started out horribly, but look where it ended up. Do you remember Jason trying to call the horses back up here after the first night?"

Bob snorted.

Jason and Thomas opened the door, and Crystal, Liz, and Bob laughed. Thomas looked down at his fly.

"What?" Jason asked. "Have you been talking about us?" He lifted his nose. "Coffee?"

Bob pointed to the tray.

Jason grabbed a cup. "Thanks. What's so funny?"

"Aren't you glad the horses weren't available to take us down the day after we arrived?" Crystal said.

"Oh, that. Not my best moment. I guess that is kind of funny, in hindsight."

Bob handed a cup to Thomas. "Here you go. First cup of coffee after your first night in a tent after your first hike to a glacier. Quite a weekend, huh?"

"Hold on," Crystal said. "Let's put some milk and sugar in there."

Once everyone had doctored their coffees just right, Bob motioned everyone together between the beds and the door and raised his cup. "To trail friends, the best kind."

After Bob and Liz sat together on their bed, Liz asked, "Who is Hannah? Do you have another girlfriend I don't know about?"

Bob was puzzled for a few seconds. "Oh, that. I must have been dreaming about last summer on the JMT. Hannah and her father brought me coffee and doughnuts on my zero day in Bishop."

"Doughnuts? Did you bring doughnuts too?" asked Jason.

Bob shook his head. He finished his coffee quickly since he had a head start in the dining room. "Thomas, I'm going to get changed, then we'll pack up the tent and everything in it. Chet said breakfast service begins in about an hour. I don't know about y'all, but I'm starving."

Thomas nodded. He raised his cup. "This is pretty good. Thanks."

"Jason, you all seem to have enjoyed yourselves the last couple of days. Have you considered what might be next?" asked Liz.

"Not really, but Crystal's been talking about going to Yosemite for years now. Maybe it's time to take her and Thomas there."

Crystal's jaw dropped. "Really! I'd love that." She put her arm around him and kissed him, the first sign of affection Bob had seen between the couple.

Liz said, "I think you have a winner, Jason."

"I second that," said Bob. "I began my JMT hike there. Hike the Mist Trail up to Nevada Falls, then back down the JMT to Yosemite Valley. It's fantastic. Crowded, but fantastic. Yosemite is one of my favorite National Parks."

40

Switch

As Bob removed the rainfly from the tent, he noticed Tony and Abbie leaving the dormitory building with their packs on their backs.

"There you are," Tony said. "We were hoping we'd see you this morning. We didn't know what room you were staying in."

Abbie added, "Hey Thomas. How was your first night camping?"

"It was great. Looking forward to doing more of it now that Dad is more open to spending time outdoors."

Abbie approached Bob and hugged him. Bob could only pat the sides of her pack. She backed up and said, "Thanks for last night. It was wonderful."

Tony shook his hand, and they nodded to each other.

"Hold on. Let me get Liz. She'll kill me if I let you leave without giving her a chance to say goodbye. Your enthusiasm helps us old folks feel young again."

A few minutes later, Bob returned with Jason, Crystal, and Liz.

Liz headed straight for Abbie with her arms extended. After hugging her and Tony, she said, "Thank you both for helping me with Bob. I don't believe I could have done it alone."

"Glad to help. We'll never forget this trip," said Tony.

"You aren't staying for breakfast?" asked Jason.

"No," said Tony. "We're off to the Tetons now. We have a permit to hike the Teton Crest Trail, so we need to get on our way.

"Ooh. Let me know how it goes. That's another hike on Cathy's bucket list, so I'll be there soon."

* * *

Thomas dropped the half-full backpack at the foot of the bed. "All done."

Bob pointed to the pile of gear on the floor. "Not quite. Liz and I still need to put all that stuff in our packs, but thanks for the help."

Liz pulled Bob's hand and patted the bed next to her. "Bob, sit down. We have a proposal for you."

"Uh-oh. What did I do now?"

Thomas laughed. Bob winked at him. "What did I tell you last night?"

"Thomas, this involves you too, so listen up," said Crystal. Thomas lost his smile instantly.

Liz put her hand on Bob's thigh and smiled. "Jason and Crystal have offered to let us ride their horses down to the trailhead. They'd like to do a bit more hiking and figured we might like to try something new and let our exhausted bodies recuperate."

Thomas jumped up, faced his parents, and yelled, "Really! Cool."

Bob didn't smile. "I haven't ridden a horse since I was a kid. I wouldn't know what to do. And the trail is so steep."

Jason snorted. "And you think we knew what we were doing?"

Crystal laughed.

Liz now sat on the edge of the bed, about to slide off. "Bob, please. I've never ridden a horse, and I may never get another opportunity like this."

"I'm still very sore from the fall." But as he said so, he peered into Liz's eyes. He saw an adventurer. He saw the enthusiasm Cathy had before her JMT hike. He saw someone who cared about him.

Bob put his arm around her. "Sure. It will be an experience. Good or bad, we won't be able to say we didn't try."

Liz rested her head against Bob's shoulder and wrapped her arms around his waist. "Thanks, Bob. Look at it this way; your butt may hurt more, but your pack won't bang on your sore back. Plus, it would take you all day to get down with one hiking pole."

Crystal smiled. "Like the pack leader warned us before we started, it's just a matter of where you want your blisters."

Liz laughed, and Bob couldn't help but grin. That was a good one. The pack leader probably used that saying with all his groups.

"Jason, I thought you had enough hiking after yesterday," said Bob.

"It's amazing how fast the body recovers after a hearty meal and a good night's sleep."

"Are you saying I didn't snore much last night?" asked Bob.

Liz glanced at him, tilted her head down, and raised her eyes. Jason smiled, and Crystal giggled.

"What?"

"Maybe just a little," said Crystal.

"You can use my hiking poles to help your knees," said Liz. "They won't be any help to the horse."

"Thanks. I'll take you up on that."

Thomas must have tired of the old person chatter and said, "Bob, can I carry your backpack down too?"

"Ooh. I don't know. You should ease into that. How about you load up your day pack with some of the things your mules carried up here so you can get a taste of what it's like?"

"OK. Good idea. Thanks."

"The horses should arrive around nine, so we have plenty of time to enjoy breakfast and get ready," Jason said.

41

Payback

Bob had to admit he could get used to this. Each step his horse took reminded him of his rough slide down the waterfall, but his pack banging on his back for another day would have been intolerable. His knees rejoiced, especially after being told they would be down a hiking pole for the six-mile, 3300-foot descent. His shoulders were unburdened by the heavy backpack. And best of all, Liz was having a blast. She was squealing, giggling, and talking nonstop. She deserved the fun after a day and a half of caring for him. Today, she delegated her responsibilities to Bob's horse and the pack leader, and fully immersed herself in the first-time experience of riding a horse on a trail. And not just any trail, but in Glacier National Park.

Jason, Crystal, and Thomas had started their hike after Jason discussed the change of plans with the pack leader. Since the rude and disrespectful Jason was fresh in the pack leader's mind, he welcomed the change. Jason's family had not packed lightly for their excursion, so they sent most of their gear down with the mules, carrying only what they needed for a day hike, and in Thomas's case, a little extra to simulate a backpack. Bob and Liz's gear was also in the bags carried by the mules at the end of the train.

His horse slowed.

"Are we taking a break already?" Bob called to the pack leader ahead of Liz.

The pack leader turned to the side. "Slow traffic ahead."

When Bob leaned to the right, he saw Jason's backside, with Crystal right in front of him. Thomas was not in sight.

"Slower traffic to the right, please," Bob shouted.

Liz laughed. "Bob, it's Jason."

"I know that. There's something I didn't tell you about my hike up. Just play along."

"If you say so."

Jason stopped and stood in the middle of the trail. "We could change our mind and take those horses back."

"Come on, Jason. Move over. He's just making fun of what you did on the ride up. Seems like forever ago, but you deserve it."

"I can't wait to hear this story," said Liz.

"Alright, alright." Jason moved to the side, next to Crystal.

"How's it going, Jason?" asked Bob.

"Thomas is having a blast. We can't even see him any longer. Me, I'm not so sure, but I'm going to prove I can do this. But thanks for the hiking poles; without them, I'd be jumping on one of those pack horses right now."

The pack leader joined in the fun. "Now that, I'd like to see!"

Crystal asked Liz, "Is it what you hoped for?"

"And more. I'm having a blast. And Bob hasn't complained one bit."

"That's a pleasant surprise," said Jason.

"Hey, I'm right here, you know."

The pack leader urged his horse to pass Jason and Crystal, and the others followed. He must have tired of the banter or didn't want to give the other Jason an opportunity to return.

"See y'all later. Giddy up!" yelled Bob.

The pack leader shook his head.

42

Reward

The pack leader and Liz dismounted their horses shortly before the Sperry Trailhead. They had agreed at their one and only break that they would be dropped off at the turnoff for the Lake McDonald corral. Civilization, in the form of the Lake McDonald Lodge, was across the road from the trailhead. In another bit of trail magic, Liz had left her car at the lodge. Bob's car was at the other end of the trail, over an hour away on the Going to the Sun Road.

"One of you better be ready to catch me," said Bob, still on the saddle.

The pack leader chuckled and walked over. He grabbed Bob's hips after Bob swung his far leg over the horse and helped him to the ground. Bob used a full minute to straighten up, then took one tentative step after another, like a one-year-old taking his first steps.

Liz placed her hands on her hips. "Bob, aren't you being a bit dramatic?"

"Maybe a little. But I was stiff from the fall before I even got on this damn animal, and now everything else down there hurts."

Liz smiled. "Everything?"

Bob shuffled after her, but gave up quickly, realizing his odds of catching her were about the same as catching the goat that had run off with his hiking pole.

"And don't be too hard on the horse. At least he saved your knees from hours of agony."

The pack leader removed Bob and Liz's stowed bags. "I need to take care of the horses and mules. It's been a pleasure taking you down. I don't know what you did to Jason, but nice job."

"Thanks," Bob said. "But it wasn't us. Thank Thomas when you see him."

Bob and Liz shook his hand.

Bob led the way to the trailhead at the road, looking from side to side. "I expected a ranger to be here checking for Walter and Jude."

"Maybe they already caught them. They left awfully early, according to Chet."

"Yeah, you're probably right–there he is, sitting by the trailhead sign."

It wasn't Bart, but another ranger sat in a folding canvas chair. He stood up as they approached.

"You must be Bob and Liz."

Bob nodded.

"I'm Jacob. You've become quite famous."

Liz blushed. "Really?"

Bob added, "Why? We were just doing the right thing."

"You'd be surprised what some people view as 'the right thing' these days."

"Hey, has anyone caught those guys who started the fire?" asked Bob.

The ranger looked at his feet, as if embarrassed to disappoint them, then shook his head. "No, I've been down here since Bart called the station. No one matching their description has come down the trail or walked along the road."

"Where else could they have gone?"

"I guess they could have gone off trail as they approached the trailhead, but you saw how steep the trail was. That wouldn't be easy. Then they'd have to walk along the road, which is even scarier. We've notified all the rangers and shuttle drivers. Someone should spot them eventually."

Bob nodded. "I guess they could also hang out off the trail to hike out this evening or tomorrow."

"Bob, I don't believe the rangers will give up anytime soon. Let them do their job. I don't know about you, but I want to get cleaned up."

"Thanks, ma'am."

"Sorry, you're right. Jacob, call us if you need anything more from us. Bart has our contact information."

"Oh. I almost forgot. I have a message for you." He took a business card out of his shirt pocket. "This man stopped by and said it was important for you to call as soon as you got off the trail."

Bob took the card. "Jonathan Rymer, Belton Chalets."

"They operate the chalets in the park. He probably just wants to thank you."

"Thanks."

Bob and Liz picked up their packs. Liz put hers on her back. Bob felt a twinge in his back as he watched, so he carried his in front of him like Tony had done on the climb to Gunsight Pass. They looked both ways before crossing the busy road to the hotel parking lot. They had already bid farewell to Jason's family when they set off and when they passed them on the trail.

They put their packs in the trunk of Liz's rental car and hobbled to the bathrooms. While Bob was waiting for Liz to return, he took his phone out of airplane mode and heard a ping. He had no voicemails, but one text message.

"This is Jonathan from Belton Chalets. We operate the Sperry Chalet. Please call me at this number as soon as you receive this message. I want to express our appreciation."

"Is anything wrong?" Liz asked.

Bob hadn't seen her coming and flinched. "I don't think so, but Jonathan left me a text as well. I guess I better call him."

Bob spoke into his phone. "Jonathan?"

"Yes."

"This is Bob Riley. I received two messages to call you. Is everything OK?"

"Hi. Mr. Riley–"

"Please, call me Bob."

"OK, sure. Bob, Chet thanked you up at the chalet, but I wanted to do so personally. We operate both chalets in the park, and as you might imagine, we are a bit sensitive to any fires."

"It was only a small one, Jonathan, and the folks at the chalet knew exactly what to do."

"Thanks. Glad to hear that. But you found it early. That was the key. Anyway, I would like to offer you and Liz a stay at the Belton Chalet, right down the road in West Glacier, and also to join me for dinner tonight."

"What a generous offer. You don't need to do that."

"I insist. Where were you and Liz planning to stay tonight?"

"Liz was headed to a hotel in Kalispell. She's flying home tomorrow. I was planning to stay at the Many Glacier Hotel for the next few days."

"That's a long drive. Do you have a car at the trailhead?"

"Yes. We were just getting into Liz's car at Lake McDonald Lodge. Mine is parked at Jackson Glacier Overlook."

"How about this? Have Liz drive you both here; it's about twenty minutes away. You can get cleaned up, meet me for dinner, and I'll drive you to your car in the morning."

"Sounds good, but let me discuss it with Liz. Hold on."

Bob summarized the discussion for Liz. She agreed immediately.

"Sounds great. Thank you so much. We'll see you soon."

Liz's eyes sparkled. "How exciting? Another chalet to add to the list. I guess we are becoming famous."

She opened the driver's door. "Let's go."

After Bob was seated, she continued. "I have to admit; I wasn't looking forward to the long drive across the park and back again. A nice bit of trail magic to finish the trip."

"You earned it."

43

Parting

As they pulled up to the hotel, Liz leaned forward over the steering wheel so she could see the top of the three-story chalet building. With easier access to building materials, Belton Chalet was a grander facility than Sperry, where everything had to be flown in on a helicopter or carried by stock. Stone pillars supported a full-length patio, on which sat several umbrella-shaded tables. The balconies above became narrower as they approached the apex of the roof. Intricate designs were carved into the wide slats of the balcony railing, and antlers and skull bones were mounted to the rails. As they pulled further ahead, Bob noticed a couple of adorable cottages which must provide plenty of room for large families to spread out.

"Wow. I didn't even notice this place on the drive into the park. I guess I was too anxious to get to Many Glacier. I hope the inside is as nice as the outside," Bob said.

"As long as they have running water, I'll be happy."

"I second that. After a backpacking trip, I usually crave a burger or pizza, but with the hearty meals at Sperry Chalet, the craving is not so strong."

"Based on what I see, we're in for much better than burgers tonight."

Bob opened the lobby door for Liz, and she stopped after one step inside. "Oh, my gosh. What a place."

Bob was disappointed he couldn't see her face. He squeezed around her pack, stepped beside her, and surveyed the furnishings of the lobby as closely as he had at Muir Hut on the JMT.

"We're in for a treat tonight. This is fantastic," said Bob.

They approached the front desk where a middle-aged man talked to the clerk behind the counter. The man smiled as they approached. His bright white teeth broke up his brown mustache and beard, and a red tie brightened up his white shirt and navy pants.

"You must be Bob and Liz."

He grabbed a few things off of the counter and held out his hand. "I'm Jonathan, and this is Patty."

Liz shook his hand. "Nice to meet you. Thank you for your generosity. What a magnificent place." She smiled at Patty.

Bob followed.

Jonathan waved his hand at the lobby. "Oh, it is. I hope you enjoy your stay. I'm sure you're anxious to get cleaned up, so I won't belabor things now. He handed each of them a room key."

Bob and Liz glanced at each other. Liz grinned, but said nothing. She looked like she was expecting him to speak, but he didn't want to seem ungrateful to their generous host.

"I imagine you're hungry as well. How about we meet on the patio for drinks in about an hour, then we can move to the restaurant for dinner?"

Bob and Liz both nodded, still admiring the lobby.

Liz looked down at her clothes and held her palms up. "I'm not sure I have the proper attire to match the exquisite furnishings. This lobby is beautiful."

"Don't worry. There is no dress code." Jonathan looked down at his tie. "This is just my work attire."

At least Liz must have left some clean, normal clothes in her car. Bob had nothing other than what was on his body and in his pack, all of which were dirty and smelly.

Both rooms were on the second floor. The old wood creaked as they climbed the stairs, their toughest uphill climb of the day. They paused at the top of the stairs, then sauntered down the runner covering the center of the maple-floored hallway.

"Well, let's clean up separately so we're not late for dinner," said Bob.

Liz appeared puzzled, shrugged, then entered her room.

Bob walked into his room, dropped his pack on the floor, and immediately went back downstairs. He asked Patty if there was a shop nearby where he could buy some clean clothes. She said he might find Glacier- and Western-themed clothes at one of the nearby gift shops. He rushed around the corner and spotted a rack of t-shirts and sweatshirts outside one of the shops. He grabbed a navy blue sweatshirt with a moose imprinted on the front and went inside in search of pants. All he found were gray sweatpants with Glacier National Park embroidered over one of the pockets–not up to even his low fashion standards for eating out, but they would have to do.

* * *

Bob waited for Liz in the lobby in front of a ten-foot-wide fireplace surrounded by a variety of wood chairs and a large sofa. White curtains covered the windows framed by dark brown wood. A piano was tucked into a bookcase covering the entire wall to the left.

The stairs creaked, so he looked up with anticipation. Liz's short gray hair bounced with each step as she descended. She wore all cotton, light blue jeans and a white, untucked shirt. They looked as soft as her skin felt the other night.

"Wow! I thought you looked good on the trail." Bob couldn't imagine a wider smile. He grabbed her hand for the last two steps and gave her a quick kiss.

She took a step back. "And you clean up pretty well yourself."

"Oh, come on. Clean, yes. But I must look silly in these clothes in this setting. My only clean clothes are in my car, so I improvised."

"I think it's cute. I appreciate the effort."

Jonathan walked up to them. "Don't you look lovely."

"Why thanks." Bob grinned.

Jonathan's eyes lingered a little too long on his sweatpants. "Well, you look lovely too, Bob. But you must admit, Liz steals the show. And she was worried about trashing up the place."

"I hope I don't offend your other guests. My clean clothes are in my car."

"No worries. And by the way, they're not my guests. I work for Belton Chalets, but we don't operate Belton Chalet, only Sperry and Granite Park."

Bob lowered his chin and squinted at Jonathan.

"I know. It's confusing. But it's a great place to recognize your efforts. I called this morning to check if they had any vacancies, and they surprised me."

Jonathan led them through the tap room and onto the patio. They sat under one of the umbrellas they had seen while driving up. A steady stream of cars left the park after a long day of sightseeing and hiking.

Jonathan handed each of them a drink menu. "They have some great local beers if you are interested."

After a minute of perusing the menu, Bob said, "How can I resist something called Moose Drool?"

"Make that two," said Liz.

Jonathan waved over the server. "Good choice." He must not have been patronizing them, because he made it three.

Liz said, "I can't believe this place. I was expecting some modern imitation of a Swiss chalet, but this place appears to be as authentic as Sperry."

Jonathan nodded. "In fact, this chalet is older than Sperry. It was also built by the Great Northern Railway, but it opened in 1910."

"Wow, I would have never guessed that," said Bob.

"Obviously, it has been renovated extensively. They added modern conveniences, like the bathrooms in each guest room, but kept as much of the original fixtures and charm as they could. Did you know the Railway initially built nine chalets between here and the Glacier Park Lodge in East Glacier?"

Bob surprised Jonathan. "Actually, yes. That was part of Chet's history lesson after dinner."

"Sorry, I guess I need to get up there more often. Well, Belton Chalet was one of the nine and was sited right next to the railway station."

"Oh, Bob. Can you imagine staying in nine different chalets? I feel like we've been blessed to stay in two. What an adventure that would be."

"Yes, indeed. Though after today, I think I'd rather walk and let the horses carry my stuff. They didn't have light gear back then, much less ultralight."

The server brought their beers. Jonathan raised his glass. "To the wonderful couple who saved the chalet."

They clinked their glasses and sipped. While Bob swirled the brown ale over his tongue, Liz said, "Wonderful couple–I like the sound of that," then winked at Bob.

Bob said, "Not what I thought drool would taste like. Dark, but refreshing, with a hint of coffee."

"The color matches the rustic furnishings," said Liz.

"Jonathan, have you heard any more about the guys who started the fire? When we arrived at the trailhead, they hadn't been found yet."

"Bob, we were just there an hour ago."

"It's OK. I called a few minutes ago. They still haven't been found. I'll check back in the morning."

After telling them more about the history of the chalets and Belton's current operations, Jonathan escorted them to the dining room. The beautifully set tables indicated they wouldn't be having roast beef and canned vegetables tonight, not that the meal last night wasn't wonderful.

"How about champagne to begin with?"

Liz raised her eyebrows and smiled. "That would be wonderful."

"This is the chalet Crystal should have booked for Jason," said Bob.

Liz laughed, but Jonathan was clearly puzzled.

"A story for the long car ride tomorrow."

Jonathan smiled. "OK."

The waiter brought their menus and water.

"Everything is delicious, but I recommend the trout. Sorry, it's not from Lake Ellen Wilson, but it is sourced locally."

"You must have read my mind," Bob said. "We both tossed crumbs in the water while we sat on the beach there, watching the fish thrash to snap up the smallest morsels."

Liz added, "The food at the chalet hit the spot, but I'm ready for a change. You made that easy for us." She laid her menu on the table.

Once the champagne had been poured, Jonathan raised his glass. "Bob and Liz, you must think I'm overdoing it, but you can't imagine how concerned our entire organization gets with any threat of fire after the horrible loss in 2017. Thank you for your quick action yesterday. You not only saved the chalet, but may have saved lives."

"And lots of mountain goats," Liz added, then they tapped the rims of their glasses together.

Bob allowed the tart, fizzy champagne to tickle the roof of his mouth. "Mmm."

"Jonathan, you just said the words any safety manager lives for. That's what I did for over thirty years. I guess I've learned to be observant and respond, not wait for others to act. And your team did a fantastic job. They had the right tools and knew what to do."

Bob took another sip, bigger this time. "And while we're talking about your staff, Phillip deserves special recognition. He dealt with a rude guest very well during dinner one night."

"Much better than I did. I lit into the guy. I pitied poor Phillip," Liz said.

"Jonathan, you should have seen her. I've been a little afraid of her ever since."

Liz slapped his hand resting on the table, causing the champagne in all their glasses to slosh.

"Do I need to warn the wait staff?" asked Jonathan.

"Guys. Come on. He deserved it."

"That, he did," said Bob. "But you know what, when we came back yesterday, Jason was a different person. Must be something about the air, the trees, and the water up there."

"It sounds like you two had a wonderful trip."

"Well, you haven't heard the interesting part yet," said Liz.

"I heard about a fall, but you both appear to be fine."

"Let's just say that I rode a water slide into Lake Ellen Wilson, almost drowned, nearly froze to death, and oh yeah, faced down an angry mountain goat at Sperry Campground while trying to protect a runaway teenager."

"That's why I don't go backpacking. I'll stick to my day trips to the chalets."

"But seriously, this beautiful lady," Bob said as he raised his glass and touched Liz's glass, "is the only reason I am here tonight. I may have helped to save the chalet, but she saved my life, then helped me make the best of the rest of the trip. Thanks, Liz."

"Sounds like he owes you one, Liz," said Jonathan.

"If he only knew how much."

The fish was as juicy as the champagne. The lemon butter sauce made it just as tart as well. Bob barely used his teeth as he kept the fish on his tongue to absorb all the flavor before letting it slide into his growling stomach. Liz looked so peaceful as she savored hers. They were served green beans after all, but they didn't come from a can. They were crunchy and seasoned to perfection. But the bread had the same pillowy texture and yeasty aroma as that at the chalet. The baker up there had done a wonderful job under the circumstances.

"Liz, Bob told me you were going home tomorrow?"

"Yes, unfortunately."

"Maybe you'll reconsider after my next offer. We've had a late cancellation at the Granite Park Chalet. How would you like to hike from Logan Pass to the Many Glacier Hotel, spending the night at the chalet?"

Liz shook her head. "Jonathan, you're very generous, but I need to get home. Bob, what do you think?"

Bob paused. "I don't know. You saw how I walked after I got off that horse today. My body is beat up. I think I'll pass as well. But thanks for the offer."

Liz responded immediately. "Bob, do this. You'll feel better in the morning, and it's a pretty easy hike to the chalet on the Highline Trail."

"I was planning to relax at the Many Glacier Hotel. It looks like a marvelous place."

"I'm sure it is, but it will be waiting for you. If you won't do it for yourself, do it for Cathy. Remember how upset you were when the ranger turned us around?"

Liz hit a nerve. Bob stared at her. He remembered how excited Cathy was when she secured a last-minute reservation at Granite Park Chalet after the fire destroyed Sperry Chalet. But staying at Sperry for two nights and a surprise visit to the Belton Chalet should be enough, right?

"Cathy?"

"Long story; Bob's deceased wife."

"Oh, I'm sorry."

"You make a good point, Liz. Thanks to you, I spent two nights at Sperry Chalet, but I didn't finish the hike for Cathy. The hike from Logan Pass to Many Glacier is epic. Maybe she'll like it just as much as the Gunsight Pass Trail. Jonathan, I'll do it."

"OK, great. We'll work out the details in the morning. Let's celebrate with dessert. You trusted me on the fish, so just trust me on dessert."

After Jonathan whispered the order to their server, Bob cleared his throat. "Um. Jonathan. Do you think the hotel can wash my clothes overnight? I'd hate to start another multi-day hike in filthy clothes, and I can't hike in these." He looked down at his chest. "You know—cotton kills."

"Sure. If you bring your clothes down to Patty at the front desk and let her know about our plans, I'm sure they'll take care of it."

"Thanks."

A few minutes later, the waiter brought three slices of warm pie with a black filling and vanilla ice cream on the side.

"Mmm. Is this blackberry pie?"

"I don't think so, Bob. It's a very dark blue color. Oh, that's right. You're color blind. I guess you can't see the blue. I barely can."

"A local specialty, huckleberry pie."

Liz took a bite. "Oh, nice. A few less berries for the bears to eat."

Bob took his time to get the perfect balance of brown crust, warm filling, and soft ice cream on his spoon. Perhaps too much. It barely fit in his mouth. The ice cream smoothed out the tartness of the berries and moistened the otherwise dry crust.

"Soooo good." A blue streak oozed from the corner of his mouth as he chewed. Liz wiped it off with her napkin.

"Oh, before I forget. When you're hiring staff for Sperry Chalet next summer, keep Thomas Coates in mind. I don't know if he'll apply, but he's seriously considering it. He has great people skills."

"You should have seen what he did with his parents," Liz said. "They were barely on speaking terms when they arrived, and his father clearly didn't want to be there; hated the outdoors, in fact. But in the end, Thomas managed to get them all up to Sperry Glacier together, and now they're planning a trip to Yosemite."

Bob added. "And he seems to like learning and trying new things. You must need flexible and resilient people."

"You got that right. They're kind of isolated up there. Thanks for the tip. I'll keep an eye out for his application."

A while later, Bob placed his napkin on the table in surrender.

Liz did the same, then said, "Jonathan, we should let you go home. You have been so wonderful to us. This has been a perfect ending to quite an adventure. Thank you so much."

Bob and Jonathan stood up and shook hands. "Thank you. I'll never forget this, and neither will Cathy."

* * *

Liz held Bob's hand as they walked up the stairs. He should have felt carefree and happy beyond belief, but he dreaded the next few minutes. The ancient wood floors creaked eerily as they walked down the hall. They stopped at the door to Liz's room. She let go of his hand, rested her forearms on his neck, and clasped her hands. He rubbed the soft cotton blouse along her ribs. So soft, just like her skin two nights ago. He had been traumatized at the time, but still remembered the feeling. Soft and warm. It helped save him.

"What did we do to deserve this?" she asked.

"I don't know. We're just being ourselves. Doing the best we can."

"You're a good man, Bob. You're just what I need about now. I'm tired of being alone."

"Liz–"

Liz put her finger on his top lip and pushed it down. She stood on her toes, leaned forward and kissed him. Not a peck like they had done many times before. This was the real thing. Bob pulled her tight, tilted his head, and kissed back.

She lowered her arms and grabbed his hand. She took the room key out of her pocket, and he heard a click. She turned the knob, opened the door, and pulled his hand. As hard as it was, he leaned back. His hand slipped out of hers, and she turned around, holding the door open with her other hand, before stepping out and letting it close.

"What's wrong?"

"Nothing, really. You're wonderful. The evening has been wonderful. But I'm a mess."

"A mess? Why?"

"I think you know why?"

Liz looked down.

"I'm sorry. I need some time alone tonight. Some time with Cathy. I hope you understand."

A single tear ran down her right cheek.

"But I need you too. I need you tonight. I've waited too long already."

Bob hugged her. "I know. But please, give me time to get through this."

She leaned back, so he let her go. She opened the door, entered the room, and let the door close behind her. The click of the door latch jarred him, even as he watched it close.

What had he done?

* * *

Dear Cathy,

We're finally alone. The last few days have been so chaotic, I felt you slipping away. I can't let that happen. Too many adventures on your bucket list remain. At times, the trail seems to conspire against us; at others, it saves me. And trail friends abound. Hannah, Jessica, Brock, Mark, and Linda on the JMT. Now Tony and Abbie—and Liz. But Liz is different; she's more than a friend. I think you know that by now, but I don't know how you really feel about it. And until I know that, I don't know how I feel about her. I know how I should feel and how I want to feel, but a part of me is holding back. It's too soon. You're still close, especially on the trail.

It may be a moot point by morning. I hurt her just now. Hurt her badly. Turned her away. Maybe I don't deserve her after what I did to you. And that's OK. I committed to keep you close, to finish your adventures. But I wonder if there's room for both of you. She seems to believe so, but what about you? Tony and Abbie showed me what it could be like again. How it should have been for us.

Perhaps Liz will help me stay close to you instead of coming between us. She reminds me a lot of you. She knows what she wants and goes after it. She doesn't wait for permission. She doesn't cede to obstacles, but plows right through them. Just like you did. You didn't let me get in the way of your hikes, including the last one on the JMT. I let you go, and you didn't come back. Now I may have let Liz go, and she may not come back. She may be tired of waiting. She may move on. Please give me a sign. I can live with either one, but not in the middle.

I'm sorry we didn't finish the Gunsight Pass hike together, but I'm happy you got to experience the Sperry Chalet, not once, but twice. I could have found a way to finish the trail by sneaking around the rangers, but you wouldn't want it that way any more than I. In hindsight, perhaps my fall was a good thing. Otherwise, I would have been at Gunsight Lake Campground when the bear showed up. Or perhaps the next morning I would have encountered a bear hanging out on the trail. Who knows how those encounters would have turned out. Liz, Tony, and Abbie may not have been around to save me.

And thanks to Jonathan, we have the opportunity for an unexpected adventure, similar in many respects to the Gunsight Pass Trail. From Logan Pass to Granite Park Chalet, then over Swiftcurrent Pass, along more beautiful lakes, past more waterfalls, to Many Glacier Hotel. Let's hope this one goes according to plan. It will just be you and me this time.

Love, Bob

X

Day Seven

July 31, 2023
Glacier National Park

44

Gone

Bob awoke late. He was surprised he hadn't heard a knock on his door or a message arriving on his phone. Liz must be up by now. He had slept poorly most of the night, so when he finally fell into a deep sleep, his body clung to it. It needed every minute to continue its recovery from the abuse he had subjected it to.

He put on his cotton sweatshirt and sweatpants. They were so comforting after dressing in cold and dirty polyester and nylon during the previous week. Those fabrics were great for hiking because they were light, wicked moisture away from his body, and dried quickly, but cotton was so soft and warm.

His stiff legs hobbled down the stairs, but Liz had been right, he felt better today. He scanned the large chairs and sofa around the massive fireplace. The area was cozy, so he could imagine Liz waiting patiently for him while being mesmerized by the fire. But she wasn't. He continued to the dining room and peered around the room. Their waiter from last night spotted him and told him to take any table. Bob asked if he had seen Liz. He shook his head.

He went back upstairs and knocked on her door. Then knocked again. He listened for running water; perhaps she couldn't hear his knocking while taking a shower. No answer. No shower. Back downstairs, he stopped by the front desk where Patty greeted him.

"Excuse me, have you seen Liz this morning?"

Patty shook her head and typed on the keyboard on the counter. "Mr. Riley, she has already checked out."

Bob's shoulders slouched and his head sunk into his neck while his stomach rose. He still managed to utter, "Thanks."

He walked back into the restaurant and sat at the first empty table. In minutes, a glass of water and a cup of coffee appeared. He sipped the coffee and winced. He had forgotten to add the cream. He always had cream or milk in his coffee.

The waiter came by again. "Will you be using the buffet, or would you like a menu?"

Bob felt incapable of making a selection from a menu, so he pointed toward the buffet. He had another sip of coffee, walked to the buffet, and filled his plate, taking a little of everything, more than he would ever eat. He picked up a piece of bacon and nibbled on the end.

Jonathan walked up to the table. "Good morning. May I join you?"

Bob held his hand out toward the chair across the table.

"Did you sleep well?"

Bob shrugged. "It's always hard to get used to a soft bed again after such a trip."

"Where is Liz?"

Bob's chest felt as if Jonathan had reached across the table and punched him. "She checked out already. She's gone."

"Oh, that's a shame. I wish she had said goodbye."

Bob thought, *Me too!*, but hid the words from Jonathan.

"About your trip today, we have some logistics to iron out."

"Yes."

"Are you OK? Are you still up for the hike?"

"Yeah, sorry. My legs and back feel much better today."

"The Granite Park Chalet doesn't serve meals like Sperry, so I imagine you need to restock your food before you leave."

Bob nodded.

"And you have a reservation at the Many Glacier Hotel for tomorrow night?”

“Yes, I was supposed to begin my stay yesterday, but when you offered to have us stay here, I modified the reservation.”

“Great. How about this? You can stock up at the market down the street. When you get back, I’ll grab one of my team members, and we’ll drop you off at Logan Pass so you can begin your hike. We’ll shuttle your car to the hotel so it will be waiting for you at the end of your hike.”

“Wow. You are so nice, but that will take up half of your day. I can retrieve my car when I’m done.”

“I insist.”

Bob shrugged. “OK.”

Jonathan stood up. “Call me when you are ready to go.”

The distraction got Bob eating again. He needed to get his act together. Liz probably needed some time alone, like he did. This little adventure should be straightforward since he wouldn’t be camping, but he needed to get the right amount of food and separate his gear. He had no reason to haul his tent and sleeping pad all that way. He would set those aside for Jonathan to leave in the trunk of his car.

On the way back to his room, he saw hiking poles hanging on the wall of the gift shop. Maybe his fortunes were changing. They weren’t as sturdy as his previous ones, but they would be worth the $79 even for one use, especially on the steep descent from Swiftcurrent Pass. As he walked toward the front desk to pay for them, something on the racks of souvenirs caught his eye. Amongst the plush bears and moose stood a mountain goat about the size of Marty. As much as he tried to set aside thoughts of Liz for the morning, they flooded back. He remembered how much Cathy loved Marty. Bob grabbed the bright white toy with hard black horns and paid for it and the poles at the front desk.

45

Caught

Jonathan pulled up in front of the Logan Pass Visitor Center and turned off the engine. He and Bob met at the trunk, where Jonathan lifted his backpack and handed it to him. He would now have to carry his own gear for a change. The pack weighed down his shoulders and pressed on his sore lower back and hips, but he felt better than yesterday–physically. Mentally–not so much.

A sign on the side of the Visitor Center pointed to the Hidden Lake Overlook Trail. He looked at his watch. *What the heck! It's only ten o'clock, and I have all day to get to the chalet.* He consulted the downloaded topo map on his phone since this was not on his original itinerary. The trail was only 2.5 miles round trip, with about 500 feet of elevation gain. *Piece of cake. I'm going for it.* Liz's adventurous spirit lingered within him.

The concrete sidewalk turned into a boardwalk and eventually into a rocky trail. Goats milling about the wide trail caused traffic jams as people seeing them for the first time took their photos. Perhaps he should have headed straight for the chalet after all. He wasn't in the wilderness any longer.

After thirty minutes of brisk walking, Bob arrived at a wooden platform overlooking Hidden Lake. The blue water wrapped around Bearhat Mountain, which dominated the view. Off to his right, the trail continued toward the lake itself, about 700 feet below where he stood now. Though he was tempted to dart down to the lake and back, he still had a 7.5 mile hike to the chalet and wanted to save some energy and time for a spur trail or two.

He looked again at the first part of the trail to the lake. A couple of hikers with backpacks struggled up the final incline before the trail junction. Their gaits seemed familiar. No! It couldn't be. Walter and Jude? They had been wearing yellow and blue hooded shirts the last two times he had seen them. These two were both in gray. Maybe they were wearing their sleeping shirts. Instead, he concentrated on their faces. Yes! That was Walter. He would never forget that smug look at the permit office.

But how did they get way over here? Bob couldn't recall any backpacking trails that started or finished here. There was no time to worry about that now. He had to act quickly. They couldn't get away this time.

The fugitives were still hundreds of feet away, and Bob was confident they hadn't seen him yet. They appeared to be fixated on the trail in front of them. They must be exhausted, but he'd never feel sorry for them after what they did and who they endangered.

Bob rushed back toward the Visitor Center. There must be a ranger there who can help. Several tourists seemed displeased with him as he entered the frames of photos and scared the goats and sheep further from the trail. He tried to apologize to them as a group silently. *Sorry, but I need to find a ranger before those guys get to the top.*

When he got to the trailhead, he looked back. No sign of them yet, but they would probably make good time on the downhill finish.

He entered the Visitor Center around the corner. The place was packed! He scanned the room for the gray and green uniform of a park ranger. He spotted one behind an information desk with a line of three in front of her.

Bob walked along the side of the line, not making eye contact with anyone.

"Excuse me, the end of the line is back there."

"Hey, wait your turn like the rest of us."

Bob ignored the remarks. He interrupted the ranger while she pointed to a map and talked to a guest. He nearly yelled, "Ranger, someone needs help outside. Hurry."

Bob rushed to the door to reinforce the urgency to the ranger. When he looked back, he saw her step around the counter and follow him to the door.

He held the door open for her and stepped to the side.

"OK. It's not quite an emergency, but it is important and urgent. Have you heard about the campfire that nearly got out of control at Sperry Campground?"

"Yes. We received a message to watch out for the two guys who started it. I heard they evaded the ranger at Sperry Chalet."

"I just saw them coming up the Hidden Lake Trail."

"Are you sure? We're so far away from there–"

"Listen. I'm sure."

"How do you know what they look like?"

"I'm the one who found the fire, and I pointed them out to Bart when they showed up at Sperry Chalet two nights ago."

She raised her hands and turned her palms toward him. "Calm down, sir–"

"Calm down! They're coming down the trail now. They'll be here any minute. If you won't do anything about it, I will." He started walking toward the trailhead sign.

"Hold on, sir. Let me get some help inside. I'll just be a couple of minutes."

The ranger rushed back through the door.

Bob looked up the sidewalk, but saw no sign of them yet. He stepped away from the trailhead so they wouldn't see him right away when they arrived.

He turned his head from the trailhead to the glass windows of the Visitor Center. The ranger was not visible.

Where did she go? What's taking her so long? Don't they want to catch these guys?

He looked back down the sidewalk.

There they are. Come on. Where are you? Hurry up.

Despite what he told the ranger, Bob was reluctant to confront Walter and Jude because they must know he was the reason they were caught the first time. They might try to shut him up or bolt again.

They passed the trailhead sign. He looked in the Visitor Center. Still no rangers on the way.

They appeared to be headed to the shuttle stop in the parking lot. That makes sense. They said their car was at Jackson Glacier Overlook. The bus stopped there.

If they get on the shuttle, they're gone.

A shuttle arrived, and two dozen people exited the bus. Bob looked back into the Visitor Center, then turned back toward the bus loading area. Walter and Jude smiled and raised their hands for a high five. They believe they've escaped. They're proud of themselves. They boarded the shuttle bus.

No. They won't escape. I won't let them. I'm tired of waiting.

He started toward the bus and heard, "Have you seen them?"

The ranger caught up and walked beside him.

"Yes, they just got on the shuttle bus. Two guys with gray shirts and backpacks."

The ranger sped up. Bob followed behind. The driver stepped off the bus. "No need to hurry. I'm not going anywhere. They told us to watch out for those two guys. Nobody messes with my park."

The ranger entered the bus.

Bob held his hand out to the shuttle driver. The driver reluctantly raised his. Bob squeezed his hand hard and shook vigorously. The driver's arm flopped up and down. He yanked it back when Bob loosened his grip.

"Sorry. Long story. But thanks. Those guys almost ruined my trip and a lot more."

The shuttle driver muttered, "OK," but still stared at him with narrowed eyes.

Another ranger, a male who obviously spent some time in a gym, passed Bob and peeked inside the bus. He backed up when the two guys exited the bus, followed by the female ranger. She pointed them toward the Visitor Center.

When they passed Bob, their heads sank. Bob could almost hear them thinking, "Not you, again!"

And you thought you had gotten away with it. Not on my watch!

Bob watched them until they entered the Visitor Center, then turned back to the shuttle driver.

"Hey, sorry about that, but thanks, thanks so much. I found the fire they set near Sperry Chalet and helped the ranger up there apprehend them the first time. But they snuck away in the night, and I thought they were gone for good. I was so mad. But you just stopped them cold in their tracks. Thanks."

The driver lifted his shoulders and thrust his chest out. He held out his hand. Bob gladly took it and let him lead this time. "Just doing my job, man. This is a special place. I love it. Thank you, as well."

The driver looked back at the bus. "I better get going. Sounds like the passengers are getting restless."

"Have a great day."

Bob headed back toward the Visitor Center and sat on a bench in case the rangers needed any information from him. Plus, he wanted to know how they got here and be assured they were taken into custody.

Twenty minutes later, the male ranger led them to a white sedan and held the back door open while they entered. As he drove off, the other ranger sat next to him.

"You won't believe what they went through to try to get away. Convinced me they're guilty. Why else would they go through all that?"

"All what?"

"There's an off-trail route, called the Floral Park Traverse, which runs from Sperry Glacier, over a pass next to Bearhat Mountain, then down to Hidden Lake. They took that route and camped near Hidden Lake last night so they could exit while blending in with the morning crowd. I guess they didn't realize how many people were looking for them, or that you would be here. What are the odds?"

"I don't call it odds; I call it trail magic. I hope they get what they deserve. Thanks for the help. I was getting worried."

"Thank you for being in the right place at the right time. Where are you headed for the rest of your day?"

"Granite Park Chalet for some R&R."

"Great. I hope you don't have to play park ranger again today. Be careful out there."

46

Overlook

Bob was so wound up by the capture of the irresponsible jerks, his heart rate actually subsided as he began hiking the relatively flat, 7.5-mile Highline Trail to Granite Park Chalet. Those visiting the chalet for the day had twice the mileage to walk, or they could take the shorter and steeper Loop Trail back to the Going to the Sun Road, where they would need a shuttle to return to Logan Pass. Either way, a very long day.

He was starting his hike much later than normal. The hike shouldn't take long, but he anticipated taking many photo breaks as the trail followed the Garden Wall, the sharp ridge on his right that was part of the Continental Divide. On the other side of the Wall were many of the excellent hikes that could be reached from Many Glacier, such as the Grinnell Glacier Trail. The tiny people he had seen on the ridge above the lake had hiked a one mile spur trail off the Highline Trail to get to that vantage point. They paid for the iconic view by climbing one thousand feet in that short distance. He hoped his worn down body would allow him to view the gorgeous green lake from a different perspective. Actually, it wasn't his body but his mind that had to overcome the aches and pains in his muscles, joints–and heart.

He carried a heavy pack for the first time in days. The weight of the gear he left behind was offset by new stocks of food. The selection at the market wasn't great, but he didn't need much: a freeze-dried meal for dinner tonight, an instant coffee mix, dried sausages, nuts, chips, granola bars, and

M&M's.

Mt. Oberlin dominated the view to his left and hovered over the Going to the Sun Road. Green bands interrupted the steep mountainside as trees tried to maintain their purchase on rocky ledges. He loved trails that began so high in elevation. The views were already worthy of a destination hike of five miles.

In less than a mile, the trail became a five-foot-wide shelf cut into the vertical face of the Garden Wall. A steel cable strung along the wall provided security for those scared of heights. Bob continued using his poles instead of the cable as he passed other hikers holding on for dear life. He peeked over the side and saw cars navigating the road below. A fall from here would be fatal, but the trail was wide enough that he'd fall on the trail, not over the edge. Or was that complacency creeping in, something he had fought every day at the plant? He veered back to the far right side of the trail after passing the other hikers.

Haystack Butte obscured his view ahead. The most notable elevation gain on the trail was climbing the neck which connected it to the Garden Wall. Shortly afterwards, he should see the chalet in the distance. At the summit of the neck, mountain goats hung out on the ledges above, nibbling on tufts of grass struggling to grow between the cracks in the rocks. Unlike most of the others he had encountered the past few days, these goats were satisfied to watch the hikers below while chewing. He moved to the left side of the trail to avoid any rocks they might dislodge.

By the time he arrived at the turnoff for the Grinnell Glacier Overlook, he could see Granite Park Chalet in the distance. While the mountainside to his right was still composed of sedimentary rock, the chalet sat on a mound of basalt (or of volcanic origin) speckled with trees and mostly covered in grass. Heaven's Peak stood proud in the background at almost nine thousand feet.

The decision he had put off earlier could wait no longer. He could continue on to the chalet, eat a snack, maybe even take a nap, then come back to the overlook. But that involved an extra two miles of hiking, and he knew he would never leave the chalet once he was comfortable there. He took the right turn and examined the steep slope ahead. His legs and lungs had been spoiled by the mostly flat trail so far, so they were sure to protest if he began to climb now. Perhaps he should leave his pack here, like some JMT hikers did before their final ascent of Mt. Whitney. He saw no marmots or goats in the area, but they could appear at any time. Then he recalled the incident at Lincoln Peak where Liz's pack had been pulled down the mountainside by a salt-craving marmot. He'd have to take his pack, so he told his legs, 'just deal with it.'

Since it was getting late for day hikers to be this far from the trailhead, he was nearly alone on the trail. A solo hiker and an elderly couple headed down, but he was the only one heading up. When he reached the overlook, he was alone, just as he had been when arriving at the lake days earlier. The white icebergs stood out even more against the green water from this distance. Salamander Glacier clung to the mountainside high above the lake. He located the spot on the shoreline where he had eaten his snack. Tiny people still crawled all over the scoured rock next to the lake. What were the odds of enjoying the lake from both perspectives in solitude in such a popular park? Another magical experience!

47

Alone

Bob's new hiking poles were worth every penny on the descent from the overlook. With no one else climbing the trail, he had likely been the last one to visit the high perch for the day. He then coasted on a mile of easy trail to his resting spot for the night. The two-story main building of the chalet reeled him in. He would have to cook his own dinner, but to prepare his shelter, he only had to throw his sleeping bag on a mattress and inflate his pillow.

The main entrance was around the building from the trail. The picnic tables and benches surrounding the chalet were mostly empty, but he figured the place must bustle with day hikers at midday. Bob entered a room not too unlike the Sperry Chalet dining room. He was relieved when the young attendant didn't recognize him. She introduced herself as Tess and welcomed him with a smile, not an overly enthusiastic handshake, a hug, or a shrill voice. He just wanted to be treated like the other guests, not some hero. He was hardly a hero after abandoning his wife before her big adventure and ruining the hikes of Liz, Tony, and Abbie with a careless fall into a lake.

"I understand you stayed at Sperry earlier this week, so let me explain the differences." She pointed to the tables and chairs behind him. "This room may look familiar, but neither my coworker, Bernie, nor I will be serving your dinner. Jonathan told you that, right?"

"Yes. I brought my own food. All I need is some boiling water. I also brought my camp stove."

"Great. You're welcome to eat in here or at a table outside. We have no running water, like you found at Sperry." She led him into the kitchen. "We have a small amount of treated water for you here, plus a container to store your food. You can use the propane stove over here to boil your water. If you need more water, you'll have to go down the hill to fetch your own."

"Thanks. I should be good between this and what I brought."

They walked out the back door, which was the one nearest the trail. A sign directed new arrivals to the front door.

"You can use this door since you're a guest."

Tess pointed to the right. "The pit toilets are down there. You probably passed them on the way in. Once again, no running water, but you should find hand sanitizer in there."

They continued walking to a separate one-story building which appeared to have four rooms on each side. The construction was similar to that at Sperry. The roof had an extreme pitch, probably to shed snow during the harsh winters. White curtains covered some of the windows, and two of the doors were open.

Tess led him around to the back side. "This is your room here." She opened the first door, and Bob followed her in. "Pretty basic."

"All I need. Much better than pitching a tent."

The room contained two bunk beds, a small table, and a canvas folding chair. Bob set his pack next to the chair and sat down.

Tess laughed at his sound effects. "Long day, huh?"

"Long week. Today was easy."

Tess pointed to the battery-powered lantern hanging on the bedpost. "You can use that to get around tonight, especially if you need to go to the bathroom."

"That's a certainty."

Why did he say that? Surely she's heard the lame remark too many times before.

"I'll let you get settled. We have a sign-up sheet for cooking times since it can get kind of crowded in the kitchen. What time can I sign you up for?"

Bob looked at his watch: 4:30. "How about 5:00?"

She waved him off. "No worries, then. You may be alone." She walked out the door.

Bob liked the sound of that. He needed some time alone. He left the door open to lighten up the room and let in some fresh air as he unpacked his gear to get to the sleeping bag at the bottom of his pack. He laid his clean sleeping clothes on the top bunk and set his headlamp on the floor, just under the bed where his head would rest.

Bob thought about lying down for a while before eating dinner, but his stomach protested loudly. He had missed lunch again. The sun would set late at this high latitude, so he figured he would eat now, lie down for a while, then return to the rocks on the west side of the chalet for sunset. He grabbed his entire bear canister and headed back to the kitchen.

Bob stopped in his tracks about halfway to the kitchen when he thought of his marmot friend. He had neglected Marty all day after being rattled by the apprehension of Walter and Jude. And come to think of it, he hadn't seen him when he was unpacking earlier. He went back to his room and rummaged through what was left in his pack. Not there. He searched all the external pockets. Not there either. The top bunk. Nope.

Uh-Oh.

He looked on the table, under the bed, and under the chair. Nowhere!

Oh my gosh, I lost Marty. How could that be? He's always with me. Cathy's going to kill me.

Bob tried to remember when he last saw Marty. He had given him to Thomas to keep him company in his tent two nights ago. Did Thomas leave him at the chalet? Take him home inadvertently … or on purpose? No, not on purpose; Thomas wouldn't do that. Or maybe he got rolled up in the tent? He liked that option best, but could do nothing about it now. His tent was waiting for him in the trunk of his car at the Many Glacier Hotel. He'd have to wait until tomorrow to narrow down the possibilities.

Marty, here you go again!

Bob ate his rehydrated chicken fried rice at one of the picnic tables on the side of the chalet–not bad, but quite a let down after the meals at Sperry Chalet and Belton Chalet. He missed the champagne, and his M&M's were a poor substitute for the fresh huckleberry pie. Back to the compromises of backpacking.

Since the glare from the afternoon sun shrouded the view of the endless mountains to the west, he faced the trail. The path to Grinnell Glacier Overlook didn't appear as steep from here as it did earlier. He followed the Highline Trail until it disappeared behind a bulge in the Garden Wall.

He attempted to locate the trail he would depart on tomorrow. It wasn't visible, but he could barely make out the fire lookout tower on the top of Swiftcurrent Mountain. Another spur trail, much steeper than the one to Grinnell Glacier Overlook, led from Swiftcurrent Pass to the top. Swiftcurrent Pass was only 500 feet higher than where he sat now; the top of the peak was another 1200 feet higher. With fresh legs in the morning, he might have the energy for that, but he would make the decision when he reached the turnoff.

* * *

Bob opened his eyes but only saw black. How could that be? It was only 6:00 when he took off his shoes and belt and lay on top of his sleeping bag. Just like at Sperry, the walls here provided a poor barrier to sound. His last memory was of his neighbors gathering their dinner supplies shortly after he lay down. He looked out of his window. Not only was the sun gone, but its lingering glow was as well. So much for sunset! With such a head start on his sleep for the night, he should be able to catch the alpenglow on Heaven's Peak and her neighbors in the morning.

He put his headlamp on, grabbed his toothpaste, toothbrush, and a bottle of water, and headed toward the bathroom. He brushed his teeth among the trees behind the bathroom, rinsing and spitting on the ground. The pit toilet was stocked with hand sanitizer, just as Tess had described.

His fresh-smelling sleeping clothes were a pleasure to put on. When he lay down this time, he got into his sleeping bag and zipped it up to his hips.

He picked his phone up from the floor under the bed and opened the voice recorder app. He began speaking, but then remembered how clearly he could hear his neighbor's conversations. *Better use the Notes app instead.*

* * *

Dear Cathy,

I've been such a hermit today. I hiked alone, ate dinner alone, and took a three-hour nap. I even had Grinnell Glacier to myself, again! I was tired of being the center of attention. It's not my style. You know that.

But being alone has brought me closer to you. I felt your presence. I tried to share the beauty of the trail and the quaint chalet with you. I may have exceeded your expectations for a change by showing you three chalets instead of just the one on your list. Granite Park has a much different feel than Sperry. The buildings are similar, but the atmosphere is much more airy. The views from Sperry Chalet are a bit confined, except for the view of Lake McDonald. But here, you can see mountains in all directions. The view to the west seems to go on forever.

We have one small problem; I lost Marty! Well, maybe not so small. I'm hopeful he is with Thomas or rolled up in my tent. I can't afford to lose that little guy. He helps keep my memories of you fresh.

Have you thought about what I said last night? About me and you and Liz? This has been my first day without her by my side in four days. And you and the trail have helped keep her in the back of my mind. I also can't face how much I disappointed and hurt her. But tomorrow, I'll be back in civilization, and soon thereafter, at home. I can't hide from it much longer. I need to know what to do. Please help. Please speak to me.

Love, Bob

* * *

Bob sat on a rock ledge with his feet swinging in the air, one thousand feet over the green water and small icebergs below. Marty sat at his side with a tiny leash connecting him to Bob's belt. "Sorry, Marty. I don't trust you up here. You've already used up all your marmot lives."

The glow to the east over the lake grew brighter. Cathy grabbed his shoulder and sat next to him.

"Bob, it's OK."

"It's more than OK. It's beautiful. The orange sky surrounding dark clouds, the green water speckled with white, the remnants of glaciers clinging to the mountainside, the ribbons of water falling into the lake."

"No, Bob. It's OK."

"What's OK?"

"It's OK. I'm OK. You'll be OK."

He took his eyes off the water and looked to his right, but she was gone. He looked to his left. Marty was gone too.

"Cathy?"

He opened his eyes; it was pitch black.

But the sun just rose. What's going on? Where am I?

He reached up and touched the bottom of the upper bunk. Oh! A dream. It was just a dream. Had he said Cathy's name out loud? Had he screamed? He cringed at the thought of waking up his neighbors.

But she said it was OK!

XI

Day Eight

August 1, 2023
Glacier National Park

48

Alarm

Bob sat on a bench behind the chalet with Tess, sipping his coffee. He had woken up for good just after four o'clock, but for the sake of his neighbors, he waited until first light to leave the room and prepare his coffee. They had been quiet for him, or perhaps he slept so soundly he wouldn't have heard them anyway.

His puffy coat, fleece hat, and gloves kept him warm, though the bench sucked heat from his bottom. Their words were sparse. Tess stared at the mountainside above the resident ranger's cabin in front of them. Bob followed her lead. She spent all summer out here; she must be expecting something wonderful. He would play along a bit longer, then move to the other side of the chalet to witness the rising sun playing its pastel light show on Heaven's Peak.

Tess whispered, "There. Do you see it?"

"What? Where?"

Tess brought her finger to her lips, then put her hand back in her pocket.

"Up there. Right above the ranger's cabin. In the distance."

He looked into the increasing light from the east and saw nothing but shadow. The spruces and firs appeared to be black triangles.

"It's too dark."

"Stare at the mountainside, not the sky. Your eyes will adjust."

"I hear it, but I still can't see it."

"Above the chimney and to the right." She pointed her nose in that direction.

Bob leaned toward Tess to get a different angle. "Oh. I see it. I see them."

"Softly."

A large bear and a small bear pulled rocks out of the ground about three hundred yards away.

"Grizzlies?"

Tess nodded.

"Wow!"

"Shhh."

"Sorry. What are they doing?"

"Looking for bugs–breakfast."

Bob grimaced.

"Do you see them every day?"

"No, but more often than not. I had a feeling this morning. I'm usually alone, but I'm glad I have someone to share it with today."

"Not as glad as me. I would have never found them."

"I've learned to enjoy the small things up here."

"Are you ever scared?"

She shook her head. "They'll run off soon. Watch."

Bob pulled his phone out of his pocket. The lighting was awful, but he took a few photos and a minute or so of video. Tess faced him and grinned.

"What?"

"When you're out here enough, you don't need photos. The experiences are etched in your brain."

The door of the ranger's cabin opened. The ranger walked toward the back of the chalet and noticed them looking over his head. He turned around. "Great!"

The ranger shook his head, returned to his cabin, and came out with a large pot and a three-foot wooden stake. He headed through the brush up the mountainside, banging the bottom of the pot with the stick.

Bob jumped with the first few blows.

Tess didn't move. "That will be everyone's wake-up call–except for you and me and Bernie inside."

The mama bear and her cub looked back at the ranger and lumbered uphill after the third bang. The ranger kept approaching, and the bears kept retreating. When he stopped, they pawed at the ground until he started banging again. Finally, they were no longer visible through the trees.

"That's just great," Bob said. "I think he chased them toward Swiftcurrent Pass."

"Is that where you're headed?"

"Yep."

"Good. You'll get to see them again. Make sure your bear spray is handy." She smiled.

Tess walked into the kitchen, but Bob walked around the chalet and sat on the rocks in front of the patio facing west. He enjoyed the solitude, but knew it wouldn't last long with the ranger's antics. Heaven's Peak was purple, morphing into pink. At least, that's what his color blind eyes and brain told him. He didn't really care what the colors were called. They were just beautiful.

✳ ✳ ✳

Dear Cathy,

Can you see this? I wish I could see what your eyes see. It's beautiful, but I don't know what I'm missing. I've always been this way.

And the bears? Many bear encounters are traumatic, but this one was so peaceful. They were searching for breakfast, just like us. I wonder what the other guests thought when the ranger banged on that pot. Tess thinks we'll see them again on the way out. Get ready!

Finally, thanks. Thanks for showing me the way. I'll always love you.

Love, Bob

49

Mission

"Tess. Time to go see those bears again. Thanks for everything, but especially for not making me feel like a VIP. Jonathan and the staff at Belton Chalet treated me and Liz like royalty. Don't get me wrong, it was wonderful, but I have to admit I was a little uncomfortable the entire time. You made me feel at home–except for the no running water thing."

Tess winked and waved. "Have a great hike. Are you headed to Many Glacier?"

"That's the plan. But I also had a plan to finish the Gunsight Pass Trail, and that didn't turn out so well."

"Chet would disagree. Have fun. And keep your bear spray handy."

Bob headed up the trail. The slope was gradual and allowed his stiff body to loosen up. His bruises were healing, so he felt less pain. His head was on a swivel as he walked near where he lost sight of the bears earlier.

He yelled, "Hey bear. Hey bear. Don't worry about me. I don't have a pot and a stick."

The trail steepened gradually, and before he knew it, he was on Swiftcurrent Pass. A trail sign pointed up the steep slope to the left. His legs were limbered up, and his back felt much better. But something kept him moving forward. Was it the anticipation of the beautiful hike down the Swiftcurrent Valley, or the dread of an additional 1200 feet of descent, or anxiety about beginning his reconciliation with Liz? Cathy's message had lightened his load. Not the one on his back, that was only a few ounces lighter than yesterday, but the load on his soul. He decided to skip the climb to the lookout tower.

Bob tried to keep up his vigilance for spotting bears, but he now had to focus on the path directly in front of him as gravity carried him down the mountain more quickly. He could slow down, but that would just add to the stress on his knees.

A thin, shirtless hiker with a tiny backpack approached him. His fast pace and gruff appearance made Bob think he was nearing the end of his thru-hike of the Continental Divide Trail, of which the Highline Trail was a small part. He must be able to taste Canada now after six months of hiking. The hiker slowed down as he neared Bob.

"Cool, bears," he said nonchalantly, as he pointed to Bob's left with his hiking poles, then kept walking. He was on a mission. Not even bears would get in the way.

Bob was also on a mission, but he had time to admire the creatures and take their photos in better light than he had before. They still searched for insects under rocks and logs and didn't even smile for the camera. He couldn't imagine insects ever satisfying their tremendous appetites.

While he was stopped, he soaked in the 180-degree view around him. Straight ahead were a series of lakes, from long and slender Bullhead Lake in front of him, to Swiftcurrent Lake, where the Many Glacier Hotel was located, to the reservoir formed by Lake Sherburne further to the east. Several of the lakes in between were unnamed on the map despite their beauty. To the right, a glacier hung to the steep slopes of Mt. Grinnell, feeding a thin waterfall that first fell down a steep rock face, then through a massive pile of talus. That must be a large source of the water in the lakes ahead. He would have to cross that stream at some point, perhaps multiple times. He hoped he could do so without Liz's reassurance.

At the end of the main descent, the stream crossing he feared was uneventful, thanks to a sturdy split log bridge resting on large rocks on each bank. He took the opportunity to replenish his water supply and eat a snack. He had eaten only a couple of granola bars for breakfast versus feasting on the hearty spread at Sperry Chalet. He ate a couple of sausages, some nuts, and finished with a few M&M's–more like an early lunch than a snack.

He marched along Bullhead Lake. It was longer than Bullfrog Lake near the JMT, but was otherwise similar–deep blue water with a convoluted shoreline. Views of the lake came and went as the trail weaved in and out of the trees on the north side of the lake. After a couple of unnamed lakes, he arrived at Redrock Falls, a popular day hike from the Many Glacier area. He must be getting close now. The crowds increased as he made his way down the valley. Day hikers in short shorts, halter tops, and sandals climbed on the jagged rocks around the falls, trying to pose for an epic photo to post on social media. Bob had been surrounded by water falling a thousand feet versus tens of feet, so he snapped a single photo contaminated with day hikers and moved on.

Just ahead was, you guessed it, Redrock Lake. On the far end of the lake, he noticed a wide but empty rock beach. He picked up the pace and cut through the trees to find it still free of people. They must either be hurrying to the waterfall or back to the hotel and hiking right by this gem. Even though he was only a few miles from the Many Glacier Hotel, he sat on his foam pad, took off his shoes and socks, and soaked his feet. This trip had been so chaotic, this was only his second opportunity to do so–if you didn't count his slide into the lake. The first was with Liz at Lake Ellen Wilson. Oh Liz. How he wished she were here now. But Cathy was. He stared at the ripples of water breaking on his ankles and relished the cool wind blowing on his face. Only the loud voices from Redrock Falls disturbed the serenity.

* * *

Dear Cathy,

I think we're going to make it this time. Only a few more miles. With so many day hikers on the trail, they won't be able to close it until I'm done. I know we didn't finish the Gunsight Pass Trail together–that hike seemed to be cursed–but we got to spend FOUR nights in chalets, which must be way beyond your wildest expectations. And we're about to finish a hike just as beautiful as the first one we set out on. I hope you enjoyed the bonus miles and chalet stays. As long as you have waited, you deserve it.

Love, Bob

50

Moose

One lake remained. Fishercap Lake was a few hundred yards off the trail and a well-known feeding ground for moose, especially in the early morning and evening. However, since he was passing so close and no climbing was involved, he would give it a shot. After a short walk through the dense forest, he arrived at a small rock beach similar to the one he had just left. He was alone again; no tourists, but no moose either.

On the east side of the lake, the steady outflow had created a large marsh, which contained more and more willows further to the east. At the far end of the marsh, two dark brown objects moved just over the top of the light green bushes, occasionally disappearing. Perhaps his color blind eyes deceived him again. Greens and browns were the hardest colors for him to distinguish. Cathy had sometimes surprised him with comments like, "Did you know the grass is dying?"

Bob heard laughter from the main trail, and a giant head with two large antlers popped up above the bushes. A moose! His small gamble had paid off. As the laughter faded, Bob was relieved he could continue to have the beach to himself. The moose relaxed as well and began lumbering through the marsh toward the lake. When he arrived at the ill-defined shoreline, he looked over at Bob and seemed to nod, as if to say, *You mind your business; I'll mind mine.*

The moose's spindly legs sliced through the water like a warm knife through soft butter. He paused when the water reached his torso, enjoying the opportunity to cool down and chase away the irritating flies. But he was there to eat, so he submerged his head to feed on the succulent plants below. When he raised his head out of the water, he looked over at Bob again to check if he was holding up his end of the bargain. Bob sat still with his phone on his knee, capturing the magic on video. Still photos would not capture the water running down his antlers, across his face, and down the long dewlap dangling from his jaw.

* * *

Dear Cathy,

Are you seeing this? What a way to end the hike. We're going to make it, even if I have to crawl back to the trailhead. I'm so happy for you. Can I cross this one off your bucket list?

Love, Bob

51

Majesty

Bob sat on the beach for over an hour. He was anxious to reach the hotel, but didn't want this magical time to end. However, watching the moose snack on juicy green plants revealed his hunger pangs. And he imagined quenching his thirst with a cold beer. Plenty of food remained in his pack, but he preferred to wait and gorge himself on a hamburger and fries at the Many Glacier Hotel. When he heard loud voices approaching, he knew his solitude would end soon, no matter what he did. When he stood up, the bull moose looked his way. Bob waved and could have sworn the moose nodded, causing his dewlap to swing. *Thank you, sir!*

Ten minutes later, he saw parked cars through the trees. The hotel was near, and with it, a shower, burger, beer, and the ability to contact Liz. Fortunately, they had exchanged email addresses and phone numbers at dinner before they went their separate ways for the night.

When he set foot on pavement, he saw a small single-story motel instead of the massive and majestic Many Glacier Hotel. This was where he had stayed the first two nights of the trip, the Swiftcurrent Motor Inn. The map on the trailhead sign knocked the wind out of him. The Many Glacier Hotel was still a mile away.

Now he wondered where Jonathan had left his car. He had told Jonathan he was staying at the Many Glacier Hotel, but perhaps he left it here, near the trailhead. Jonathan had taken care of everything else so perfectly; perhaps he had anticipated the disappointment Bob now felt. His sliver of hope withered as he searched the parking lot twice, not finding his car. He gritted his teeth and continued walking along the road toward his destination. He passed the campground hidden away in the dense trees and the backcountry permit office where he had his first scare of the trip several days ago.

Cars spilled out of the parking lot for the trailhead of the Grinnell Glacier Trail. As he walked down a trail headed toward the lake, the trees thinned, and he saw his home for the next few nights. A small marina floated on the lake between him and the hotel, no doubt the source of the canoes and kayaks exploring the lake. The massive, five-story hotel was dark brown with bright white paint outlining the windows and doors. The first floor consisted of a tan rock wall, on top of which sat a huge balcony. He pictured himself lounging there with a cold beer this afternoon and a hot coffee in the morning.

A line of cars extended up the road ahead, waiting to make a left turn toward the hotel. As Bob turned the corner around the marina, he identified the cause of the traffic jam. A small herd of bighorn sheep grazed along both sides of the entrance road to the hotel. Fearing he might become trapped between the large animals and the shoreline, he detoured around the herd.

He stopped as soon as he entered the hotel to allow his eyes to adjust to the interior finished with dark wood. After being bumped from behind twice, he stepped ahead and admired the enormous lobby. The crowds would take a day or two to get accustomed to, part of his readjustment to the real world.

A huge fireplace, wider than he was tall, formed the centerpiece of the lobby and sat on a slab of rock about twenty-feet square. Rustic-themed chairs and sofas encircled the fireplace on the floor, and multiple balconies surrounded it above. A large skylight let in enough natural light for the wood interior to glow. At one end of the lobby, a wide, spiral staircase ascended to the second floor.

He saw deep lines of people at the other end of the lobby and looked at his watch: 1:35 PM. Signs indicated check-in time was 3:00 PM. He'd probably need to come back later anyway, so instead of waiting in line twice, he headed toward the line of bright windows across the lobby. Doors led to the balcony he had seen from across the lake. As he did at the end of most backpacking trips or resupply stops, he paused to consider the priorities of his needs. The shower would have to wait until his room was ready. He needed to gather his thoughts before he attempted to contact Liz. A beer on the patio sounded good. Then, a burger. By the time he was done eating, he should be able to check in and clean up.

But he had an additional priority this time—Marty! One that rose to the top, even above a beer.

He located the concierge and explained that his friend should have left car keys for him. The concierge checked his logbook, then walked over to the check-in area. He returned with the keys to his rental car.

"Thank you, so much."

He rushed out the door and up the long series of steps to the massive parking lot. Despite its size, a dozen cars circled the lot to find parking. Now what? Where would Jonathan have parked the car? He glanced at the key ring and noticed something scribbled on the information tag: '2nd row, far right.' That man thought of everything. He pressed the unlock button repeatedly while walking down the row, then pressed the trunk release button when he saw flashing lights.

The trunk was open by the time he arrived, falsely raising the hopes of the drivers in the passing cars. He pressed down on the roughly rolled tent.

Yes! It feels a little lumpy.

He took the tent out, unrolled it, and shook. No marmots jumped out. He laid out the tent in the parking lot, opened the zipper, and swiped his hands back and forth.

Yes, there he is.

He yanked the marmot out of the tent and pressed him against his face.

You must be thirsty and starving. Let's go fix that.

Now that one burden on his mind had been lifted, he sought his beer. Once in hand, he stepped out onto the crowded patio and stood against the railing. Swiftcurrent Lake extended in front of the long, narrow hotel. The deep blue color was muted by the bright glare from the afternoon sun. The massive, triangular Grinnell Point dominated the view above the lake, but dozens of other peaks provided a dramatic backdrop. He found a couple of adjacent empty chairs, sat in one, and set Marty in the other. He held his glass next to Marty's mouth.

Here you go, buddy. You must be parched. Sorry for abandoning you for a couple of days.

He took his own sip and closed his eyes as he focused on the cold liquid traveling to his stomach and the alcohol-laced blood making its way up to his brain. Thinking of the sunset he had missed last night, he forced his eyes back open. He put his sunglasses on and stared at Grinnell Point, trying to tune out the dozens of others around him.

52

Advice

Bob was pulling the phone away from his ear when he heard the voice he sought comfort from.

"Hello."

"Hi Hannah!"

"Bob! How are you? Are you still in Glacier?"

Bob didn't have a daughter or son to worry about him, but he had a trail friend about that age. Much more than a trail friend actually, a real friend. They bonded quickly and tightly while sharing the good times and bad times on the JMT. He needed help. He needed advice. Who else was he going to call? Perhaps Jessica, who was another close friend from the trail, but not quite old enough to possess the life experience he needed to draw upon.

"Yes. I'm sitting on the patio of the Many Glacier Hotel, staring at a mountain over a lake and sipping a beer. How are you doing?"

"Working hard. Waiting for you to return so we can hop on the JMT again, but I managed to day hike to Kearsarge Pass last weekend. Trying to keep my legs in hiking shape. Now I understand why you liked that area so much. Did you and Cathy enjoy the Gunsight Pass Trail?"

"That's a long story. I had a little accident–"

"Accident? Are you OK?"

"Yeah, I'm sore, but I'm fine. I've done a lot of hiking since then. But I didn't get to finish due to bear activity on the other end of the trail."

274

"Oh. Sorry, Bob."

"However, I got to stay at Sperry Chalet twice, without a reservation. Mostly due to a wonderful lady I met–"

"Lady?"

"Yes."

"Like a lady trail friend or–"

"More than a trail friend."

"Good for you, Bob. I can't wait to hear more."

"Well, that's why I called. I need some help. Some advice about her–Liz."

"Remember, I might not be the best one to ask about relationships."

"But I trust you. You know me and Cathy, even though you never met her."

Bob paused, but Hannah must have been waiting for him to continue.

"I think I made an awful mistake. She's so wonderful to me. Adventurous, generous, caring. Kind of like you–and Cathy. She saved my life. She wants to be more than a trail friend, much more. But Cathy is still close. I still owe her so much. I don't know what to do. I may have pushed her away. She may never come back."

"Oh, Bob. I wish I could be there. You must be hurting so bad. Maybe worse than on the JMT."

"It's been hard, but also wonderful. Maybe this is what I could have had all along with Cathy. What should I do?"

"What do you think, Bob?"

"I don't know. That's why I called. I asked Cathy for help last night, and I had a dream. All she said was, 'It's OK.'"

"There you go. It's simple. You already know the answer."

"Simple? But she slips away when I spend time with Liz."

"She'll always be there for you. Remember, she's the one who wanted you to retire and live life to the fullest before it was too late. Don't you think she still wants you to do that?"

"I don't know, but Liz is that way as well. She goes after what she wants. And I think she may want me."

"Do you want her?"

"Yes."

"Then go for it."

His heart thumped. His breathing quickened.

"Thanks, Hannah. You're a wonderful friend."

"You're welcome. Hurry up, so we can get back on the JMT before the snows come. Maybe Liz can come with us."

Bob pictured a smirk on her face. What a great way to end the call. "Bye, Hannah."

53

Surprise

One beer was all he could handle in his famished state, so he walked back inside in search of a restaurant. A sign directed him to the second floor. His legs wobbled as he looked up the spiral staircase. But heck, if he had survived the ledge on the Highline Trail yesterday and climbed the narrow chute to Comeau Pass, he could do this. He had just enough coherence left to hold the handrail all the way up. He continued to follow the signs to the restaurants. A small bar and grill sat off to the right. Just ahead, hotel staff were putting linens and cutlery on the tables and vacuuming the floors in the Ptarmigan Dining Room. A sign in front of the restaurant confirmed it was closed until 5 PM. He retreated to the dark bar and grill and ordered another beer and a bacon cheeseburger and fries.

After satisfying his hunger, he headed back down the spiral staircase. His knees complained after the long descent from Swiftcurrent Pass. His decision to forgo the climb of Swiftcurrent Peak seemed brilliant about now.

The lines to check in were just as long as before, but he should only need to wait once since it was past 3 PM. The beer and full belly made the long wait tolerable.

"Hi. Welcome to the Many Glacier Hotel. Checking in?"

"Yes. Name is Riley, Bob Riley. R-I-L-E-Y."

The clerk's name tag indicated her name was Amanda. Her tilted head

277

and narrowing eyes began to worry Bob.

"Just a second, Mr. Riley. I'll be right back."

Uh-oh.

Was his wonderful day of hiking going to be capped by a mad scramble for alternative accommodations?

The young clerk discussed something with an older lady in the back. The lady peeked over her reading glasses at Bob and smiled. That was a good sign, wasn't it?

The clerk came back to her station. "Good news, Mr. Riley. You have received a complimentary upgrade to a lakeside room. Here is your key."

"Thank you very much. This trip has been full of surprises."

Complimentary upgrade? Did Jonathan have influence over this hotel as well? He didn't think so. Who else could have made this happen? Or was it just more magic?

Bob took the stairs to the fifth floor. Not only would his room face the lake, but he would be well above the bustle on the patio below.

Bob opened the door to his room, prepared to be impressed. Not only did he have a lakeside view, but he noticed he had two rooms and a balcony. A cool breeze blew through the open balcony door. The housekeepers must have forgotten to close it when they left. He imagined they preferred working in the fresh air when they could. He dropped his filthy backpack on the floor against the wall and walked onto the balcony.

What a view! What an upgrade!

"Bob! You're here."

He turned to the right. An even better view awaited him there. Liz rose from one of the two chairs, opened her arms wide, and said, "Surprise!"

She waved one of her arms toward Grinnell Point, but Bob's eyes stayed on her. She was all he wanted to see–and hold. He walked to her and hugged her tightly. He leaned back, gazed into her eyes, and kissed her.

"So I guess the hotel didn't upgrade me after all?"

"No."

"I thought you had to go home? I was disappointed I didn't get to tell you goodbye, but I guess I deserved that."

Liz nodded. "My flight was a couple of hours late. While I waited, I realized I wasn't being true to myself. I was giving up. I don't give up pursuing what I want. I want you, Bob. And I'm willing to help you through your struggle."

She put her face against his chest, hugged him, then led him inside.

Bob raised his index finger. "Oh, hold on for one second. I got you something."

"Really! When? Where?"

"Hold on."

Bob unzipped his backpack and reached in. He pulled out the white furry animal and tossed it to Liz.

"A goat. You got me a goat. What a great way to help me remember this trip. Plus, Marty will have a companion when we hike together in the future."

"Hike together? I like the sound of that." She pointed to the door of the extra bedroom. They walked inside.

"I asked for a lakeside room with two beds, but they had this suite available. I wanted to give you the space you needed."

They walked back into the main room, and Bob closed the door to the extra bedroom.

"I'm sorry you overpaid, but I don't believe we'll be needing the extra room."

The End

To see other books in the Bucket List Hike series, download a FREE novella, or get a copy of the photo album for this book, visit my website here.
(https://strivingforsafety.mailerpage.com/fiction)

Author's Note

I sincerely hope you enjoyed the story and that it motivates you to get outside and experience your own adventures. Please **leave a review** where you bought this book. They really help others discover and enjoy it as well. Thank you in advance.

As a bonus for you, I have created a **Photo Album** showing many of the key scenes in the book and some of the intriguing wildlife the characters encountered, including the Grinnell Glacier, Sperry Chalet, Granite Park Chalet, Lake Ellen Wilson, Gunsight Pass, Many Glacier Hotel, and Swiftcurrent Valley, plus bears, goats, and marmots. To obtain the photo album or a free novella in the Bucket List Hike series, please visit my website. (https://strivingforsafety.mailerpage.com/fiction)

For updates on new releases, free bonus material, and highlights from my own travels, please sign up for my newsletter here. (https://strivingforsafety.mailerpage.com)

My website is https://strivingforsafety.mailerpage.com/.

You can also follow me on:
Facebook
(https://www.facebook.com/profile.php?id=100087842125447)
LinkedIn
(https://www.linkedin.com/in/arnold-marsden-14170180)

You can email me at arnold@strivingforsafety.com. I love to receive feedback from readers on my books and their travels.

Acknowledgments

Thanks to the following generous people for providing valuable feedback on drafts of this book to make it a better read and help me become a better author: Lori Downs, Debbie McSwain Teal, Mary Hamilton, Lee Lovelace, David Galloway, and Joan M. Griffin.

About the Author

Arnold lives in Fulshear, Texas, USA, just outside of Houston. He worked as a Health, Safety, and Environment (HSE) professional for over thirty-five years helping to prevent injuries, save lives, and protect the environment. Since retiring, he continues to hike and backpack in some of the most beautiful parks and wilderness areas in the country and has begun an author career, writing both fiction and nonfiction.

Glacier Chalet Surprise is his second novel in the Bucket List Hike series and was inspired by his own visit to Glacier National Park in 2019. *Muir Trail Magic* was the first novel in the series, inspired by his own hike of the trail in 2021 and 2022. Stay tuned for future releases following Bob, Cathy, and others on hiking, backpacking, and sightseeing adventures in the National Parks and other nature preserves. Though fictional, he hopes that the books help you prepare for your own adventure, relive a past adventure, or experience the area from the comfort of your own home.

In his nonfiction books on industrial safety management, he shares valuable lessons learned from his career to help others save lives. His first book was *Don't Let It Fall: Stop Dropped Objects, Save Lives*. His second, *Safety First! Really?*, was published in February 2023.